# "You Must Carry My Message To Whomever You Meet."

Nuela stared at the keeper, at her unbetraying face. Finally she said, "Who do you expect me to meet?"

Polamaire shook her head.

"So I'm to go alone and if I meet someone, I'm to give him a message I don't understand. I—"

"That is precisely what you are to do. And if you are wise, you must not challenge yourself unduly along the way. Aurlanis becomes small when you leave its near-waters. The dreams are far more compelling upon the open sea."

Stiffening, Nuela met the keeper's eyes. "You have had the same dream I had," she said.

"I have had that dream. And others."

"You have lived when you should have drowned."

"I have lived."

*Other Avon Books by*
**Sydney J. Van Scyoc**

FEATHER STROKE

# DEEPWATER DREAMS

## SYDNEY J. VAN SCYOC

AVON BOOKS ◆ NEW YORK

DEEPWATER DREAMS is an original publication of Avon Books.
This work has never before appeared in book form. This work is a
novel. Any similarity to actual persons or events is purely coinci-
dental.

AVON BOOKS
A division of
The Hearst Corporation
105 Madison Avenue
New York, New York 10016

Copyright © 1991 by Sydney Joyce Van Scyoc
Cover art by Keith Parkinson
Published by arrangement with the author
Library of Congress Catalog Card Number: 90-93622
ISBN: 0-380-76003-7

First Avon Books Printing: June 1991

AVON TRADEMARK REG. U.S. PAT. OFF. AND IN OTHER COUNTRIES,
MARCA REGISTRADA, HECHO EN U.S.A.

Printed in the U.S.A.

RA 10 9 8 7 6 5 4 3 2 1

For Bret,
Jake and Eric

# Prologue

LeCler passed a trembling hand over the primary control panel. The ship's structure had been damaged by sentry satellite fire in the ascent from Chaheras, and he had pushed the vessel well beyond design limits in the brief but fierce pursuit that had followed. Later, programming the controls for the plunge into Flearstream, sealing himself into the stasis suit, he had only half expected to wake again.

*To wake, to free Sulienne, to swim again with the free Chahera . . .*

Desperate dreams. Desperate measures. But the suittimer had roused him on schedule. Light-headed, disbelieving, he had gazed out the faceplate to confirm that the gel-seal had closed the punctured skin, that the cabin held pressure, that the injured vessel indeed neared its programmed destination. And when he had emerged from the suit, he had found ship and body little worse than he had left them.

But of course he had not left them well. And now, after an anxious, hovering hour at the panel, it no longer seemed to matter what adjustment he made to the control settings. The surface of the warning panel remained hectic with lights, the interior of the cabin shrill with an ongoing series of alarms. And the body—

Silencing the latest volley of alarms, LeCler stepped back from the console and clasped the trembling hands together, trying to quiet them. In the confusion of throwing off stasis, of assimilating instrument data, of attempting to program a safe descent in a damaged ship, every alarm that blinked, that squealed, that flashed seemed to echo some mindstate of his own. Anger, will, conviction, sorrow . . .

LeCler frowned down at the square, strong hands, and the fingers contracted again. An involuntary spasm? Or a deliberate effort by his host to regain control? There was something accusing in the pulses and tremors of the body as it struggled to reject him.

And indeed LeCler felt compunction over his theft of it. He felt regret for the man named Morrow, who had sold him a month of its time—only to have him tear it away to a nameless world five charts from the clinic on Beldarme where he was to have surrendered the body after settling his affairs.

But his affairs were not yet settled, and LeCler felt no compunction over his theft of the ship. Because the cargo he had stolen with it was claimed flesh, the carrier itself the registered property of a flesh dealer. His uncle. And no one had the right to claim the living flesh of a willed people.

Certainly no one had the right to deal in the Chahera.

The hands clenched—with LeCler's anger or his host's? Did the body's increasing restiveness indicate a return of awareness? Or was the struggle purely reflexive? LeCler had studied the host face closely before contracting for the imprint: close-cropped dark hair, reticent mouth, black eyes that held wariness and restrained challenge.

The physical details of the face had evoked no sense of identity, but the veiled challenge in the other man's eyes had touched him. Was it simply the defiance of a man driven by circumstance to sell body-time? Or the deeper anger of a man who had examined the human race and its institutions too closely? Might Morrow have done the same thing LeCler had done, given knowledge and opportunity?

If LeCler had been strong enough to return to Chaheras a whole man—

But he had not been. The disease that had caught him on Piiridaar, his plans only half formulated, had progressed so rapidly that he had barely survived the passage as far as Beldarme.

A new alarm sounded in the cabin, growling for attention. Silencing it, LeCler glanced tensely over the readouts. Saw that they had entered the upper atmosphere.

The entire host body tightened in response, as if mobilizing for action. But it was useless to waste time on air-to-surface observations. The reports said the waters below were suitable for the Chahera and their lucticetes, and he had no second destination of choice if they were not.

And he must not abandon the cabin during descent, must not go to the holds now to release the Chahera. He would free them later, when the ship was safely down.

But if it broke upon impact, if the holds flooded, if he could not reach the Chahera—

Taut fingers trembled at his temples. An image of the girl came to quick focus in his mind, feathery golden lashes shadowing still cheeks. This was the image he had carried away from Chahera so many years before, the image that had finally drawn him back. To risk her survival now, when he had stolen ship, cargo, and body to save her, when he had crossed five charts in a crippled vessel— LeCler turned from the cabin and ran down the passageway that led to the holds.

The Chahera were secured in the first hold, chained to the bunks that were bolted in stacks along the bulkheads. They lay slack and disarranged, stasis-masked but not suited up. And they were young—children. Taken from their pods as infants, they had never known the open sea or the company of lucticetes. They had known only his uncle's stock ponds.

This time LeCler identified the clenching of the hands as his own. As anger. He made his way among the bunks until he stood over the girl he had named Sulienne—for the girl who had been Sulienne.

For a moment, looking down at her, he forgot the ship, forgot the body, forgot everything but the gold of her hair. He had combed it across her shoulders before suiting for stasis. Incredibly, it still lay there in a smooth sheet.

As Sulienne's hair had once spread like liquid silk across bare tan shoulders.

Kneeling, LeCler gently raised her eyelids. Gazing into the gold-rimmed pupils, he shuddered with the hunger to swim with her again. To draw dark tracks across the moonlight that sheeted the water. To break starlight into bright spectra with the water that clung to his eyelashes. To touch her hand beneath the water.

To do things he had once done. To do things he had not done.

But this girl was not Sulienne, and he was no longer the boy who had slipped away from his uncle's pond ranch to swim with the free Chahera as they passed in migration. He was only an imprint now, the surviving memory trace of a man who had died in the clinic on Beldarme.

A man who had died, now, many years ago.

He swallowed back bitterness, regret, grief. There was no time for those things. Drawing the mask from the girl's face, he did not touch her again until the others were unmasked as well. Then he returned and felt carefully for the pulse at her neck. When it fluttered softly to life, he released her chains so that only snap-webs and safety bumpers confined her. If they reached the water safely, if she chose then to swim with him—

He had released most of the Chahera when a new series of alarms screamed through the vessel. Startled, LeCler bolted for the control cabin.

From the frantic blinking and squalling of the systems alerts, it seemed that everything that could go wrong suddenly had gone wrong. They had reached the lower atmosphere, and the braking system had gone into partial failure. They were descending too quickly, driving too hard through the air. Scarred skin panels were heating, ripping. Hold and cabin temperatures were already rising.

LeCler stared at the panel, and very quickly the last thing that could go wrong did. The hand he thrust at the controls shook violently, then retracted. Simultaneously the entire host body stiffened, the shoulders snapping back painfully, the jaw clenching, the muscles of the thighs and calves drawing suddenly so tight they cramped. Slowly, rigidly, the head turned. A sound came from the throat, half query, half protest. Startled eyes—Morrow's now, Morrow's *again*—stared around the cabin and found just one thing they knew.

LeCler screamed silently. *Morrow—no!* He could not relinquish control of the body now. He must get the ship safely down. He must release the Chahera and their 'cetes. And when they were in the water, he must orient them. They were children, pond raised. To simply set them loose in a strange sea—

But the body's rightful occupant had reclaimed it. LeCler tried to turn back to the control panel. There was a secondary deceleration system, but it hadn't kicked in. If he could set it now—

The body refused his command. Carried him toward the stasis suit instead. It stepped into the suit. Because there, only there, Morrow recognized safety.

LeCler screamed again, feeling everything the body

felt: the painful tension of muscles, the rushing tingle of adrenaline, the wild battering of the heart against the ribs. But he was as powerless now as Morrow had been earlier. He could do no more than make the hand that closed the suit quiver slightly.

*No! Morrow— If we set the secondary slow-system, we can get the ship down whole. We can turn the Chahera free in the water. We can—*

If Morrow heard the silent plea, he did not respond. Fasteners hissed shut. The faceplate slid into place. Swiftly an enveloping darkness closed around LeCler. He went into it with a name silent on the lips that no longer spoke for him.

*Sulienne . . .*

The dream grew momentarily brighter, more desperate, then yielded to darkness.

# Chapter One

THE EVENING WAS WARM, THE SEA QUIET, ITS VOICE no more than a whisper within palace walls. Sunset was an hour past. The sky was star-pierced with light. The wiskis shell moaned a solitary wind note from its column in the courtyard, drawing Nuela to the window again. She had watched there since dusk-horn for Sinjanne. Still there was no sign of her in the tiled courtyard below or on the moonlit beach beyond.

Troubled, Nuela turned back to the small, sparsely furnished room. Two bedmats with blankets neatly rolled, two chests of woven wiregrass, a low lamp stand, the lamp itself casting pastel light against the grainy wall . . . Only the candidate's sash did not belong to this familiar setting. It lay coiled like an unanswered question on her bedmat. Would she return tonight to the room she had shared for so many years with her sister, to things she knew? Or would she be among those who followed the sea trail?

She would not know until Polamaire drew the tiles. Frowning, Nuela took up the sash. She looped the fine-grained white fabric at her waist and tied it there. The loose ends hung cool and silken against her bare thigh, making her shiver. Her fingers fumbling, cold, she formed her pale hair into a single braid and bound it with white cord.

Still Sinjanne did not come. If she had gone again to the men's beach, if she had forgotten that this was the night tiles were to be drawn . . .

She had only to look up to be reminded. The moons had run their separate courses for forty-two days, Lomaire drifting in golden silence, Tuanne first fleeing, then pursuing, small and copper. Tonight they stood disk upon disk again, their fifth conjunction for the Year of the Sia-kepi. Soon after Tuanne's small disk centered itself upon Lomaire's larger one, the tides would fall and the sea trail would open.

Polamaire would not wait much longer before drawing the tiles. People were already emerging from the dinner hall, their hand-lamps speckling the courtyard with light. And as Nuela watched them spread across the pavement, the first night-horn sounded from the torch-tower, and the wiskis shell wailed again as if in answer.

Nuela closed her eyes and repeated a smallchant beneath her breath. She could wait no longer for Sinjanne.

Heart pounding, she left the room and made her way down three flights of stairs. She hesitated at the arched door to the main hall, knowing that people turned to look, suddenly caring that they saw her begin her walk alone, without even a sister at her side. Whispering a second smallchant, she drew a long breath and paced slowly across the white pressed-shell tile of the courtyard, head bowed.

Reaching the edge of the courtyard, she crossed the sand and chose a place at the beach's edge, slightly apart from the candidates who had already gathered. The sea rushed gently at the shore, the waves light tipped, sparkling. Cold, anxious, her eyes averted, Nuela settled to the vigil she had kept seven times before: first in the Year of the Haspipi, then once, sometimes twice each year since. At the end of each of those previous vigils, she had returned to her room. Her tile had not been drawn. But tonight?

Digging her toes into the sand, Nuela glanced at the other candidates. They were younger than she, more Sinjanne's age than her own. They sat with their families and friends, talking too feverishly, laughing too loudly, their eyes darting anxiously at the sea when they thought no one noticed. Some of them would go tonight. The others must gather again for the drawing next year—and Sinjanne would sit among them then, wearing sash and braid.

Sinjanne would sit among the candidates, whether or not Nuela went to Pahla's Nipple tonight, whether or not she returned to help her prepare.

But she would return. She would never leave Sinjanne to prepare alone for her own kalinerre, her time at Pahla's breast. She vowed that with a cold shiver of will. There were so many things she had not yet impressed upon Sinjanne—not because she had not said them but because Sinjanne had not listened. And so she must return to say them again. And again. She must return to say them until Sinjanne heard.

"Nuela."

Nuela turned with a sharply drawn breath. But it was only Delfinne, Belina squirming in her arms.

Delfinne dropped to the sand beside Nuela and shook her hair back from her plump, bold features. "Well, do you think this little wriggle fish would stay with Allinarde tonight?" She clasped the child firmly between her legs, whispering into her ear. The child subsided slowly, staring wide-eyed at Nuela's bound braid.

Nuela touched Belina's foot, awed that her friend, a child herself so few years before, had a child of her own now, small and perfect and self-willed. She counted tiny, warm toes, making Belina laugh. "Have you seen Sinjanne, Del? I thought she would come to wait with me.''

Delfinne's lashes fell, screening her eyes. "She's always come before, Nuela.''

Nuela frowned at the change in her friend's voice. Disapproval? Or simply anticipation of the question Nuela always asked on the night of the drawing? Brushing sand from Belina's foot, releasing it, she asked once more. "Delfinne, will you look out for her if I go tonight?''

Delfinne's lips tightened. "You know she won't come to me if she needs help, Nu.''

Yes, disapproval. "But if she gets into trouble—''

"Going to the men's beach when she hasn't completed kalinerre? Swimming out to the edge of the nearwaters when the wiskis is crying? Singing broadchants in the corridors in the middle of the night, waking everyone on the floor?''

Nuela sighed. Sinjanne had done all those things since her last birthday—and more. Yet Nuela still thought of her as a child running on the beach, sand rising in golden wings from her bare heels, or bobbing in the morning pool, tiny brightly colored acafa nibbling her fingers. Sinjanne had always been bright, sparkling, intense. She had seldom had time to pause, to listen, even as a small child. But it was only in the last year that she had become openly defiant.

"It's my fault. If I'd known what to do for her, if I had guessed when she was young that she would be so wild—'' But what could she have done, only five years older than Sinjanne, barely grown herself when their parents drowned?

She had supervised her sister's physical care, had exercised a fierce, persistent protectiveness on her behalf. She had seen that Sinjanne came out of the water for meals, that she joined the others in the courtyard for evenchant, that she had fresh clothes and clean bedding.

She had done everything she knew to do. Obviously it had not been enough.

"Nu, it isn't your fault," Delfinne said almost angrily. "If Sinjanne is wild, it's her nature. She'll go to the Nipple next year or the year after, and if she comes back—"

*If?* Nuela drew a sharp breath.

"If she comes back, then she will settle down just like the rest of us," Delfinne continued relentlessly. "And you should think of yourself tonight, not Sinjanne. Nuela, if you go this time . . ."

Nuela met her friend's eyes and saw apprehension. "I'll come back, Delfinne. I'll be as careful as I know how."

Delfinne shook her head. "You'll come back if you're meant to come back, Nuela. If you're not—"

"But I will come back." The candidates whose tiles were drawn must go to Pahla's Nipple without nets, without spears, without even carrybags or a change of clothing. For the period of kalinerre, forty-two days, they must feed themselves entirely from the open sea. There were no reef gardens on Pahla's Nipple. There was no netting pool. There was no protecting arc reef. Nor was there any palace to offer shelter, any pharmacy to treat illnesses and wounds, any experienced person to offer guidance and counsel.

No one who returned was permitted to discuss his or her experience. And no one spoke of the two or three who failed to return each year. But Nuela was five years past the age when most candidates went to the Nipple, and in that five years she had learned judgment and caution.

"Then you'll find us waiting," Delfinne said. "Me for my friend, Rinarde for his mate, and Belina for a little play-sister."

Nuela expelled a sharp breath. "Rinarde isn't waiting for me, Del." Although sometimes he walked so close beside her in the evenings that she was forced to draw away. And sometimes there was a question in his glance that she refused to let him speak aloud. If he thought he could speak that question when she returned . . .

And a child? When she had done so poorly with Sinjanne? Nuela glanced down at Belina and met a solemn, judging stare.

The other candidates stirred and gazed toward the palace. Nuela turned.

Polamaire strode across the sand toward them, tall and austere in her white gown. Her hair was wreathed about her head. She clasped the candidates' basket in both hands. A final candidate walked behind her, her head bowed but her eyes avid upon the sea.

A final candidate, her hair braided and bound, her body slight in the abbreviated swimshift, her eyes much too bright. Meeting Nuela's, they widened in triumph.

Nuela rose, her heart leaping against her chest wall. "Sinjanne!"

The others rose at the same time, families and friends withdrawing several paces, candidates stepping nearer the water. Nuela stared at her sister, stricken, unable to move.

Reaching her side, Sinjanne extended one hand. "Are you surprised, Nua? Polamaire didn't want to accept my tile, but I threw it into the basket and she had no grounds to remove it."

Nuela shook her head numbly. Polamaire had accepted Sinjanne's tile? When Nuela had not guessed Sinjanne had cut one? When she had not guessed she had even thought of cutting one? And when there had been no time to prepare her, no time to make her understand that she could not dance carelessly at the edges of danger when she went to Pahla's Nipple? The sea was not tolerant; it would not forgive heedlessness or error. "Polamaire knows you haven't had your birthday."

"And she knows I'll have it before the year is out."

"On the last day of the year," Nuela said. "If you had told me you intended to do this— Sinjanne, if you had come to me—"

"Then you would have been upset all day."

And this was how she spared her? With this last minute appearance in sash and braid? When she was eligible for the drawing in the Year of the Sia-kepi by a matter of two hours? Nuela stared at her sister, at the delicate face that burned by moonlight. There was a fire in Sinjanne, a flame somewhere just beneath the surface. She had always been brighter, more intent than anyone else, even as a tiny child. If only Nuela had found some way to tame the fire . . .

Sinjanne tugged at her hand, drawing her toward the tide line. "Don't worry, Nua. I'm ready. I've been swimming at the edge of the near-waters every morning and every night. I caught a bia-kia with my hands last night, and I ate it raw. I touched a harka night before last. I almost caught it. And I've let my nails grow so I can peel polipods and skin linsofi without a blade. I sharpened them this afternoon, see?"

Nuela stared at the honed nails, then glanced at Polamaire. There was no time for appeal. The keeper had raised her basket. The first measured syllables of her chant were already in the air.

Nuela shuddered, tensing herself against the gentle power of the chant. But the syllables rose, and the beat of the sea grew louder, became the beat of her own heart. Breathlessly she flowed from the confines of her body and was drawn into Pahla's arms.

Pahla, first mother, boundless, powerful, little caring.

Pahla, the sea that fed them, the water that carried them on its crest.

Pahla, who once had been so lonely that she had mated with the sia-kepi, the oso, the torahon, with the others of the twelve consort breeds, and brought forth human offspring.

Pahla, who nourished but did not forgive. The moons shone down upon her, gliding toward the moment of perfect union. Then they stood joined in the sky, Tuanne centered precisely against Lomaire's golden disk. The chant rose for a moment, then died. Slipping from ephemeral arms, Nuela closed her eyes and listened for the names Polamaire spoke as she drew the nine tiles.

None of the names she spoke was Nuela's.

But: "I'm going," Sinjanne said softly, with the seventh tile.

Then the drawing was done, the chant ended, the spell broken. Nuela found the muscles of her arms, of her legs drawn so tight they cramped. Reluctantly she opened her eyes.

"I'm going," Sinjanne said again, her voice different this time. Her smile had frozen; it seemed to hurt her face. Her eyes glittered with mingled excitement and fear. She caught Nuela's hand. "Don't worry, Nua. It won't be long. I'm strong. I'm ready. You know that if I stayed here without you, I'd only get into trouble."

Strong? When she was as slight as a child? Ready? When she had obviously frightened even herself this time?

But surely if she was capable of fear, she was capable of caution too.

And there was no turning back. Her tile had been drawn, her name called. "You must be careful," Nuela said with fierce, trembling conviction, as if she had not said it hundreds of times before. "If there are games in the water, don't be the one to swim farthest from shore. If you see something you can't name, don't go near it. If there is storm weather, don't leave the Nipple. If—if you must choose between going hungry and going into rough waters—"

"I'll go hungry," Sinjanne promised. "And I'm sorry. I'm sorry I haven't been better. I've tried. Really, I've tried, Nua, but—

"Do you remember when I was young? That day when you were pounding drakirre pods for the pharmacy and I drank the juice from the bowl? I feel like that this year. All year I've felt like I just drank a bowl of drakirre. I can't be still. My heart beats too fast. My thoughts run through my head and I can't catch them. And something is calling me and I can't find it. Not here. Even at night, Nua, I wake and I hear it. I go down to the beach and I watch the water and I listen.

"I think it's Pahla."

Nuela shuddered. The sea—who had drowned both their parents. "Sinjanne, don't expect the sea to be kind," she said sharply. "Don't expect the sea to forgive you if you're careless. Don't expect—"

*Don't expect to survive when you nurse at Pahla's breast. Even if you are very careful, never expect to survive the sea. Only hope for it.* Their father's words, spoken one night when moonlight fell over his face. Spoken as they sat together on the beach watching for Nuela's mother to come from the sea.

There had been many nights like that one, too many to count—until the night when they had waited and Tuleja had not returned at all. Leaning against her father, Nuela had felt the increasing tension of his muscles as the hours passed. Had grown more tense herself, trying not to say aloud what both of them were thinking.

Finally the unspoken fear had grown too potent. He had taken to his feet, gazing down at her from shadowed eyes. "Look after your sister, Nuela." And he was gone too. Gone to search for his mate.

Never to return.

Nuela had honored his last words. She had watched alone while Sinjanne slept on the sand beside her. She had watched, and when eventually the sun had risen over an empty sea, she had carried Sinjanne back to the palace—and continued to watch.

She had never spent another night as cold, as long as that one.

"I'll never expect her to be as good as you," Sinjanne said, throwing her arms around Nuela, holding tight to her. Then she broke away. "You have to go back. We're to be alone now while the trail opens. Nua, I'll come home. I'll come back to you, and then you'll go and come back to me. And we'll never have to worry about anything again.

"I'll come back."

Nuela tried to laugh but what emerged was a torn sob. Through tears she saw that she was the only one who had not turned away from the water's edge. She caught Sinjanne's shoulders and held her at arm's length, filling herself with images of her sister: the small, perfectly aligned teeth; the wide, heavily lashed eyes; the fine, flaring line of her brows. Then she turned away, overpowered with cold.

Helpless.

Empty.

Delfinne waited for her. They walked back to the palace silently. Belina bobbing on Delfinne's shoulder.

"You did everything you could," Delfinne said when they reached the main courtyard. "You did, Nu. There was nothing else you could have done. Come and sit with me for evenchant."

"No." If she had done everything, Sinjanne would not have stirred so restlessly through the last year. She would not be sitting at the edge of the water now, waiting for the sea trail to open. She would not have cut her tile when she was barely qualified for kalinerre.

If she had done everything, Sinjanne would be settling in the courtyard with the others for evenchant. She would be safe.

The first stanzas had already begun. They stalked softly across the courtyard, making heads droop, making eyelids fall. Evading their gentle spell, Nuela broke away from Delfinne and ran across the cut-tile flaggings and into the palace.

The corridors, the staircases, the room she shared with Sinjanne were deserted. Snatching up her blanket, pulling it around her, she ran to her window and stared over the beach.

She quickly let the blanket fall. The cold she felt was too deeply rooted; no blanket could touch it. And Sinjanne had nothing to warm herself with as she sat at the tide line watching the moons set.

Nuela kept vigil at the window until the last hour before dawn. She could not see the mouth of the sea trail. Her room was not properly placed for that. She could not even see the setting of the moons.

She watched anyway, until she knew Sinjanne had long gone. Then she threw herself down on her mat and fell into a bitter, restive sleep. ''Look after your sister.'' Her father had asked nothing more of her. And she had failed.

# Chapter Two

THE DAYS PASSED WITH THEIR USUAL FORM AND STRUC-
ture. Nuela reported to the pharmacy each morning,
working alternately at the compounding table and the
recording counter. Beyond work hours, her friends
were much with her. If she went to swim, Delfinne
soon joined her. If she walked along the beach, Rinarde walked with her, tall, protective, often so closely
observant of her mood that she frowned down at her
feet and answered his questions shortly. Alwinne left
her own family to sit with Nuela at evenchant. For
once, Allinarde forgot to be jealous of Nuela's friendship with Delfinne and kissed her by proxy, lifting
Belina to her cheek.

But no matter how heavy Nuela's lids when she returned to her room from evenchant, Sinjanne's bedmat
lay vacant beside her own. She spent the nights mur-
muring smallchants, finding little ease in them.

Early on the afternoon of the forty-first day, she
climbed the narrow staircase to the upper storeroom.
No one entered the large, cluttered room to distract her.
No sound intruded from the corridor. She could not
even hear the plaintive sigh of the wiskis shell as the
early afternoon breeze swept across the courtyard five
floors below.

Still the bottles she had come to set in order remained scattered, the inventory tile unmarked. Sighing, she turned to the south window and peered down at the lower reaches of the sprawling palace: the chunky black stone of the jutting walls, the white pressed-shell tiles that paved the balconies, walkways and the half-dozen small courtyards, the gleaming white seven-chambered wiskis shell mounted upon its pillar in the main courtyard. The storeroom stood on the highest floor of the palace. Only the torch-tower stood above, commanding a superior view of the sea beyond the golden beaches that girdled Aurlanis.

The sea from which Sinjanne would return night after this, if she was to return.

The nearer water lay quietly in the protecting arms of the arc reef. Beyond the concentric arms of the reef, the sea rocked in restless sheets: silver, violet, green. The sea trail lay at the eastern extremity of the island, past the morning pool and beyond the arc of the reef. It was lost in the water now, but tomorrow when the tides fell, Neula would wait near its mouth, watching for Sinjanne.

If she could name one thing those who came back from Pahla's Nipple had in common . . .

She could not. Each year weak swimmers, careless swimmers, fearful swimmers returned safely. Each year there were strong swimmers who did not.

Nuela turned back to the worktable. Her fingers trembled as she arranged rows of jars. She felt guilty relief when she found the licatana jar empty. The smaller jar in the pharmacy was almost empty too. She must go into the garden to replenish the supply.

She paused only to change into her swimshift and to select a fine-mesh carrybag. Then she ran quickly down the stairs, hardly feeling the smooth-worn tiles beneath her feet.

The wiskis shell groaned loudly with a gust of wind

as she hurried across the main courtyard. She paused, its wind note touching her with misgiving. If the sea was rough tomorrow . . .

She shook her head and waved to the cluster of children perched on the courtyard wall shelling tiny white crustaceans. They leaned together in shuttered concentration, their heads bobbing with the soft syllables of the shelling chant. Only Delfinne's brother Chanarde, sitting at the edge of the group, raised one hand in greeting.

Relieved to escape the company of her thoughts, Nuela ran down the courtyard steps and crossed the beach. Then she was in the water, sand flowing between her toes, wet and smooth.

The shallows were warm. Nuela walked until the water reached her hips. Then she lay forward and floated, gazing down open-eyed at the still bottom. Turning to her back, blinking water from her eyes, she peered back at the sea palace jutting massive and black from the flank of the dead spill-cone that had spewed Aurlanis into the sea. No one could say when the cone's mouth had sealed over, but there was a live cone to the west. Nuela had seen its plume in the sky in the Year of the Malin-ji.

She had reached the inner garden now. Protected from the surge and tug of the sea by the curving arms of the arc reef, bottom plants anchored themselves in the sand and sent streamers and floating bulbs groping to the surface. Nuela picked her way along the harvest lanes, careful not to become entangled. Small crustaceans grazed on the vegetation, their shells shimmering in the sunlit water. Occasionally a school of acafa or oso flashed past.

Nuela started as Rinarde surfaced barely an arm's length from the harvest lane. "Nuela—where are you bound?"

"To the outer gardens for licatana." She raised her

carrybag. "Can I bring you something for dinner?" Rinarde had just been chosen second master of the kitchen.

Briefly submerging, he rose again and shook his head, letting the wet hair stream back from his forehead. His shoulders were broad, his eyes the color of dry sand, brown flecked with gold. "I saw a pair of grippie earlier, but we don't need them tonight." His eyes narrowed. "Who's swimming your wake?"

Nuela stiffened. "I'm meeting Delfinne." This once, surely, she could go unescorted.

He frowned. "The sea has been rough today. There's heavy splash over the far wall."

"Then we won't go near the far wall." Nuela ducked beneath the water and swam swiftly away, before he could offer to swim with her. When she surfaced and glanced back, Rinarde stood watching, frowning into the sun. She raised a reassuring hand and submerged again.

The far curve of the inner garden was planted with fiber plants. The water grew deeper there, and Nuela skipped along, bouncing off the sandy bottom and scissoring herself forward.

She approached the garden stile, smooth-worn steps chiseled into the arc reef itself, cautiously. The grey, rocky material of the reef was jagged, but the steps of the stile were wide and deep. Within a moment she stood safely at the top, water washing her ankles.

She shook her hair back and gazed out over the deep garden. Here the vegetation was coarser, the water darker and more active, moving with caged restlessness to the rhythms of the sea beyond. White-capped waves slapped at the wall and spilled freely over it. Occasional dull shapes glided among swaying leaves and stems.

Biting back a moment's unease, Nuela dived into the garden and glided along the harvest lanes.

She had bagged three tiny, spiral-shelled licatana when a harsh grating sound ripped through the water and she was suddenly sucked from the path and dragged across the growing beds. Staring down, too confused at first to seek the surface, she saw that the plantings no longer stood upright in the water. They lay almost flat against the sandy bottom. And the surface layers of the sand itself were boiling rapidly away, drawn in the same direction she was.

Nuela fought to the surface long enough to catch a strangling breath and to see—incredulously—that she was being drawn toward a breach in the far wall. Uncomprehending, she tried to fight her way back toward the inner garden wall. The force that carried her toward the opening was too strong. Drawn under again, she tumbled in the water, sand rising in clouds around her.

Briefly she touched bottom and was dragged through a flattened mat of vegetation. Desperately she clutched at a cluster of polipods. Instead of anchoring her against the current, the heavy stems ripped free and tumbled with her. Leaves wrapped themselves like wet fingers around her. She felt a sharp pain in her left arm, and she spilled through the breach in the wall into the sea.

But where was the sea? The gushing current of water from the garden threw her almost casually aside as it spread across the exposed seabed. Nuela lay stunned in a tangle of collapsed sea growth.

Sitting, coughing water and sand, she stared back at the reef wall—jagged, grey, exposed. Water rushed from a wide, irregular breach and spurted and sprayed from a dozen smaller breaks and crevices.

But it rushed into an empty seabed. The sea itself had drawn back, leaving behind tangled vegetation and stranded fish and marine creatures. A black-spined kaskas flopped convulsively. A milminesa lay shapeless among the flattened plants, its fragile external membranes unable to support the weight of its internal organs. Tiny shelled animals extended cautious sensors.

Nuela stood. Strangely, the thin stream of blood that ran down her arm felt colder than the water that dripped from her hair. She fingered the long gash in her upper arm, then jumped back with a gasp as the spreading water of the garden deposited a wriggling pispis at her feet. It lashed out with spiny legs, grappling at her ankle.

She shook it loose and retreated as the water of the outer garden continued to rush through the breach.

Finally, looking out across the empty seabed, Nuela began to understand where the sea had gone.

And, understanding, she knew that it would return. It would return in a very few minutes, taller and more destructive than she had ever seen it. It would return with such force that it would overrun the outer garden, the inner garden, the beach beyond. It would thrash at the main courtyard, knocking the wiskis shell from its pillar. Then it would pound at the lower floors of the palace itself, seeking prey. Whomever it caught, it would break.

The drowning wave was coming, and she stood in its path.

If she could climb the broken reef wall, fight her way back to the stile, reach the beach and then the palace before the crest struck . . .

She knew she could not. She had only minutes—two, perhaps three—before the water came rushing back and dashed her against the jagged reef.

Her first impulse was to huddle at the foot of the wall, her second to burrow into the sand. Her third—

She and Sinjanne had sometimes flushed shy dinadin from crevices in the inner garden wall. Desperately Nuela studied the length of the exposed outer reef wall. If she could find a cavity large enough to shelter in, if the drowning wave came and went before she drowned . . .

She knew it would not. The violence would last longer than she could possibly survive.

Still, when she spotted the first dark orifice, she ran toward it, slipping on wet leaves.

Her shoulders were too wide, the cavity too small. Nuela jumped up, listening for the thunder of the returning sea as she ran toward the next cavity.

The second cavity was barely wider than her body but, probing with one hand, she found that it widened and swelled upward into the wall of the reef. Nuela crouched and hunched her shoulders. Squeezing her eyes shut, she squirmed upward into the close, dark space.

The interior of the cavity was smooth, wide enough that Nuela was able to raise her arms from her sides and press them against the cold emptiness of her chest. She wondered, as she pulled her knees up and braced her feet, what her parents had thought of in their last moments. Had they thought of her? Of Sinjanne? Or had their minds simply flashed—as hers did now—with random images and impressions: the glint of sand at midday, the soft wail of the wiskis shell when the breeze rose from the sea, Lomaire's face rippling upon the surface of the midnight waters.

Nuela pressed hard fists against her chest and listened to the terror rush of blood in her ears. Soon the sound grew louder, and she knew she no longer listened to her own breath.

She drew a sobbing breath and held it as the sea howled back toward Aurlanis. Even hidden within the wall, she felt the slamming fury of its impact. Water drove into the small cavity with such force that it crushed the breath from her lungs. Half stunned, Nuela inhaled. Choking, flailing uselessly at the cavity wall, she was only distantly aware of the harsh grinding of reef rock as the drowning wave tore at the wall—and of the far louder rush and cry of the sea itself.

Her lungs were heavy. She tried to expel seawater but the heaviness did not ease. Crushing pressure grew within her skull. A white light appeared behind her eyes. It grew brighter, more intense—became pain as the rush of blood in her ears, the throb of her heart in her throat grew into a panic chant. Still struggling, she fell deep into herself—deep into darkness.

And then she stood upon a beach of fine white sand. It was night. A single large moon bathed the sand with silver light, and the air was warm, calm, fragrant. It touched her bare arms lightly, bringing the flesh to life.

She turned slowly, almost without willing it, and gazed in confusion at the shining white palace that rambled across the raised crest of the island. The perimeters of its wide courtyard were overgrown with vegetation, plants that stood tall and straight without the supporting presence of water. Nuela watched, wondering, as leaves and fronds swayed in the light breeze, casting moving shadows upon the sand.

A figure, tall, caped in black, stepped from the shadows and glided toward her. Nuela tried to retreat, but she had no command of her legs. A touch at her arm distracted her. She turned back to the sea—turned, again, without willing it.

The water was quiet. Silver ripples nibbled at the shore and withdrew with supple grace. As Nuela watched, a poorly defined patch of light brightened upon the water's surface near the horizon. She thought at first that it was the moon's reflection. But the moon remained in its place high in the sky, its silver face brightly distended, while the luminescence drifted toward her.

A light pressure at her back urged her toward the water.

*Heed now your waking dream, Chahera.* The words

came in a whisper, bodiless but compelling. *In our lives, there is a time to walk upon the land and a time to go upon the sea. For the one is solid and safe and offers a reassuring firmness to our feet, while the other is vast and fluid, presenting vistas and challenges that demand each last grain of our valor.*

*There is a time to feed the senses of the land, to offer them flavors and fragrances that can be found nowhere else. There is a time to taste the perfumes of wood smoke and honeyed blossoms, a time to hear the beat of drums against the warm night air, to dance upon the cool stone of the courtyard—to feel the full weight of our bodies and to take pleasure in that weight. There is a time to remember the places that we come from, the places that first formed us.*

*There is a time as well to feed the senses of the sea, to cast off the weight of our bodies and to reach for cool, dark depths. There is a time for loneliness, for silence, for danger, for these things make us strong.*

*Heed this above all: the one constant of life is change. The stars move in the sky. The water moves upon the sea. And you move always toward your next breath, your next heartbeat, your next horizon.*

*And so if you have been long upon the land, you must go now into the sea. And if you have been long in the sea, you must seek land.*

*Heed this lesson and come now upon your waking journey.*

Though her mind balked, Nuela's feet heeded the whispered command, carrying her forward. Silver, cool, the water reached her knees, her thighs, her navel. Lying forward, surrendering her weight, she moved without effort toward the brightness.

It took form slowly. First she saw a pair of half-inflated sacs lying upon the surface of the water, glowing with a brilliance that matched the moon's. Suspended between them she saw a dark, smooth-fleshed body. As she drew near, she distinguished a knobbed spine, a broad tail fluke, and the glint of recessed eyes hovering just above the surface of the water.

The creature was large, its body many times longer, many times bulkier than her own. Curiosity and the dream carried her near. Reaching the trailing edge of one partially inflated sac, Nuela drifted downward through the brightly lit water and approached the creature's white underside.

The creature settled slightly and regarded her with lightly filmed eyes. They were dark, depthless, completely dispassionate, but when Nuela stroked the creature's smooth underside, she knew its shivering response signalled pleasure. And when one sac parted slightly from the creature's body wall and a broad, flat flipper reached to gently guide her into the opening, she did not resist—though she did wonder.

Was this how her dying mind saw death? As a dark creature that invited her into a place of light?

But if the creature represented death, why did the touch of her fingers give it pleasure?

Confused, Nuela found herself first in a small, membranous cell. From there she passed through a second opening into the sac itself. She emerged on her stomach, her arms at her sides. Rippling, the sac quickly contracted to fit itself to the shape of her body. The air within the sac was moist, its scent faintly oily.

Then they were moving through the water, Nuela folded securely against the creature's side. She drew exploring fingertips across the interior surface of the sac. The sac's luminescence was directed almost entirely outward, lighting the water through which they passed. The interior of the sac was dim, its inner surface warm and slightly rough.

The creature left the water's surface, sliding deep into the sea. Baffled marine creatures were caught briefly in its light, then vanished into the surrounding darkness.

Although the sac did not distend again, Nuela breathed easily.

From somewhere a distant, rhythmic reverberation reached her, jarring softly through the tissues of her body—the creature's heartbeat. She closed her eyes, pressing close to the creature's flesh, and after a while her own heart slowed to meet the creature's slower, deeper rhythm.

She did not know how long she slept in the cradling sac. Nor did she know what woke her. But one moment she rocked in the warmth of the sac—and the next she was curled again in the reef wall, water flooding her mouth and nostrils.

Her eyes flew open upon darkness. A moment's disorientation and then, panicked, she clawed her way from the cavity and kicked to the surface. She vomited seawater, choking, coughing, fighting to suck air into water-logged lungs. Her eyes stung. Her flesh was numb, her hands and feet so cold they ached.

When finally she breathed freely again, she peered around. It was night. The sea was still. Beyond the arc reef, torchlight burned from the tower. Stunned, uncomprehending—what had happened to the afternoon? how had she survived the wave?—Nuela stared at the distant flames. Then, because she could not think what else to do, she swam toward them.

She passed through the rent in the outer reef wall. The sea washed into the outer garden and broke upon the inner wall. She climbed the stile on quivering legs and slid into the shallower water of the inner garden.

She swam until the water became shallow. Then she walked on legs so weak they trembled. She paused occasionally, lying back in the water to rest. At last she reached the shore, her body so heavy she could no longer stand. She slumped to the damp sand and lay with her arms outstretched, staring at the stars in uncomprehending shock.

She did not understand. She did not understand at all. She had taken seawater into her lungs, and reality had turned away. Now it had turned back, but the face it wore was alien. The drowning wave had come and the drowning wave had gone. She was alive and nothing in her experience told her why.

Her eyes closed. For a long time she thought of nothing at all.

# Chapter Three

THE MOONS STOOD NEAR THE HORIZON WHEN NUELA shivered back to awareness. Unsteadily she took her feet. Her legs were stronger; but her ears rang, her throat was raw, and her shift clung to her in damp strings. Her hair was stiff with sand.

She hardly saw the litter of uprooted vegetation, cast-off shells, and exoskeletons on the beach as she made her way to the courtyard. Sand and debris had already been swept into heaps, but the pale tiles were gritty underfoot. Nuela met no one as she approached the small side courtyard that held the spring pool.

The wave had driven sand and debris over the low pool wall, silting the tile floor. A small school of oso swept in from the sea darted nervously among suspended shreds of vegetation. A single ra-meki swam at the far end of the pool, its long, thin body vividly patterned with scarlet stripes.

Nuela stripped off her torn shift and lowered herself into the pool. The cold water shocked her senses briefly to life, making cuts sting and bruises ache. She bathed cursorily, then emerged and stood dripping on the gritty tiles.

Except for the torches in the tower, no light burned in the palace. Somewhere someone cried quietly as

Nuela made her way down empty halls. Even the shell-chimes that normally sang in every window were still.

It was not until she reached her own room and stood staring at two bare bedmats that fear closed cold fingers on her throat. *Where was Sinjanne?*

Nuela turned to the window. Lomaire lingered above the western horizon, her golden face tarnished by thin clouds. Tuanne had almost closed the distance between them. Tomorrow night the sea trail would open. She would go to the beach to watch for Sinjanne's return.

But would Sinjanne return? There was no palace on the Nipple. She knew just that much—no more. Did any point of the cone itself stand above reach of the drowning wave? Nuela stepped from the window, pulled on a loose gown, and turned tensely back.

Then she was in the corridor, her bare feet slapping the cold floor. Delfinne could not speak of her kalinerre. But surely she could at least tell Nuela if there was any place on the Nipple where Sinjanne could have hidden.

Nuela hesitated at the door, afraid at the last moment of what she might learn. If there was no safe place, if the sea had taken her . . . Tense, anxious, she slipped across the dim room and dropped to her knees beside her friend's mat.

With a start, she realized that Delfinne peered up at her with wide, sleepless eyes, her face puffy and discolored, her cheeks wet. Nuela caught a sharp breath and glanced toward the smaller mat where Belina slept. It was empty.

Nor did Allinarde sleep at Delfinne's side.

"Not—not both of them," Nuela whispered, disbelieving. "Delfinne, not both."

Delfinne blinked fresh tears from her eyes. "Both of them, Nuela. Bel went to play in the morning pool. When the water drew back, Allinarde ran to get her. But it came too soon. The wave came too soon. I saw it from the window. I was in the workroom on the fourth floor, and I saw it. Nuela—'' Sitting, she pressed her face against Nuela's shoulder, her arms tightening around her. ''What will I do without them? What will I do, Nuela?''

Nuela stroked her hair, stricken. ''You'll go on,'' she said, but the words reassured her friend no more than they reassured her. How could they be gone? She had seen Belina playing in the sand only the day before. She stared at the empty mats, stunned, then threw herself down beside Delfinne and held her, patting and stroking her while she sobbed convulsively. After a while, Delfinne quieted into sleep.

Nuela lay wide-eyed beside her, bruised, sore, alive for no reason she could name. Alive and torn with worry, disbelief, grief. If the sea had snatched Allinarde and Belina from the very sands of Aurlanis, how could Sinjanne be safe?

She must have slept because she woke with a start and saw sunlight at the window. Delfinne slept heavily beside her, frowning in her sleep. Sitting, Nuela stared down at her friend's ravaged face, and the raw force of her own fear rose hot and sour in her throat.

Slipping from the mat, returning to her own chamber, she stood at the window, staring down over the courtyard. The wiskis shell was gone, the pillar it had stood upon a broken stub. No children perched on the courtyard wall. Nor did they play at the edges of the water. A few adults moved along the beach sorting debris into piles. Heads bobbed in the inner garden, but no one swam in the breached outer garden.

Footsteps approached the door. ''Nuela?'' Coranne, Polamaire's runner, stared at her in surprise, pushing straying hair from her forehead. ''Your room was reported empty when we made count last night. We thought you were lost until Wilarde saw you standing here." She frowned at Nuela's lacerated arm, at her bruised legs.

Startled, Nuela stepped from the window. "No, I've been here. I was—I was on the lower floor when the wave came. The water caught me on the stair and threw me against the wall." How could she tell anyone what had really happened? "I should have gone down to help after I changed, but I fell asleep. I—"

"No, no, Polamaire sent everyone who was hurt directly to quarters. If we had known you were here, Elfina would have come to you when she made her rounds. Polamaire wants to speak with you in quarters, but you'll want Elfina to bind your arm first."

Polamaire wanted to see her? Would the keeper summon her if there were good news? Her heart beat an anxious rhythm in her throat. "No, I washed the cut myself. It doesn't need binding."

"Immediately then," Coranne said. She lingered, the moment's sympathy in her glance impaling Nuela, driving away her breath, then stepped into the corridor.

Nuela's hands clenched, nails biting the palms. Did Polamaire know already what had happened to Sinjanne, to the others?

If they had returned safely, Sinjanne would be sleeping on her mat.

Nuela forced herself to draw a deep breath, to release it. Cold, rigid, she drew on a fresh shift and stepped into the corridor.

People spoke as she passed. Blind to them, deaf, she did not respond.

The keeper's quarters were located on the northern wall at the top of the palace. Nuela entered stiffly, as if her legs rebelled against carrying her there. Polamaire stood at the window gazing down the bare black slope of the spill-cone. "Keeper," Nuela said, her voice thin.

Tall, unsmiling, the keeper turned. Her greying hair was freshly braided and her gown crisp from the laundry, but her dark eyes were deeply shadowed, the flesh beneath them crumpled and discolored.

Nuela recoiled from the piercing bitterness she met in the keeper's eyes. She licked her lips. "Coranne said you wanted to see me."

Polamaire glanced briefly back at the spill-cone and then paced across the chamber. The keeper's quarters were as sparsely furnished as any in the palace. There was a low table, padded mats arranged beside it, a bed-mat in one corner, a long, low wiregrass chest. The room was still, completely innocent of the sounds of wind and water.

Nuela glanced toward the window and caught a sharp breath. When she had last visited the keeper's quarters, a long double strand of shell-chimes had chattered at the window. Today the chimes were gone. "Rinarde—Rinarde was in the garden when the wave came," she said, stricken. Rinarde, Polamaire's only child, her own self-appointed guardian—and she had forgotten.

"He was in the garden and now he is gone. The wave was not so lenient with him as with you."

Nuela recoiled. "No," she said, unwilling to believe. "I was in the palace when the wave came. It caught me on the staircase. I—" She bit her lip, her grief sharp, bitter. Rinarde had warned her of the water, and it had taken him instead. If she had stayed to talk, if she had been with him when the outer wall broke . . .

She could have done nothing. They would have turned back to the beach together, but neither of them would have reached the palace before the wave struck.

Belina, Allinarde, now Rinarde.

Polamaire shook her head. "No, don't make a story of it. You were not here. Several people saw you go to the garden shortly before the wave struck. No one saw you return. And you were not in your quarters when we took the count last night."

"I—"

"I explored the reef wall myself when I was young. There are dozens of cavities large enough to shelter in. I tested myself there without even knowing what I did, long before my tile was drawn. Now you have tested yourself. If I had let you go to the Nipple the first year you were eligible—"

"Let me go?" Nuela said in confusion. She had tested herself? By hiding in a cavity in the garden wall? And if Polamaire had *let* her go to the Nipple . . .

Only chance governed when she would go to the Nipple. "My tile has never been drawn. I dropped it in the basket five years ago."

"Yes, and I culled it out and set it aside. I did not return it to the basket until this morning."

"But—why?" Nuela demanded, astonished. "I could have gone with Delfinne and Challa. I could have gone in my first year."

"Yes, but neither Delfinne nor Challa left behind a young sister with no other family. Sinjanne needed you. There were people who would have taken her for the period between conjunctions, if I had let you go. But kalinerre is forever if you do not return."

Nuela stared at her, stunned. "Keeper, I would never have left Sinjanne to grow up alone. Whatever care I had to take, whatever precautions, I would have come back. I—"

Polamaire's expression, the slow shake of her head silenced Nuela. "Care? Precautions? What have your friends told you about kalinerre? What have they told you about the testing?"

"They have told me exactly what they were sworn to tell." Nothing.

"You respected their silence?"

"What was I to ask them?" Nuela's hands tightened, nails crimped to her palms. "Please, is there shelter on the Nipple? Is there a place where Sinjanne and the others could have hidden from the wave?''

Slowly Polamaire shook her head. ''No. If your sister was on the Nipple when the wave struck, she was swept to sea.''

*If* she was on the Nipple? ''But—where else could she have been?''

Polamaire met her eyes with a slowly narrowing gaze. ''That I cannot tell you. I took the same vow your friends took: not to speak here of what passes beyond our own near-waters. But I can tell you that there are other places than Aurlanis and other people than our own. If Sinjanne was in one of those places, she may have survived. If she was not—'' The keeper turned back to the window, her broad shoulders taut. She stared down the black flank of the spill-cone.

Other places? Other people? Nuela shook her head, confused, angry at her confusion. ''If she was not in one of those places—then she is dead.''

Polamaire turned back. She studied Nuela, level-eyed, silent. ''I did not say that. There are a dozen things that may have happened, a dozen ways she and the others may have survived the wave. But they will never return to Aurlanis if we don't take the correct steps from this point. There are terms, conditions—I cannot leave Aurlanis now. We lost more than seventy people to the wave. I must stay to call the last chants. If Aliapara were here—''

But she was not. The second keeper had drowned earlier in the year, and no one had yet taken her robes.

Polamaire shook her head impatiently. ''I must call the chants myself. But if I do not get a message to the schools before year's end—'' She stepped across the room and took the candidates' basket from the table. Without ceremony, she drew a single tile and extended it to Nuela. ''You began your kalinerre when you tested yourself against the wave. Now you must take the sea trail when it opens tonight and carry my message to whomever you meet.

"Tell him this: these young people are not findings, and they are not to be treated as such. Even though they were unable to return to Aurlanis at the time prescribed, they are to be given free choice, and they are to be permitted to make their choice with land beneath their feet. I expect the intent of the pacts to be observed even though the circumstances are exceptional."

Nuela accepted the tile she had cut so many years before and turned it in cold fingers. "No one goes to Pahla's Nipple at the last conjunction of the year."

"No. And I would not send you if it could wait. If you prefer not to complete the testing, you can invoke the messenger's privilege and return to Aurlanis once you have delivered my message. But I think . . ." Polamaire studied Nuela, a long, deliberate gaze. Slowly she shook her head.

Denying what? Nuela stared at the keeper, at her unbetraying face. Finally she said, "Who do you expect me to meet?" Who—on a deserted spill-cone somewhere in the sea? *Other people.*

Polamaire shook her head.

"Then—what are the pacts?" With whom had they been made? Why had Nuela never heard of them before?

Again Polamaire shook her head. Her gaze remained level, fixed.

"So I'm to go alone and if I meet someone, I'm to give him a message I don't understand. I—"

"That is precisely what you are to do. And if you are wise, you will not challenge yourself unduly along the way. Aurlanis becomes small when you leave its near-waters. The dreams are far more compelling upon the open sea."

Stiffening, Nuela met the keeper's eyes. "You have

had the same dream I had," she realized. "The beach, the light on the water—" The great, dark creature.

"I have had that dream. And others."

"You have lived when you should have drowned."

"I have lived."

And, Nuela recognized, she did not intend to betray anything more. She intended only to stand waiting for Nuela's response.

Nuela drew a deep breath, consciously setting aside anger and confusion, trying to think with absolute clarity. There was only one possible answer, no matter how poorly she understood the consequences of it. "I will go." But not as a candidate and not as a messenger, although she would carry Polamaire's message. She would go to find Sinjanne.

Polamaire did not seem surprised by her answer. She nodded. "Then I will meet you at the mouth of the trail tonight and tell you how to find the Nipple. If you choose to complete your kalinerre, you may return at the next conjunction or anytime before. Should you remain beyond the boundary of our near-waters past the day of conjunction, you will be entered into the keeper's log as drowned and you may not put foot to our shore again. By the terms of the pacts, only the keeper and her second may come and go freely from Aurlanis."

Nuela drew a sharp breath. She would be entered as drowned? When she had survived the wave? "Keeper— how do you know that Rinarde is dead? How do you know . . ." That he had not simply been swept to sea? That he would not return later just as she had? Tired, water-logged—living.

Polamaire's eyes glinted. She turned sharply away, her voice flat. "I do not need to see his body to know that Rinarde is dead. There is no question."

So some people could survive an ordeal like hers and others could not. And if Sinjanne was no more vulnerable to drowning than she was, then it did not matter that there was no shelter on the Nipple. She could well be alive.

But alive where? *Places other than Aurlanis.* What kinds of places? Inhabited by what kinds of peoples? Nuela clenched her fists, trying to control an inner tremor.

Polamaire stepped to the table and opened a tiled box. She removed an object that hung from a lanyard of braided twine. "Wear this. It will verify the authority of your message."

Nuela accepted the object with unsteady fingers. It was of a hard, smooth silver material she had not seen before, close-grained and lustrous. It lay lightly upon the palm of her hand, flat and square, a quarter the thickness of her small finger. A rectangle and two round holes had been cut through it. "What is it?"

"It came ashore during a storm when my great-grandmother was young. I wear it when I leave our near-waters. It is recognized as my device."

Nodding, Nuela slid the lanyard over her head and tucked the object inside her shift. She glanced up again, wanting to question the keeper further, knowing there would be no answers.

Polamaire's gaze was steady, weighing. "You must rest today," she said finally. "And you must tell no one where you are bound. I will instruct the families that they are not to wait at the mouth of the trail tonight."

So at least Nuela could slip away down the trail unobserved. She already felt a profound unease. By the time the tides fell, fear would sit plainly upon her face. "Thank you."

"Tonight then."

Reluctantly Nuela withdrew. She hesitated in the corridor, not prepared to return to the solitude of her room, not ready to confront Sinjanne's empty bedmat again. Impulsively she turned to the tower staircase.

The tower was deserted. Its six broad apertures looked upon the water in every direction. Nuela turned from window to window, Polamaire's device cold against her chest. Wide sand beaches, bright morning sun, rocking sea of silver, violet, and green . . .

Sinjanne was lost there somewhere. And in just one day everything had changed. She had learned the answers to questions she had never thought to ask. Other questions, harder, more perplexing, had been raised in their place. Rinarde, Allinarde, and Belina were gone, snatched without warning.

Nothing was as she had thought. Yet beyond the tower windows, the sea had not changed at all.

# Chapter Four

NIGHT, WHEN IT CAME, HAD THE QUALITY OF DREAM: detached, episodic, undirected. Briefly the last light stained the western horizon, and the images of day were replaced by the softer images of dusk, then night. Nuela watched from her chamber window as Tuanne glided slowly across Lomaire's golden face. Coranne had brought the candidate's sash shortly before dinner. Nuela braided her hair and bound the braid but left the sash where it lay. She was not a candidate. Not in any real sense.

Three hours after sunset, the moons stood near perfect conjunction. Nuela left her chamber then and felt nothing, not even surprise at the profoundness of the numbness that had settled upon her with night.

The palace stood strangely silent, mobiles and wind chimes stripped from every window. The corridors were deserted. Families, groups of friends had withdrawn to chambers to tell long bittersweet stories of the dead. Nuela met no one as she crossed the courtyard and made her way down the beach past the protecting curve of the arc reef.

The trail mouth had not yet emerged from the tide. Nuela sat at the edge of the water, letting it taste her toes, stroke her calves, flutter foamy fingers at her thighs. This was not the tamed water of the walled gardens. This was the open sea, and although it was quiet tonight, it caught at the beach, making sand shift and spill.

Eventually the rhythmic touch of the water lulled her into a nodding sleep. When she shivered awake, the moons sat near the horizon and the sea trail lay open before her, a fragile ribbon of naked, wet sand leading out into the sea. Glancing back toward the palace, she saw Polamaire descend the courtyard steps. Her throat constricting, Nuela stood.

At another time, another mood upon her, she might have listened with tightly focused attention to Polamaire's directions. Tonight she heard them with bowed head, a stunned frown on her face. When finally Polamaire fell silent, Nuela turned and gazed down the exposed trail, and for the first time since the sun had set, she felt the full force of fear. It struck at her chest and made her heart leap and then pause. She licked her lips.

"It is almost year's end," Polamaire said. "There are—things that happen in school waters at this time of year, but my message cannot wait. If you would like me to repeat my directions—"

"No, I'll remember." The trail would lie exposed until sunrise. Following it, she would eventually find herself upon a wide bar of sand that would stand above the water even after the tide rose again. She was to sleep there until noon. Then she must walk eastward into the sea again. When the water reached her chin, she was to loose herself upon the current and let it carry her to Pahla's Nipple. Reluctantly Nuela met the keeper's eyes.

"Remember that you leave our near-waters under the terms of the pacts. If you do not return before the next conjunction, you cannot return at all."

"I—understand," Nuela said, understanding only that she could not return until she found Sinjanne.

But *there*—in all the vastness of the sea? She drew a long, aching breath and turned quickly to the trail that led eastward into the darkness of the sea.

The sea trail was little more than a wavering track of sand exposed by the steeply fallen tide. The restless rush of the water drowned the slighter sound of Nuela's feet against packed sand as she started down the trail. Walking briskly, then running, she did not turn to look back until her breath came short.

The palace had already grown small. Polamaire stood at the edge of the water, a bowed figure.

Nuela ran again, until a sharp pain caught her in the side. She paused, one hand pressed to her abdomen, and gazed back again. The keeper had vanished, as had the bulk of the palace. Only torchlight remained, floating above the water. Nuela's footprints stretched in a distinct line behind her, disappearing into the darkness.

Frozen, she watched as Lomaire's upper rim slowly subsided beneath the horizon. Then she turned and ran again, starlight guiding her.

Night no longer held the quality of dream. She had passed beyond the near-waters. She ran along a twisting, elongated ridge of sand—what held it there, above the fallen water?—the sea rocking restlessly at either side. Fear shortened her breath. Desperately Nuela narrowed her attention, focusing upon the shining paleness of the path, upon the pumping of her legs, upon the impact of bare feet against wet sand. Even when she paused to catch her breath, she sent her thoughts racing ahead.

She would find Sinjanne. She would bring her home.

Once, from the corner of her eye, she thought she glimpsed the surge of pale bodies in the sea. She halted, suppressing an involuntary cry, and stared across the water. She saw nothing except the sea itself.

She saw nothing, yet she dared not glance toward the water again. Head low, Nuela bolted down the trail.

When finally the trail widened and she found herself running upon dry sand, she threw herself down.

She was alone on the wide sandbar to which Polamaire had directed her. She saw no moving paleness beyond an occasional spilling wave. Embarrassed, Nuela sat. Shoulders hunched, arms barricading her chest, she watched until she saw the first brightening of dawn at the horizon.

The tide had begun to rise again. She retreated to a point where the water could not reach her. After a while, the steadiness of the rising waves lulled her and her head dropped to her bent knees.

She woke slowly, sunlight warming her face, the sound of the sea near. Stretching, she opened her eyes and started fully awake. The sun stood directly overhead.

She stood, brushing sand from her shift, and turned in a full circle. The sea trail had vanished. She stood upon a long, narrow crest of sand. To her east and to her west, the sea itself lay little more than a hundred paces from where she stood.

The surface of the sea itself was featureless. Nuela licked her lips, pulling the device Polamaire had given her from her shift. Clasping it in one hand, she returned to the water, walking eastward. Sand spilled between her toes, wet and fine.

By the time the water reached her shoulders, she could no longer see the sandbar. Nuela pulled up her feet and frowned as the current moved her back toward the sandbar. Had she misunderstood Polamaire's directions? She extended her feet, gazing back in the direction she had come.

Again, from the corner of one eye, she saw a surging body in the water. She turned, her pulse leaping with alarm.

There was a sharp tug at her knees, and suddenly she was beneath the surface of the water. She struggled, trying to strike out, but her arms were caught and drawn sharply back. She uttered a gurgling protest and water flooded her mouth and nose. She doubled forward, trying to wrench free—instead simply taking in more water. She struck the bottom on bent knees, sand rising in clouds. With fierce effort, she half turned in her attacker's grasp.

For a moment his face wavered before her in the cloudy water, and its familiarity startled her into numbed confusion. She shook her head, trying to clear the growing pressure. Then her assailant's features vanished in the sudden explosion of light within her skull. Her blood, her heart beat a rushing chant in her ears.

And she stood upon a beach of fine white sand. It was daylight. A sun slightly smaller, slightly brighter than the sun she knew stood overhead. A blanched white crescent moon drifted near the horizon. The sand had a slow, winking glitter, as if the grains shifted fitfully to expose alternating facets to the sun. Slowly Nuela turned.

The palace stood blazing white at the raised crest of the island, the plants that bordered the courtyard starkly green. Blossoms—scarlet, yellow, white—glowed against strange, stiff foliage. The vegetation cast shadows that lay upon the white sand as if painted there, crisp and distinct. As Nuela watched, a tall figure cloaked in black emerged from the shadows and glided toward her.

*Concern for our resources is the living bond that joins us. For each of us, for all of us* . . . The voice, again, was whispering, bodiless.

Nuela fought with failing limbs against her assailant. Forcing her eyes open, she twisted and stared into sandgold eyes. He recoiled slightly, then spun her in the water and forced her flat on her back against the sandy bottom. He knelt over her, meeting her waning struggles with a clinical frown.

*As important to us as any resource, more closely allied to us than any other creature . . .*

*. . . these great beasts, these leviathans who bear us willingly across the deep basins of the sea . . .*

The words continued raggedly, drawing Nuela into the dream. The dark-cloaked figure had advanced to stand directly before her. Helplessly she stared into the pallor of his face, into the piercing black of his eyes. Her own face, strangely distorted, peered back at her from the glistening surfaces of his pupils.

His brow was high and vaulted, bisected by a single deep vertical crease. Black hair swept back from his forehead in a full, coarse mane and shone against the black of his cloak. His brows were steeply arched, his lips full. They did not move as he began to speak.

LISTEN, CHAHERA, FOR I AM NEPTILIS, WHO HAS TAKEN YOU FROM THE CONTINENTS WHERE DEATH SETS DOWN HEAVY BOOTS AND FREED YOU TO THE SEA. I AM NEPTILIS, FATHER OF YOUR RACE, ALTHOUGH NOTHING OF MY BLOOD IS IN YOU. INSTEAD, I HAVE BESTOWED UPON YOU THE MORE POTENT HERITAGE OF MY VISION AND MY EXPERTISE. His voice was deep, as black as his eyes, as full as his mane.

CALL ME GOD IF YOU WILL. I HAVE NAMED MYSELF FOR A GOD. OR CALL ME SIMPLY HE WHO HAS SHAPED YOU TO GO ON IN A CHANGED WORLD.

LISTEN, FOR I AM NEPTILIS, AND THESE THINGS HAVE I GIVEN YOU:

BODIES ONCE SUITABLE ONLY TO WALK UPON THE LAND, ALTERED NOW TO MEET THE DEMANDS OF THE SEA.

GREAT MOON-BEASTS, ALTERED FROM THEIR ORIGINAL FORM, TO BEAR YOU IN SAFETY WHEN YOU GO UPON THE WATERS.

LIVING DREAMS, CAREFULLY CRAFTED INSTINCTS THAT SPEAK ALOUD TO GUIDE YOU.

THE INNOCENCE OF A PEOPLE BORN NEW.

HEED THE DREAMS THAT I HAVE GIVEN YOU AND YOU
WILL KNOW WHAT THINGS YOU MUST DO.

HEED THE WISDOM OF THE DREAMS AND CARRY THE
BANNER OF NEW LIFE PROUDLY WITH YOU. AND TO ANY
WHO ASK, SAY THIS: WE ARE THE CHAHERA; THE SEA
IS OUR MOTHER, NEPTILIS OUR FATHER.

For a moment longer, Nuela stared into her own distorted face. Then the tall figure drew heavy lids over
his reflective pupils and was gone. Leadenly Nuela
turned and peered back toward the palace. Neptilis
stood again in the shadows, his black cloak flaring
around him.

*Concern for our resources is the living bond that joins
us,* the whispering voice said again. *For each of us, for
all of us, the concern is the same. None can be excused
from the imperative that bids us never to waste and
never to lay waste. For all the sea is sacred, as is the
land that rises from its ancient beds. We will enjoy its
riches only as long as we respect and conserve those
same riches.*

*Primary among the directives we live by is this: in
our lives there is a time to walk upon the land and a
time to go upon the sea. For there is fragility in both
places, and we risk abuse by remaining overlong in any
place. Dependence upon the environment too swiftly
becomes overdependence. Familiarity breeds the con-
tempt of attempted mastery. We cannot permit ourselves
this fallacy, for we are not made to be masters of land
or sea. We are made only to be masters of ourselves.*

*As important to us as any resource, more closely al-
lied to us than any other creature, it is the lucticete that
enables us to go as we must from place to place. These
great beasts, these moon-whales who bear us willingly
across the deep basins of the sea . . .*

Briefly Nuela opened her eyes and gazed up at her
captor. He no longer restrained her. She lay on her back

on the sandy bottom and he hung above her, grasping her wrists lightly. Again she was struck by the confusing familiarity of his features. Before she could do more than frown, the whispering voice drew her back.

She turned at its instruction and saw the great beast that came on the sea. By daylight its distended sacs were opaquely white. The dark body that lay between them was even larger and darker than it had appeared before. It drew near the shore, and this time Nuela did not have to be urged into the surf.

She swam to the creature and dived beneath it. Two impassive eyes regarded her. Tentatively Nuela stroked the smooth white belly and the eyes closed. A single flipper reached to guide her toward the open sac.

Once she had entered, the creature drew most of the air from the sac, folding Nuela to its underside. She lay quietly, and after a few moments the creature's great heart began to beat in her own chest.

Shuddering, the creature slid away into the daylit sea. They glided at first in the bright surface waters. Startled sea creatures hung before them, then vanished. Others, more curious than frightened, leaped aside and then wheeled to study them. None of the creatures they saw were familiar to Nuela.

Then they passed into the deeper water and daylight drowned behind them. Sometimes the creature's sacs glowed, lighting the water around them as if it had drawn moonlight to the depths. Other times they moved in a darkness broken only by fleeting patches of phosphorescence. Vivid streaks of color flared briefly before them and winked out. Occasionally Nuela looked out into a pair of glowing eyes.

*These great beasts who rise like moons from the night waters, these leviathans who bear us so willingly on their journeys and migrations, require little beyond our friendship and occasional protection against the sea's more vicious predators. In this we enter into surrogacy*

*with them. They serve as nurturing parents to us, we
as protecting parents to them, each of us as affectionate
child to the other.*

*Behave toward the lucticete as you would toward be-
loved human kin. Express your affection in ways that
give pleasure. Offer care and protection as required.
And accept graciously the gifts offered in return.*

*Do not attempt to assert mastery. You are not the
intended master of the lucticetes, nor is the lucticete
master to you. If there is any master, it is Neptilis, and
his bidding is that you heed the dreams he has given
us.*

*Live then the dreams. . . .*

But the lucticete held her too closely to its beating
heart. The warm, moist air within the sac was sopo-
rific. Nuela was only faintly aware of the slow march
of images and instructions as she drifted into sleep.

She woke in slow confusion, bobbing alone on the
quiet water. Opening her eyes, she gazed up vacantly
at the late afternoon sun and waited for voice or heartbeat to summon her back into the dream. When neither
came, she rolled over in the water and took her feet.

She stood just fifty paces from a sparse black beach.
The blunt spill-cone that rose from the beach did not
stand even as tall as the first floor of the palace on
Aurlanis. Someone had cut irregular steps into the
cone's flank, leading to its low, cratered summit.

Nuela glanced back toward the open sea and saw
nothing. Frowning, she stepped from the water and
paced the sandy beach. It took her only minutes to
completely circle the projecting cone.

So she had found Pahla's Nipple—small, desolate,
barely tall enough to stand above the water when the
tide came high. If there had been anything to mark
Sinjanne's presence here, it had been swept away by
the drowning wave. There was only rock and sand—
and the sea beyond.

And somewhere there was a man who bore a startling resemblance to Rinarde. A man who had deliberately held her under the water. Nuela reached to touch the device Polamaire had given her. It no longer hung at her neck.

Disturbed, she pulled back her hand—and stared, startled, at the inner wrist. It was marked with three irregular scarlet stripes. The other wrist held the same pattern. Nuela rubbed the marks with a fingertip. There was no pain, no raising or thickening of the skin. The scarlet did not rub away.

Nuela stared for a long time at the pattern on her wrists. Then, thoughtfully, she climbed the flank of the cone. She glanced briefly into the dark water that filled its crater, then looked out over the sea again.

Were there really great animals called lucticetes living there? Was there really a people called the Chahera, created by a man named Neptilis? And the candidates who failed to return each year—had they been lost? Or had they gone away with the lucticetes?

But if there were moon-whales in the sea, why had she never seen them? And why—she frowned—had the sky of her dreams held just one large white moon?

Each question raised another. Nuela pressed her stomach, suddenly hungry.

There were no reef gardens and no netting pool to forage from. Approaching the water cautiously, going no farther from the beach than necessary, Nuela browsed through the scattered bottom growth for edible stems and pods. Once a linsofi the size of her hand drifted past, fat and succulent. She snatched at it instinctively, then released it, realizing she had no appetite for raw meat.

Later, when the sun stood near the horizon, Nuela stood and made a restless circuit of the spill-cone. Had Polamaire released her tile five years earlier, she would have come to Pahla's Nipple not to find Sinjanne but to meet her own kalinerre. She would have come to be tested. But for what? Her ability to withstand drowning? Her ability to dream?

Or for her ability to learn from the dreams?

*If there is any master, it is Neptilis, and his bidding is that you heed the dreams.*

Nuela made another circuit of the spill-cone, her tongue pressed between her teeth. She did not know how to find her way back to Aurlanis. She did not know how to find Sinjanne. But she knew how to find the dreams.

And dreaming, she would ride again at the lucticete's heart.

She felt a stir of excitement at the prospect. She waited, tense, not completely decided, until the sun had set. Then, when pale-capped waves rolled restlessly out of a dark sea, she entered the surf and stretched out against the water.

Her hands struck something smooth and hard. She jumped up, shook water from her face, and dropped to her knees in the surf. Peering through the shallow water, she saw a dark object resting on the sand. It had the size, the shape of a human body at rest, legs extended, arms at its side. The head was smoothly contoured into the bulk of the shoulders. The object seemed to be made of some opaque material. Yet moonlight showed her that it bore human features. She stared at the face floating indistinctly so near her own. It was male, with dark brows, deep-set eyes, lips slightly parted.

She reached to touch it, but her fingers struck a smooth, transparent surface. She drew back, puzzled.

And saw an indistinct phosphorescence gliding across the surface of the water. Nuela came quickly to her feet, her heart leaping.

The dully glowing form was not large enough, not brilliant enough to be a lucticete. She watched with held breath anyway as the paleness approached, resolving into a series of dully glowing objects, each borne upon the outstretched hands of a single person.

Six people stepped from the sea bearing glowing bladders—led by a seventh who paced ceremonially through the shallow surf toward Nuela. He halted a dozen paces from where she stood, arms extended from his waist, his gaze direct, concentrated.

"Rinarde," Nuela said softly. But that could not be. Was not.

Because even by the failing light she could see that the man who stood before her slowly raising his arms, palms upturned, was older and taller than Rinarde. His bare chest was patterned with stripes, the color indistinct. His eyes held Nuela's as he began to chant.

He spoke alone, spoke so quietly his voice was little more than a whisper against the louder voice of the sea. The syllables he uttered unfolded with easy rhythm, falling into phrases, into lines and stanzas, finally into one long song. Caught, Nuela shivered with uncomprehending anticipation.

When the chant ended, Nuela found she had stepped toward the singer. Found that her own arms had risen from her sides. They floated before her, palms upturned, displaying the scarlet pattern on her wrists.

The man inclined his head, briefly freeing her from his spell. Nuela drew a long breath, numbed and shaken by the power of his chant, and peered past him at the six people who stood ranked behind him, glowing bladders in their outstretched hands. If he was the head of some great ceremonial beast, she saw, his followers were the ribs that supported the body of the beast. The glowing bladders formed the lucticete's luminous sacs.

He raised his head, his eyes recapturing hers, and began to chant again. The others joined him, and this time, as the long song unfolded against the rush of the sea, Nuela heard what she had only dimly perceived the first time: the beat of a great heart. Her own heart first rushed ahead, then slowed to meet the rhythm of that other, larger heart.

She felt a great warmth. She tasted a familiar scent. The leader of the group paced backward, leading her into the rib cage of the beast. Because now it *was* a beast. The leader's chant made it so, and it opened and took her to its side.

Took her. Enfolded her. Cradled her. She did not resist until the last moment, when she rebelled blindly against the enveloping power of the chant. She had come into the water to dream. This was no dream. This was something else—some ritual she did not understand, some ceremony she had not consented to.

She had come to find Sinjanne, not to be carried away in a fantasy beast made of sea findings and human flesh.

She struggled, but the pounding of the great heart possessed her. Slowly the fantasy beast withdrew into the sea, bearing Nuela with it, lost in its glow.

# Chapter Five

THE FANTASY BEAST COURSED THROUGH THE SEA, CAR-
rying Nuela on a journey as real as the beast itself—a
journey that had the power and conviction of truth, if
not the substance.

They traveled first in the open water, sometimes
alone, sometimes in the company of shining silver creatures that leaped and spun joyously in their wake. When
the sun shone, rainbows of tiny fish darted in the upper
layers of the water. When only the moon shone—the
single large moon—quizzical eyes peered cautiously
from the silvered water and then vanished. Once a company of creatures with bodies like large, iridescent tear-
drops jumped in quick succession from the water,
creating a living arch.

The spell that grew from the chant was complete,
enveloping. Nuela felt the texture of flesh against her
bare arm. She heard the rush of the moon-beast's
breath. The slow, jarring beat of its heart was her own.

They passed through the living arch and, after a
while, glided in slow review past a series of islands.
People gathered on wide white beaches, talking, playing, performing small tasks. They paused and raised
their hands in greeting, exposing the bright patterns

that marked their wrists and arms. Low white palaces gleamed from among ranks of vegetation.

*We have created this brightness, this peace, through the counsel of Neptilis. If we honor the guidelines he has set for us, our islands will always shine this way, like jewels in the matrix of the sea,* a quiet voice instructed Nuela.

Moving on, they came after a while to an elongated limb of land set with a succession of pale, gleaming palaces. Groups of young people sped through the shallow near-waters and briefly flanked them. Their bodies were brightly patterned, as if they were so many schools of oso or acafa. Each group had its own characteristic pattern; each swam its own stroke.

*In preparing us for the sea, Neptilis made us to pattern ourselves after the creatures of the waters and to join together in schools and in smaller groups we have named pods. Within each school there is one who can summon wisdom beyond the ordinary, and within each pod there are a few who can call the stroke for those who swim with them. Thus are we protected against unwisdom and disunity, and even those who cannot find the stroke go safely in the sea.*

The sun arced across the sky, vanished for a moment, and reappeared overhead. Leaving the islands then, the beast brought Nuela to a long limb of land that reached out into the sea. Silently it disgorged her. She hesitated, bobbing at the beast's side, until one broad flipper urged her away.

*Come now and see the land that was our home and our killing ground. You will not lose your way. You are under guardianship of the living voice.*

Reluctantly Nuela loosed herself to the current and drifted toward the limb of land. When she looked back, the beast had submerged, leaving only its spine exposed.

Then she stood upon the shore, dry although she had

just stepped from the water. Moving effortlessly, she crossed sand that winked in the sun, climbed rocks, drew herself over the jagged rim of the cliffs that rose from the sea.

*Now you see the land, great and vulnerable at once.*

Nuela stood upon a shelf of stone that protruded from a hillside matted with green growth. From that vantage point, she saw the land in its completeness. She saw places where crags of rock reared from the earth in jagged peaks, where great flows of brown water rushed down enormous gorges, where a cold whiteness lay upon the ground, masking every irregularity. She saw places where stalks of vegetation stood a hundred times taller than she, stood in bands so dense sunlight could not penetrate to the ground.

Present in each of her five senses, yet not present at all, she saw the land first in its vastness and then in its vulnerability. As she watched, what had been whole shattered, burned, and was swiftly disfigured by craters and pits. She saw palaces so large, so extensive she could not imagine how many people inhabited them. She saw them whole, and she saw them broken and burning. A drifting darkness covered the land, masking the red glow of fire.

*This we inflicted upon the land, dependent upon it though we were. We laid waste to it with fire and with explosives so potent they turned the day to a long night of smoke and dusk. We killed our own kind in great numbers and caused the death of other kinds as well. Even the fish and the beasts of the sea suffered with our wars.*

*Three generations passed before Neptilis found us sickened and savage upon our poisoned lands. He refashioned us to go into the sea. He refashioned the lucticete to bear us with it, and he forbade us to return to the warlands for sixty generations.*

*Accordingly, for that time, we ranged with the great*

*moon-pods or we confined ourselves to the islands and to those few lands that were not poisoned. And we learned to heed—as we must always heed—his instructions that we must never again fashion weapons for use against each other or destroy each other with fire and explosives.*

Once, briefly, the spell wavered and Nuela found herself in the sea, beating the water with arms and legs heavy with fatigue. For a few moments, the beast that bore her was no more than seven people gathered close around her. They masked the glowing bladders with their bodies, peering into the dark with straining eyes. Then the leader resumed his chant and the beat of the great heart sounded again. Nuela swam once more within the protective sac.

She swam until the beat faded, until the spell dissolved—until she woke to see the luminous bladders drifting loose on the sea. Startled, Nuela glanced up. Moons and stars told her she had been in the water half the night.

The bladders drifted to the east. Peering after them, Nuela saw a faint, wavering light. *Other places, other people.* Had she found them? She hesitated for a long time. Finally, cold, exhausted, afraid, she swam toward the light.

She found only a floating platform illuminated by a flickering bowl-lantern. She clung to the side of the platform, peering over the edge. It was perhaps twenty paces wide, a few paces longer. It sat steadily in the water, not dipping or swaying when Nuela finally pulled herself over the side.

Someone had raised a small shelter of woven pilchis fronds at the center of the platform. The shelter was furnished with a bedmat and a single blanket. Nuela hesitated at the edge of the platform, water streaming from her shift and her braid. Finally she crept forward and wrapped herself in the blanket.

A basket sat beside the sleeping mat. Nuela examined its contents, then peered out over the dark water. Freshly peeled polipods, smoked linsofi, flakes of dried grippie, sweet-bulbs . . .

Perhaps they were not intended for her. She ate them anyway, her fingers quivering. Then she settled at the center of the platform, the blanket pulled close around her, and peered over the water.

Her vigil was brief. The platform rose and fell. The bowl-lantern flickered. Nuela's eyelids fell. After a while she crawled into the shelter and slept, her braid cold and damp against her neck.

She woke to sunlight and confusion. Needles of light penetrated the walls of the shelter and stung her eyes. Her lips were cracked, her face gritty with salt. The man who had summoned the fantasy beast, the man who bore Rinarde's features, sat a few paces from the shelter, Polamaire's device gleaming on the palm of one hand. He regarded Nuela without welcome, his gaze clinical.

Nuela sat, brushing salt crystals from her cheeks, licking her lips—trying to concentrate an entire day's incomprehension into one coherent question. From the angle of the sun, it was late morning. "I thought I lost Polamaire's device when you pulled me under."

"No, I took it from you," he said, not glancing at the object in his hand. "Did my sister send it for me to wear in her place? Or have you come to speak as the voice of Aurlanis?"

His sister. "I don't understand. Who are you?" And how could Rinarde's sand-gold eyes study her with so little warmth?

"I'm Tirin. I call the stroke for the second pod of the Ra-meki. I speak for Aurlanis when my sister cannot. And now that I have conducted you this far into school waters, it is time for you to declare yourself. Are you candidate, messenger, or an appointed voice?"

"You're Tirinarde," she said, beginning to understand. "You're Polamaire's brother. You went to kalinerre when I was young." She frowned. "You didn't return."

"I didn't return," he said, the emphasis harder, harsher. "I went to the Nipple the day after candidate's moon expecting to meet my sister there. Instead I found you, wearing the keeper's device. Have you brought it for me? Or have you been robed as second keeper?"

Nuela raised her brows, startled at the suggestion. "No, I—No. I'm Nuela, from Tuleja and Altin." Did she imagine it, or did his eyes widen slightly? "I came to find my sister and to carry a message for Polamaire. She must stay and call the last chants for Rinarde, for the others who died in the wave."

Tirin's features stiffened. He glanced away, his eyes narrowing with a moment's pain. When he glanced back, they were cold again. "And the message?"

Nuela's eyes flickered to the scarlet pattern at his wrists. The fainter stripes on her own wrists seemed to warm in response. She licked her lips again, remembering the concentrated force of his gaze when he paced toward her through the surf the evening before, remembering how effortlessly he had summoned the fantasy beast, how real it had soon become, the beat of its heart as solid as her own.

"The candidates who came at the last conjunction are not—findings." She had never heard that word applied to living persons. "They are not to be treated as such. Even though they were unable to return to Aurlanis at the time prescribed, they are to be given free choice, and they are to be permitted to make their choice with land beneath their feet." She drew a shallow breath. "Polamaire expects the intent of the pacts to be observed even though the circumstances are exceptional." She peered up at him narrowly. Perhaps he understood the message. She did not.

His nod was terse, uninformative. "I will relay the message. The schools will choose for themselves whether to waive the terms of the pacts." He stood, the device dangling from one hand. "I'll take you back now to Aurlanis."

Back? "What do you mean?" Nuela emerged from beneath the canopy, alarmed.

"I mean that you came empowered to deliver a message. You have delivered it. Your status as messenger is no longer valid."

"*No.* I can't go back now. I've come—"

His eyes narrowed. "I marked you yesterday on behalf of my school, the Ra-meki. If you want to declare candidacy, we have the right to test you and then either to propose induction or to refuse you." He spoke formally, as if he had uttered the same formula before. "You in turn have the right to our protection during the period of kalinerre and to safe conduct back to Aurlanis if you fail—or if you refuse induction.

"But if you have come only as a messenger, you must return immediately—or you swim alone."

Nuela stared at him, then frowned past him across the water. The sea was quiet, empty, wide. Sinjanne had gone into it more than forty days before. "I didn't come as a candidate. I came to find my sister. She was too young for kalinerre. She should never have come. If I had known she intended to put her tile in the basket—" His features remained set, unresponsive. She sighed. "My sister's name is Sinjanne. All I want is to know if she is safe."

He shrugged, frowning. "I can't tell you that. The Ra-meki took no candidates this period, so your sister went to one of the other schools. If she failed her candidacy, she was returned to Pahla's Nipple several days ago."

Nuela's hands clenched. "The wave—"

"The wave caught anyone waiting on the Nipple for

conduct back to Aurlanis. Any who survived were probably swept back into school waters and claimed as findings. But if your sister succeeded in her candidacy, if she decided to join the school that tested her—''

Join a school? ''No,'' she said with conviction. ''She would never have done that. We're alone. She has no one but me. I have no one but her. The last thing she said to me—'' She peered up at him, suddenly anxious to bring some expression to his face, some understanding. ''She told me she would come back.''

A small muscle tightened in his jaw. ''What do you think I told Polamaire when I went?''

Nuela caught a painful breath. ''That you would come back? But I don't understand. Why—''

''Why did I stay? Why do I swim with the Ra-meki? Because I knew three days after Harienne marked me that if I returned to Aurlanis, I would never stay. Once you wake to Pahla, Aurlanis can call you back—but not for more than a few minutes, a few days, maybe a few years. Not unless you have a will as strong as Pola maire's. I don't.''

Nuela frowned at the pain she heard in his voice. ''But Sinjanne is too young to make a decision like that,'' she protested. ''Unless they took her from Pahla's Nipple and refused to return her.'' Unless she was being held against her will.

''No, by pact each candidate pronounces her choice with land beneath her feet. That provision is honored to the letter by every school in the waters. If she remained with one of the schools, she remained of free choice.''

Could Sinjanne have done that? ''But—I have to know.'' Couldn't he understand? She had to know if Sinjanne had been on Pahla's Nipple when the wave struck. If she had drowned. Or if she had freely chosen not to return to Aurlanis.

Chosen knowing that when she did not come back,

Nuela would think she had drowned. Could Sinjanne have made such a cruel choice?

Tirin shrugged. "I will carry Polamaire's message to the other schools. I will ask for your sister as I go. If you remain in school waters, I can bring you an answer within six days."

Nuela glanced over the empty sea. "Bring me an answer—here?"

"I can bring you an answer aboard second pod's raft if you declare candidacy."

"But I didn't come as a candidate."

He shrugged. "Then you must return to Aurlanis. You can't stay here. My mark will protect you for only a few hours after we separate."

She touched the scarlet marks on her wrists, baffled. "And then?"

"When the mark is gone, you will be findings. Whoever finds you can claim you. Not as a candidate but as a mandated subject of his school—a person without privilege or entitlement. You have entered school waters. You are subject to the terms of the pacts."

"Even if I don't know what they are?" she demanded, her voice sharp. Even if she had not heard of pacts or terms or schools five days before?

"You will learn. By the pacts, each person has a clearly defined status. These marks define you as a candidate. Without them, you are defined as findings."

She shook her head, suppressing an angry response, and stared across the featureless horizon. "Is there land near?"

"A few quiet nipples, none much larger than Pahla's Nipple. Several active spill-cones. And Aurlanis and Pelosis. Aside from those, I can't name you any land but the Great Land."

"The Great Land?"

"The land at the end of the current. But you haven't heard of that yet."

She hadn't heard of it, and his words told her nothing. But the undercurrent of feeling in his voice was clear, had been clear from the first. "Why are you angry with me? Have I caused you so much trouble?"

His eyes narrowed, the pupils contracting sharply. "I am always angry when candidates come from Aurlanis expecting—Well, tell me. What have you come expecting?"

"I don't know," she said helplessly. Just a few days before, she had thought that the greatest challenge of kalinerre would be to feed herself safely from the sea. "I didn't know—" That there were other people, other places. That there was a sky with a single white moon and lucticetes waiting in a sea of drowning dreams. That there were voices and confusions and chants she had not heard before, waiting to draw her in.

"And you don't know now. But you've come, and if I leave you to your own devices, you will end up as findings. Here—give me your hands."

She extended her hands, confusion overriding rebellion. He took them, turning them so that her wrists faced upward. With his thumbs, he found the pulse points and pressed.

Nuela stared down as the pattern of scarlet stripes blazed brightly on his wrists and arms. The fainter pattern on her own flesh spread upward to her elbows, slowly brightening until it was almost as vivid as the pattern on Tirin's forearms.

Her arms pulsed with a foreign heat, pulsed as if fevered. With a quick rise of panic, she snatched her hands from Tirin's. She held her arms before her, staring at them, watching with sharp-held breath for the pattern to fade.

Instead it continued to spread up her arms. It reached her armpits. Seared the tender flesh beneath her swimshift.

She did not see Tirin bend to retrieve the keeper's

device. She did not see him hang it at his neck. Nor did she hear when he began to chant. The first stanza was all but inaudible over the racing beat of her own heart.

But suddenly, as if reality had abruptly leaped forward, he stood before her, the pendant at his neck, his body fully patterned in bold scarlet stripes. He spoke softly, but with every syllable Nuela's heart pounded more fiercely and scarlet markings blazed alive upon some new surface of her body. She gasped with their rising heat.

Tirin's eyes met hers, and they held the fire of the sun. With the final syllables of the chant, he raised his arms, turned, and vanished over the side of the platform.

Stunned, burning, Nuela stared down into the water. She did not see him at first. She saw only the water, rocking in placid sheets. Then Tirin appeared, a ripple of scarlet speeding through the upper layers of the water. He circled the platform, his stroke swift, strong. Sunlight sheared through the water and blazed upon his back.

Nuela watched, not breathing, watched as he circled the platform twice, three times, and then vanished deep into the water.

Time leaped forward again, and she was in the water too, floundering and confused.

Tirin reappeared, driving swiftly toward her. Nuela cried out. But this time he did not pull her under. Instead, catching her hand, he drew her forward.

Her resistance was instinctive, ineffectual. His touch made the pattern burn more fiercely upon her arms and breasts, made her legs throb. But when he freed her hand and vanished beneath the surface again, her legs found a will of their own and propelled her after him.

She caught lightning glimpses of him darting between leggy polipod stems and leafy streamers. He led her deep into the tangled bottom growth, led her among schools of tiny, startled fish. A frightened pispis gathered up its spiny legs and closed its carapace around them.

Tirin's scarlet markings darkened with depth. He wheeled and peered back at Nuela, his eyes bright with a fierce joy. Then he soared toward the surface again, and she swam after him. They broke the surface together, water bursting in a glittering explosion.

Smiling with the same fierce pleasure, Tirin uttered a few soft syllables of the chant he had spoken before. He uttered them so softly Nuela had to read them from his lips. But once he had spoken them, he did not have to repeat them. They spoke themselves in the beat of her heart, in the rush of her pulses. They sounded with pounding strength in every part of her body.

They swam then. They swam in a stroke so perfectly coordinated that they might have been a single organism. They coursed along the surface of the water, sunlight beating at their vividly patterned flesh. They swam in the mid ranges of the water, gliding over the tops of tall bottom growth. They swam deep among the intertwined bottom plants, threading among stems and streamers.

Nuela realized after a while that a school of ra-meki had joined them. As long as her forearm, no thicker than her hand, the ra-meki swam with swift, darting energy. Their vividly patterned bodies stained the water with scarlet light. Their eyes were round, black, empty. Yet the uniform beat of scarlet and silver bodies suggested a keen organic awareness.

Tirin changed course and the ra-meki darted away without them. Instinctively Nuela drew close to Tirin's side. The syllables of the chant beat softly within her now, falling sometimes to a bare thread. They bound her anyway, so perfectly that she could match Tirin's stroke, his course, even with eyes closed.

She felt a distant, muted misgiving. He had usurped the beat of her heart, the rhythm of her limbs. She swam with him not through choice but because the pattern he had set upon her flesh had called her into the water. He held a power over her far greater than Polamaire had ever exerted with the keeper's chants.

He held power over her, and perhaps the most frightening measure of it was that Nuela no longer felt any compulsion to struggle free.

They swam together across the broad, rocking plane of water. The sun climbed to the peak of the sky and after a while, Nuela saw a boiling disturbance upon the horizon. Matching Tirin's stroke, she watched as the distant disruption drew near and became a large pod of mela-mela. They sped forward, alternately driving themselves through the water with the beat of broad, muscular tails and arcing into the air, their bodies gleaming silver grey in the sun.

Tirin laughed and turned to catch Nuela's hand. Thrusting their joined hands into the air, he drew her body to his. For a moment, Nuela felt the jarring of his heart—in his chest, in hers. Then they plunged beneath the surface, sinking feetfirst. His thumbs found the pulse points at her wrists again. The scarlet pattern faded rapidly from his flesh, from hers. Only the markings at her wrists remained.

Releasing her, he kicked his way to the surface. Nuela hung in the water, momentarily lost, then rose after him.

Nuela had seen an occasional solitary mela-mela playing beyond the garden wall. Once she had seen a pod of twenty, again a pod of fifty or more. Now at least a hundred sleek animals approached, their swift, powerful bodies glinting in the sun. She hung in the water, glancing uncertainly at Tirin.

He uttered a shrill three-note whistle. "Come," he

called back to her. He swam to meet the mela-mela, pausing only to whistle again.

Reaching him, the sporting animals settled back into the water and gathered around him, pressing against his bare chest, poking smooth beaks into his armpits. He glanced back at Nuela, summoning again.

Nuela approached warily, drawing up her limbs when a dozen long, muscular bodies immediately gathered around her and nudged her with inquiring silver-grey beaks. The mela-mela whistled in shrill excitement.

"They're introducing themselves. Tell them who you are. Give them a call, a few notes—a signature." He repeated his own three-note whistle. "You only have to tell them once. They'll remember."

Tentatively Nuela stroked a smooth head and turned the three syllables of her name to a whistle.

The mela-mela shrilled in enthusiastic response. They continued for a moment to press around her, bumping her with their beaks, winking at her with small, clear eyes. Then, as if by mutual agreement, they withdrew, leaving just one animal hovering in the water before her. It turned, brushing first its side, then its tail against her, and sank into the water. Only its single round nostril remained above the surface.

Nuela glanced at Tirin. With a gesture, he dismissed his own exuberant coterie. The single mela-mela that remained sank in the water. Tirin straddled it, his knees pressed to its sides. He leaned forward as the animal rose again, stroking its gleaming flesh. "We'll travel faster if you ride."

Nuela glanced uncertainly at the creature that hung in the water before her. It waggled its tail and submerged completely. When it resurfaced, it whistled again, blowing water from its nostril.

She had only to nod and the mela-mela slid beneath her and rose with her astride its back. The creature was shaped much like an elongated teardrop, swelling

quickly from its beak to its greatest girth, then tapering
to the broad horizontal tail. Beneath the water, Nuela
saw narrow flippers. The flesh of the mela-mela's back
was smooth and resilient. Instinctively Nuela clasped
its flanks with her knees and lay forward.

"Don't press her sides too hard," Tirin called back
as the animal moved forward in the water. "Relax and
let your body find its own balance. If you slip off, one
of the others will retrieve you."

Nuela's mount traveled sedately, soon falling behind
as the others leaped and swam ahead, returning in the
direction from which they had come. Tirin lingered beside her for a while, then let his mount race to the head
of the pod.

The afternoon sea practiced a strange seduction as
the mela-mela carried Nuela after the others. Water
exploded into jewels under the impact of broad tails.
Flying droplets caught sunlight and broke it into fast-
melting rainbows. Breeze and water slapped Nuela's
face. Without thinking, she pulled the bindings from
her hair and shook it free.

Tirin turned back and remained briefly at her side,
noting her progress with narrowed eyes. Baring his teeth
in a brief, challenging smile, he whistled and urged his
mount ahead again. Nuela drew herself up, suddenly
eager, and her mela-mela bolted after his.

Abruptly Tirin and his mount disappeared beneath
the surface. Nuela's mount dived after them. Nuela held
tight against rushing water. Tirin glanced back at her,
the water tearing at his hair. Then, with a beat of its
tail, Nuela's mount followed the other mela-mela back
to the surface and broke free of the water. Its arching
body curved through the air and swiftly plunged back
into the water.

Nuela clung tight, gasping for air when they were
briefly in the air, letting her breath bubble free when
they coursed beneath the water. They reached the cen-

ter of the pod in a series of leaps and plunges. Gleaming bodies darted and flew around her. Whistling, squealing mela-mela drove directly at Nuela's mount, hurtling into the air in the moment before impact, flinging water back at Nuela with cupped tails. Their broad faces were not expressive. She felt their playful derision anyway as she struggled to keep her balance.

She lost her seat several times. Each time, whistling mela-mela converged upon her, jostling for position. Once two of the sleek creatures plunged toward her from opposite directions. Slipping past each other, they wheeled and sped toward her again. They bounded into the air at the last moment, tails waggling, one skimming over the other. Before they struck the water, a third mela-mela surfaced beneath Nuela, bearing her into the air precariously balanced on its back.

The other two whistled in indignation and hurtled after the third mela-mela as it whisked Nuela away.

Gradually the pod settled to a sober, purposeful pace. After a while, Tirin brought his mount to Nuela's side again. "You'll see our raft soon. Watch to the west."

Wringing water from her hair, combing the wet strands with her fingers, she watched. She saw only sunlight and water. She frowned. "You said there were Nipples—and a place called Pelosis."

"Yes. Pelosis is comparable to Aurlanis. The Sia-kepi hold the palace there until year's end." When she looked at him blankly, he said, "There is a school named for each of Pahla's twelve consort breeds. In the year of the Sia-kepi, the Sia-kepi take the palace at Pelosis. The rest of us are permitted to go ashore at year's end, for the interim observances." He frowned. "When the year of the Greater Milminesa begins four days later, we must all leave, except for the school of the Greater Milminesa."

"Then one year out of twelve—"

"One year of twelve, each school holds Pelosis. And

when the year ends, the school returns to its rafts and another takes its place. This is by terms of the pacts." He peered across the water. "There. You can see second pod's raft now." He leaned forward and urged his mela-mela ahead.

Nuela's mount plunged after him. Soon she saw a joined collection of broad platforms rocking in the sea. They presented an irregular profile, some topped with three-sided shelters, others shaded with woven roofs, still others no more than floating platforms. People sat in the early afternoon sun shelling crustaceans, pounding fiber plants, weaving fabric, and twisting cord. Their work-chants sounded quietly across the water.

Tirin turned. "And now you must declare yourself. Either you are a candidate for the Ra-meki or you sleep the night aboard and I return you to Aurlanis tomorrow. And if you have any idea of slipping away, of going by yourself to find your sister, put it aside. You'll be findings before Lomaire rises twice."

The mela-mela had come to rest in the water. Dozens of small, clear eyes regarded Nuela, as if the mela-mela waited for her answer. As if they understood that she knew what it must be—but had not yet reconciled herself to it.

She could not go back to Aurlanis now. But to stay, to give herself voluntarily to the strange seductions she had met today, had met even before leaving Aurlanis—

"If I stay, you will help me find Sinjanne? And you will take me back to Aurlanis before the next conjunction?"

"If you choose to go back, I will take you."

She licked her lips. Turning, she peered back across the sea. Gentle, sun-silvered, it rocked to a beguiling rhythm, promising excitements and fascinations she had never guessed at.

"I'll stay," she said, her voice husky with misgiving—not because she did not want to remain but because she did. She wanted to swim again with the mela-mela. She wanted to plunge heedlessly through showers of water jewels and dart among deep beds of weed. She wanted to see all the bright, strange fish and creatures that lived only in the deepwaters.

She wanted to feel the stinging pleasure of Tirin's touch again. Wanted to swim again to his stroke.

Wanted not to. Wanted never again to yield to the bright fever he evoked in her.

She met his narrowed eyes. "I'll stay until I find my sister." But even as she slid from the mela-mela's back and swam with Tirin toward the raft, she knew her decision had less to do with Sinjanne than she wished, and she felt the distinct stir of apprehension.

# Chapter Six

DUCKING BENEATH SUN-SILVERED WAVES, NUELA followed Tirin under a series of floats and surfaced in a square of water enclosed by four long platforms that appeared to be made of layers of coarse woven material. Tirin climbed aboard the nearest platform. Shaking water from her hair, Nuela reached for his extended hand—and froze. A slight, almost childlike woman stared at her from the shadows of a roofed shelter.

Deliberately the woman set aside her work and stood. She was as small as Sinjanne, with straight, pale hair that hung loose to her hips. Her short, fitted gown was belted with braided cord. Strands of tiny shells dangled from her headdress, rattling as she stepped forward.

Nuela pulled herself up and reached to press water from her hair, then did not, self-conscious under the woman's unwelcoming frown. Water from her shift puddled on the close-woven mat that covered the floor of the float and then vanished into the weave.

Seen closely, the woman was older than Nuela had first thought, her face webbed with fine lines, her pale, straight hair as much silver as gold. Studying Nuela a moment longer, she extended both hands to Tirin. "A candidate at this time of year, Tirin?" Scarlet markings blazed alive on her forearms at the clasp of his hands.

Her eyes darted to Polamaire's device. "You've seen your sister?"

"Nuela has brought a message from Polamaire. You'll want to have someone prepare the candidate's retreat for her and see that Filien takes her into his wake while I carry Polamaire's message to the schools. She's already passed the first tests. I will administer the others when I return."

Nuela glanced at him in surprise. She had passed the first tests? When had she done that? And how? By not drowning when he pulled her under?

Pale brows drew tight. "Have you been to Anamirre with this?"

"No, Cela, I came to you first. I thought you would want to know immediately that we have a candidate."

Cela's face tightened at the irony in his tone. "Of course I have nothing better to do than to provide for a candidate when there should be none. I'll prepare the retreat when I see your candidate wearing the girdle." Her pale-lashed eyes narrowed. "There were Maku-hiki in our waters earlier. They came to trade mooring rope from us. So they said."

Small muscles tightened in Tirin's face. "Did you send them home with rope?"

"When we have our own moorings to repair? Do you think they came expecting us to give them rope three days after the wave broke all but our extenders? They didn't even bring a carrier. There were Haspipi spying around by candidate's moon. They were seen near pod three and five as well as here. And there have been Inin-nana in our waters every day. By the time our float is ready, every school in the waters will already know we're sending nothing but effigies."

Tirin's eyes darkened. "Oh? Would you rather send one of your daughters, Cela?"

Cela turned sharply away, shells rattling. "You know I would not." She turned back, meeting his gaze with bitter defiance. "But it will come to that, Tirin. Eventually it will come to that whether we choose it or not. They're watching us, all of them."

"You know Anamirre will never speak according to who comes spying in our waters."

"No, only according to who strokes her wrists and tells her sweet land-tales. Well, take your land-cousin to Anamirre and ingratiate her. Bring her back when she wears the girdle."

Tirin met her anger with a taut nod. Shrugging, he drew Nuela with him off the edge of the platform. "Your hands," he said when they surfaced. When she only stared blankly at him, he repeated, "Your hands." Taking them, he probed the pulse points with his thumbs. "Close your eyes."

Too late Nuela realized what was happening—tried to draw free. But Tirin had already uttered the first measured syllables of the chant. Heat spread up her arms and across her breasts. Her heart fluttered against her chest wall.

"Close your eyes. You must learn to match my stroke even when you can't see me. It's important."

She stiffened, briefly resisting. But the chant already rushed in her blood.

She did not know later how far they swam or how long. Eyes pressed shut, she soon matched his course almost without effort, as if some inner sense guided her, some sense that was slowly waking to life under Tirin's tutelage. Occasionally, losing the sense of his presence, she opened her eyes—and each time found herself very near his side.

Each time he sensed immediately that she faltered, and he paused to close her eyes with his fingertips and to whisper a few soft syllables. Once, tracing the line of her jaw with his fingers, he pressed his thumbs to the pulses at her throat as he spoke. Nuela's body arched and her eyes flew open again, staring up into his as the pattern of the Ra-meki blazed upon her more fiercely than before. She was caught by a moment's total, ecstatic helplessness. When Tirin released her and darted beneath the surface, she scissored after him, confused and shaken.

She did not want to be thrall to his power. She did not want to feel his will in the beat of her blood. But when he glanced back at her, she closed her eyes and her body found his of its own accord. She knew without opening her eyes that she swam again to his stroke.

They swam at the surface and sunlight fell heavily on her back, as if it had substance and weight. They swam at depth, and she discovered minute currents and temperature gradients she had never noticed before. They darted among beds of polipods, and the plants stroked her with lingering fingers.

Eventually the pattern on her flesh cooled. Yet she felt it as distinctly, as keenly as before. If she wanted, she could trace each stripe and bar with her fingertips, eyes closed.

Tirin slowed after a while, leading her back to the surface. They swam a long lazy stroke, easing through the water effortlessly. The world narrowed to the slow beat of limbs against water.

And then there were voices calling. Tirin caught her wrists and pulled her under. Startled, Nuela stared at him through the clear water as the markings vanished from his face and limbs, from hers. She lingered for a moment, disoriented, confused, after he released her.

Bobbing to the surface, she caught a long, ragged breath. They neared a second collection of floats. A group of children swam toward them, crying for attention.

"Tirin! Tirin! Call the stroke for us!"

"I'm first at your side!"

"I get heel position!"

There was a moment's disconcerted silence when the

children saw Nuela. They gaped artlessly, blinked almost in unison, and resumed their clamor.

Tirin raised one hand. "Every baby knows you can't swim with your mouth open. Pirina, it's your turn to be first. Then Korsin and Inda at my heels. The rest of you at theirs." He clasped their wrists, each pair in turn, and swept away. Seven slight, unmarked bodies darted after him, matching his stroke imperfectly. Nuela followed.

They circled the raft, the children calling triumphantly to the people who worked on the floats. Other children plunged into the water to join the formation before Tirin finally led them beneath the raft, gesturing for Nuela to follow. They emerged in an open square of water enclosed by four long platforms.

Tirin ceremonially released each child in turn, then climbed up and pulled Nuela after him. Securely lashed, the four floats were almost entirely covered by a single many-paneled enclosure. "We'll take a moment to dry. Then you will meet Anamirre."

"She's keeper for your—for your school?" Nuela wrung water from her hair and pressed it from her shift. Her flesh felt suddenly bare and cold. She stared around, recognizing some of the materials used to build floats and shelter—finding no names for others.

"No, each pod has its own keeper. Cela serves pod two. Anamirre is our true daughter. She is—our wisdom. She points out the way, and the rest of us try to go where she points. Not always successfully. You have no one comparable on Aurlanis."

"Not even Polamaire?"

Tirin laughed. "Particularly not Polamaire. A true daughter—or true son—subjects will to wisdom. Polamaire is will, pure will."

Will. He had spoken of will before. "Tirin—"

But he shook his head. "Let the fish swim to your net, Nuela."

*Let the grippie swim to your net, Nuela. If you try to chase it down, you'll come to shore with nothing.* Nuela glanced up at Tirin quizzically. "I suppose your father said that to you too."

"Every father teaches his child not to try to outrace the grippie, doesn't he? There are plenty of fish in school waters. Thousands of them. Hold your net steady, and I'll flush a few of them your way."

Don't question him. Let him guide the answers her way as opportunity permitted. She frowned down at her feet. Did he forget that more than curiosity lay behind her arrival? "I have to find my sister."

"We'll find your sister. Here—" He extended one hand. "You're as dry as you need to be."

Within, the shelter was divided by partitions into a corridor from which opened a series of small rooms. Some were clearly workrooms. Others held bedmats and personal possessions. None was occupied, but Nuela heard the murmur of voices through tightly woven partitions.

Tirin led her to a large, roofless chamber, sunlit, decorated with bright-colored streamers and chattering shell-chimes. Four frail white-haired women sat on woven mats, attended by two girls, one slight and dark, the other taller, older, copper haired. The youngest stood eagerly to meet Tirin, then drew back when she saw Nuela.

Nuela was startled by the quick radiance of the smile Tirin directed at the oldest occupant of the chamber, a tiny, shrunken woman with white hair gathered into a thin braid. "Anamirre, I've come back—and I've brought a candidate."

The old woman laughed, pleased, surprised, and turned, extending both hands. Her eyes, dark, large, nestled like heavy drops above her fragile cheekbones. "A pretty girl—from Aurlanis. Here, come, let me touch you."

Despite the crumpling of the flesh, her face was open, as bright and unguarded as a child's. Nuela stepped to take her hands, and the old woman immediately drew her down and slipped a light, almost fleshless arm around her shoulders. She patted her happily, at the same time flicking the fingers of her other hand through Nuela's wet hair.

"Yes, yes, very pretty. And you've come to be our candidate, have you? Evanne, bring the girdle. Lienne, don't you think Tirin is hungry? And thirsty. Aren't you thirsty, Tirin?"

Both girls hurried away. Tirin immediately took his place at Anamirre's other side. The three remaining women peered at Nuela with open curiosity, then nodded formally to Anamirre and withdrew.

"Now, aren't you surprised?" the old woman demanded when they were alone, releasing Nuela. "Tirin promised to bring you to meet Neptilis' true daughter, and instead you find an old crone. But Neptilis is very old himself, isn't he? Very old indeed, perhaps even older than Pahla. So I am entitled to be old too."

Nuela glanced uncertainly at Tirin. He studied the old woman with affection. "Don't you want to know this pretty girl's name, Anamirre?"

The old woman responded to his teasing tone with a pleased chortle. "She will tell me herself once her hair is dry. Evanne—" The youngest of the two girls had stepped back into the chamber. She glanced shyly at Nuela. "Leave the girdle here and take this pretty girl to dry her hair. When you bring her back, we will all have something nice to eat."

Nuela followed the girl from the chamber, confused. This childlike woman was "our wisdom"? She pointed the way for them all? Certainly she was as unlike the stern, composed Polamaire as any person could be.

Nuela heard Anamirre laughing with Tirin on the other side of the partition as Evanne rubbed pilchis grains into her hair and combed them out. "You will want a headdress," the girl said when Nuela's hair hung dry and shining on her shoulders. She met Nuela's glance for the first time, her eyes as large, as dark as Anamirre's, shy and curious at once.

"No, no," Nuela assured her, but the girl had already vanished.

She returned a few minutes later with an elaborate skull-crown of braided cord. Long strands of small white shells hung from it. "Anamirre likes this one especially. It's very much like one Cela wears. If you turn your head like this, it will speak." She turned her own head quickly from side to side. "She likes to hear the different ways people make the shells speak."

And indeed as the older girl served food and drink, Nuela was aware that each time she made the shells rattle, Anamirre turned and listened with keen interest. Tirin remained at the old woman's side, his fingers clasping hers whenever she turned to touch him. Evanne ate silently, gazing sidelong at Tirin, flushing and averting her eyes when he returned her glance. The older girl, Lienne, served food and drink with unhurried composure, handling the delicate shellware with sure fingers. When Tirin's eyes caught hers, she met his gaze with a slight frown, aloof and unabashed.

The float rose and fell, its motion constant but gentle. Finally the bowls were empty, the drinking shells dry. "I believe you were going to ask our candidate's name, Anamirre." Tirin held the old woman's hand, idly stroking her wrist.

"Ah, do you see how sly he is? He's afraid I won't remember to ask your name, and if I don't, you will think I am a forgetful old woman, won't you?"

Nuela glanced in brief fascination at the scarlet pattern that flickered palely on the old woman's wrist at Tirin's touch. "I am Nuela, from Tuleja and Altin."

Anamirre's dark eyes widened. She smiled broadly,

bobbing her head. "Ah, Altin from Peshira and Weldin. And Tuleja from Hiria and—Porsin, wasn't it? They
came into school waters when I was hardly older than
Cela, all four of them. I traveled among the schools in
those days. I met them all. Hiria went to the Torahon,
Peshira and Porsin to the Malin-ji. And Weldin came
to us. I have remembered their names all these years.
But my own grandchildren—" She tilted a rueful hand
at the two girls. "Do you know why I keep only these
two with me? Because every time I go to call one of
the others, I mistake her name."

"You must understand she is boasting when she calls
Evanne and Lienne her grandchildren," Tirin said.
"Cela is Anamirre's granddaughter, and Evanne and
Lienne are Cela's."

Nuela glanced at Evanne. "You're Cela's daughter?"
She saw no resemblance. Nor did Lienne resemble the
tiny, pale-haired woman.

"I am her granddaughter," Evanne said softly, embarrassed by the attention.

"And do you want to know more about our family?"
Anamirre demanded. She flipped her thin braid across
her shoulders. "Show her, Tirin, and see if she guesses.
Show her now. You haven't told her, have you?"

Tirin glanced narrowly at the old woman. "Have we
made you tired already, Ana?"

"No, no, I'm not tired," Anamirre said, but there
was a thin note in her voice and her hand had begun to
quiver. "Show her, Tirin."

"All right. Watch, Nuela." He stroked Anamirre's
wrist, making a feeble pattern glow on her wrinkled
arm. Reaching across her, he took Nuela's wrist. She
tensed herself against the heat that rose to his touch.
Nodding, he released her and clasped Evanne's hand.
Again the scarlet pattern glowed brightly. Tirin settled
back on the mat, a brief, smiling question in his eyes.

"Now, did you see? Do you know?" Anamirre demanded.

Nuela frowned. What did the old woman want her to say? That Tirin was the only one of them who could bring the pattern alive? That Anamirre did not respond as vividly to his touch as she and Evanne did because she was so much older?

Nuela drew a doubtful breath. Anamirre's eyes were eager, those of a child who has set a riddle. But her shoulders drooped and her head had begun to quiver. "In one of the dreams, I saw schools of people swimming together. They were marked alike, but none of them was Ra-meki."

Anamirre frowned, disappointed. "No, there are no Ra-meki in the dreams. The dreams come from the time of Neptilis, but the schools were born of Pahla and her twelve consorts, and we are much newer to her than to Neptilis. But the dreams tell us something we must all remember. 'Neptilis has made us to pattern ourselves after the creatures of the sea.' Has he spoken to you yet? Do you remember?"

"Yes. Yes. I remember."

"He made us so that when we left the world of the silver moon and were born here, we could pattern ourselves to this sea as we did to that one. Do you know why he did that?"

Nuela glanced uncertainly at Tirin. He watched Anamirre with frowning concern.

"So that we will be safe, Nuela. Neptilis made us this way so that we can go safely in the sea, whatever moon we swim under. We don't eat the ra-meki or the sia-kepi, do we? Or the haspipi or the torahon—or any of the other consort breeds. Neither do the toothfish or the wanaimi or the other predators. Some of the consort fish are poisonous to them. Others are dangerous to them, although they are not predatory upon them. So the large predators avoid us too when we take their colors. And do you know what that means?'' The old woman's eyes were suddenly bright with tears. ''Neptilis wanted good for us. Listen, child, to all the dreams and you will hear nothing else. He made us for good. He wanted good for us. Tears and pain are wrong. They are against everything Neptilis wanted when he made us.'' She leaned forward, catching both Nuela's hands in hers. ''We are not made to give each other tears. Things happen and we cry; everyone has pain. But Neptilis did not make us to bring tears to each other.

''Yet I cried every year when I was young, Nuela. I cried when we sent the floats on the current. If Neptilis wanted the floats to go, why did I cry? Why did the others cry? Do we cry when good happens?'' Her eyes brimmed with tears. They spilled over and lost themselves in the webwork of her face. ''Do we cry for good, child?''

''No, of course not,'' Nuela said, not understanding. When they sent the floats on the current?

Anamirre's lips quivered. She clutched Nuela's fingers and Nuela blinked, trying to hold back the unreasoning tears that suddenly quivered in her own eyes. She didn't understand what the old woman said, but her anguish touched a nerve.

Tirin stood. Bending over Anamirre, he gently uncurled her fingers. ''You're tired, Ana. You must lie down. Evanne— Come, Ana.''

Evanne jumped up and helped Anamirre to her feet. ''Come and I'll comb out your hair,'' she promised. ''I'll make a fresh braid, and then I'll sit with you while you sleep.''

Anamirre shook her head. ''We must not make each other cry.''

Evanne bowed her head. ''I know. I know. Please, Grandmother, you'll feel better when you've slept.'' She glanced anxiously at Nuela, tears glinting in her dark eyes. "She only needs to rest. You can talk to her again tomorrow."

Together the dark-haired girl and Tirin led the old woman from the chamber. Shell-chimes rattled emptily after them. Nuela sat back on the mat, confused, then glanced at Lienne.

The older girl's coppery eyes met Nuela's, aloof and undisturbed. "She wanted you to notice that I was the only one he didn't touch," she said, each word cool and precise.

"Oh." So the riddle had been as simple as that. Tirin had touched Evanne, Anamirre, and herself but not Lienne. Frowning, Nuela eased the headdress from her head and spread it on the mat. Her head had begun to ache.

"Don't you want to know why he didn't touch me?"

"Oh," Nuela said again, disconcerted. She not only had not noticed what Anamirre had wanted her to see, she had not wondered at its significance. "Why didn't he touch you?"

"He is not permitted to rouse me with his caller's touch because he is not permitted to mate with me. I am his daughter."

It took Nuela a moment to react. She stared into the girl's level copper eyes, uncomprehending, then flushed violently. "He is not permitted to mate with me either."

"Because you haven't harvested pilchis fronds together and woven them into crowns? Because you haven't worn your crowns into the morning pool when the night-horn blows? Because you haven't spoken your words to the sea and listened for Pahla to echo them? Those are the things the land-bred do before they mate, aren't they?"

"Because I haven't chosen him," Nuela said sharply. "Because he hasn't chosen me. Because I don't intend to stay here. Because—"

The copper eyes narrowed. "Do you always get to choose? When you live on land, do you get to choose everything that will happen to you?"

"No, of course not." But she got to choose her own mate. And she would choose him because he suited her, not because his touch brought scarlet to her flesh. Not because it roused an alien heat in her.

"We don't live the way you live. *You* don't even live the way you think you live," Lienne said with aloof precision. "I have two brothers and a sister on Aurlanis. You didn't know that, did you?"

Nuela stared at the girl and met only cool dispassion. Why then did she feel that Lienne was deliberately—successfully—trying to provoke her? "I don't see how—I don't see how you can have a family on Aurlanis."

"Do you think a child conceived in school waters can't be born on Aurlanis?"

"I don't see—"

"Do you think you could never carry a child back to Aurlanis?"

Nuela's breath hissed sharply away. She stood, her pulse racing angrily. "I didn't come for that. I came—"

She shook her head in confusion. She had come to find Sinjanne. But had she stayed because she sought her sister? Or because she had ridden a leaping mela-mela and listened to the whispered seductions of the afternoon sea?

"You came because we are here." Lienne stood, distant and cool. "If you pass the tests, then you must weigh wisdom against will if you want to return to Aurlanis. But the wisdom may not be what you want it to be. And your will may not be strong enough to stand against it." She touched her temples with splayed fingertips. "Here is our will. Only here. But here—" she ran the same fingers the length of her slender body

"—here is our wisdom. You can see which has the greater weight."

Nuela drew a long breath and forced herself to speak calmly. "I came to find my sister. When I've found her, I will go home." Home to a world of visible boundaries and known parameters. Home to a place where the floor did not rock, where her flesh did not burn. Home to the solidity and order of the palace. *Home* . . .

"You will go home if you are blind and deaf. That's what Aurlanis is, by the pacts—a sanctuary for cripples who have lost the gifts Neptilis gave us. You were born there so you are permitted to return even if you pass the tests. But you will live like a defective there. You will live like a blind woman. You—" Lienne caught a sharp breath, her eyes abruptly blazing to sharp focus.

Nuela turned. Tirin had stepped back into the chamber. He studied his daughter silently. "I think it is time you went to your mother's pod."

Lienne's cheeks burned with color. "Anamirre likes me here."

"I do not like you here. Not until Nuela has completed her candidacy. Not unless you can find better will than you've shown just now."

Lienne stared at him, her nostrils flared. "I am exercising wisdom, not will. If she thinks—"

"She is entitled to think what she thinks, and your wisdom seems much like spite to me. It seems like little more than badly directed will. Anamirre would not be pleased. You will go to your mother's pod until I call you back."

Lienne bared her teeth in a quick grimace. With a fierce gesture, she passed her hands before her face. A swift, blood-red stain spread from her hairline and washed down her features. She turned her hands palm upward, staring at them expectantly. Finally, displeased by what she saw, she tossed her copper hair. "I will go to my mother." Stepping past Nuela, she shoved aside a partition and dived into the water beyond.

Tirin frowned after her. "So there you have a lesson in will and wisdom," he said, setting the partition back into place. "Will tells Lienne that as the daughter of callers, she has the right to be a caller too. But the body has its own wisdom. It doesn't care at all what she wants or how badly she wants it."

"She wants to—to do what you do?"

"Yes, and she will make everyone as unhappy as she is until the gift comes to her—or until she gives it up for lost."

"Well, she hasn't made me unhappy," Nuela said with false conviction. She touched her forehead, rubbing at the pain that had settled just above her brows.

He flicked a wry glance at her. "It's too bad you don't lie better. She flushed an entire school of fish into your net, didn't she? Now you will try to eat them all at once—and make yourself sick."

She shook her head irritably. Which ones would he have her leave for later? A wise woman with the demeanor of an ancient child? Did the Ra-meki really permit Anamirre to govern them? Children conceived in school waters and born in the palace? And Aurlanis—a sanctuary for the defective? "When are you leaving to carry Polamaire's message?"

"Today. I'll return you to pod two first. Here, wear this." The knotted girdle Evanne had brought was of plain bleached cord. Nuela shook her head, but Tirin tied it at her waist anyway, then studied her half-averted face. "Tell me: have you found anything here that you expected to find?"

She glanced up reluctantly. "No. Must I match your stroke again?"

"I've already sounded the clappers. We will have mela-mela to carry us back to pod two."

Another thing she had not guessed. "You call them to you?"

"We have been accused of that."

"Accused?"

"Some schools consider that summoning a mela-mela, riding it amounts to attempting mastery of the sea. And we've been told we were not made to be masters of land or sea." He shrugged. "But what have I mastered if I strike a clapper and a mela-mela comes and insists upon taking me on its back? Did you feel you mastered anything today?"

Nuela remembered her slippery, bolting ride, her unceremonious dunkings. "No." The mela-mela had bounced her around like a toy.

"Then we'll ride."

By the time they made their way to the square of water, half a dozen mela-mela had congregated. They whistled shrilly, jostling for position at the edge of the platform. Nuela and Tirin slid easily to the backs of the two nearest. The mela-mela dived and carried them under the raft to open water.

Whatever seduction the sea had practiced earlier, it practiced none as they returned to pod two. Nuela rode behind Tirin, struggling to keep her balance as contentious mela-mela bumped her mount from either side, shrilling for attention. Afternoon sunlight reflected from the water and stung her eyes. The pain between her brows grew more intense. She peered across the water and saw . . .

Emptiness.

Emptiness in every direction, from one horizon to the other.

An emptiness so large she felt it like a weight upon her shoulders, so oppressive it crushed the breath from her chest. An emptiness, and she was lost at the center of it, lost among people with gifts and tempers she did not understand.

She stared up at the sky and found it even larger, even emptier than the sea. Swallowing hard, she averted her face and hunkered against the mela-mela's back. Her knees pressed so hard at its flanks that the mela-mela made a quick nervous leap.

She had come because she could not bear to think of Sinjanne lost in the sea. She had come, and in coming—had she lost herself too?

# Chapter Seven

It was late afternoon when Cela escorted Nuela across a series of interlocking floats to a small four-walled shelter at the end of a long bare platform. Lashings creaked with the rise and fall of the water. Cela stirred aside the stiff curtain that hung at the door. The interior was furnished with a bedmat and a small chest.

"You will have food later. For now you must use this." She removed a small bundle of dried stems from the chest. "Chew them and spit them away. Don't swallow them."

Nuela took the brittle stems. "What are they?" Nothing she had seen before.

"You will know tomorrow. Use them and drink all the water you want. There is a dipper in the chest. Does your head hurt?"

Nuela drew her fingers from her temple. The pain between her brows had diffused into a deep, dull ache. "No."

"Good," Cela said crisply, obviously neither deceived nor sympathetic. She studied Nuela with narrow dissatisfaction. "You will swim Filien's wake while Tirin is gone. He will come for you in the morning." She withdrew, letting the curtain fall.


89

Nuela settled into solitude with relief, closing her eyes against the points of light that penetrated the close-woven walls and, after a few minutes, stretching out on the mat. The floor rocked to a calming rhythm. The breeze rustled at the curtain. Lashings rasped.

She woke to the flicker of a bowl-lantern. She sat, startled and confused. Food and drink sat on the chest. The curtain fluttered but, when she rose, she saw no one on the platform beyond. The sun had set, and the moons passed in luminous silence among the first stars.

Nuela stood for a long time at the door. Surely the Ra-meki did the same things at sunset that her own people did: gathered, ate, talked, chanted. She heard only the wash of water against the sides of the platform and, once, the plaintive voice of a shell.

She ate without appetite and drank the single shell of plainwater left for her. Then, frowning, she chewed the brittle stems. They stung her gums and made her tongue briefly numb but had no other effect.

The chest, she discovered, held a blanket, fresh clothing, and grooming supplies. Discarding her swim-shift, she pulled on a loose gown and went to the edge of the platform to clean and braid her hair.

She sat for a long time, her feet dangling in the water. Occasionally she heard voices or the call of a shell. Once she saw pale shapes moving swiftly through the water toward the platform. She first thought they were mela-mela. But they drew nearer, six swimmers with flesh so white it glowed against the dark water. They swam to a single stroke, slipping through the water in formation, their arms raising chains of moon-gilded droplets each time they broke the surface.

Six pairs of eyes glinted up at Nuela. She drew back from the edge of the platform, her heart suddenly racing. Moonlight touched milky flesh and eyes as black, as cold as the eyes of fish. The swimmers sped toward the platform, slipped beneath the water, and vanished.

Nuela turned and waited with rigid shoulders for them to emerge at the other side of the platform. They did not.

From somewhere on the raft, she heard a brittle rattling sound. It came in rhythmic bursts, interspersed with the wail of shells. Nuela stood, tense and still, listening. Watching.

After a while the raft was quiet again. The water remained empty. Nuela returned to the shelter and curled up on the mat, pulling the blanket close around her. Finally wakefulness gave way to a long confusion of dreams.

She woke to a tentative hand at her shoulder. "Nuela, don't you want to eat? Nuela?"

Opening her eyes, Nuela stared with momentary puzzlement at Evanne.

The slight, dark-haired girl drew back with an uncertain frown. "Anamirre sent me to spend the day with you. I brought your breakfast. And I hung your swimshift to dry. Do you want me to comb out your hair while you eat?"

Nuela sat and glanced unenthusiastically at the tray of food. "No, please." Sleep had not refreshed her. Her mouth was stale, her eyes grainy. "Is it late?"

Evanne jumped up and pushed the curtain aside. Sunlight fell bright and clean into the shelter. Beyond the door, half a dozen children sat working with concentrated attention at some object Nuela could not see. They chanted softly over their work.

Evanne glanced at Nuela anxiously, then brightened. "Do you want to swim before you eat? I'll get your shift."

Before Nuela could protest, Evanne had gone. She returned with the dry shift. Nuela pulled it on and laced the candidate's girdle into place, refusing Evanne's help. "Will Anamirre be all right without you?"

"Yes, she wanted me to come. She didn't want you

to be alone. But if—if you want, one of my sisters can
come and spend the morning with you instead.'' Dark
eyes flickered across Nuela's face and shied away.
''Chierra would be glad to come. I could take care of
her baby. If you want someone else but me—''

''No, no,'' Nuela assured her. ''I'm just not used to
being cared for. If you would let me do things for myself . . .''

''Oh!'' Evanne's cheeks reddened. With an anxious
frown, she sat and clasped her hands. ''I'll be quiet.
Unless— Do you want pod-water to wash your face?
Tirin likes to wash in the morning before he eats. He
likes pod-water. It's like spring water but we take it
from crespi pods.''

''That would be good.''

Evanne hurried away again and returned a few minutes later with a container of cool plainwater. She prof-
erred a small bathing cloth and watched as Nuela
washed. ''You can drink it too if you want. Tirin does.''

Nuela poured a small quantity into a shell. It sweet-
ened the stale taste from her mouth.

''Did you chew the parching sticks?''

''I chewed the sticks Cela left for me. Have you
eaten?''

Evanne half rose, anxious and questioning. ''If you
want to eat alone . . .''

Nuela sighed. ''No, no. Here, why don't we eat outside.'' Perhaps Evanne's solicitude would be less suf-
focating there.

Evanne jumped up and whisked the tray from Nuela's
hands. Meeting Nuela's startled frown, she returned the
tray with an apologetic bob of her head and held the
curtain aside instead. When they had chosen a place
near the edge of the platform, she sat back with clasped
hands, letting Nuela serve herself.

They ate in silence, entertained by a lone mela-mela
that bobbed at the edge of the platform, whistling for

attention. When they ignored its antics, the mcla-mela slapped its tail against the water, showering them. They moved back, laughing.

When they had returned the empty serving shells to the tray, Evanne glanced shyly at Nuela. "Tirin says he never knew we lived here until he came into school waters."

"I never guessed anyone lived beyond Aurlanis," Nuela confirmed.

Evanne frowned down at her bare feet. "But we hear of Aurlanis from the time we're children. Sometimes, at night, we swim to the edge of the near-waters to look at the palace." She met Nuela's startled glance with an eager nod. "I've heard the wiskis shell. Once I thought I heard evenchant, but Tirin said it was only the sound of the water. He's told me where everything lies on Aurlanis, so I can close my eyes and walk wherever I want. I've chosen a room in the palace. I go there sometimes and look down into the courtyard. I—I keep things there. Gowns, shifts, necklets I make from shells I pick up on the sand."

Imaginary possessions stored in a room she had never seen. "But why can't you come ashore?" And why was the very existence of the schools such a closely kept secret?

Evanne stared at her from large eyes. "No, Nuela. No one who belongs to a school can go ashore on Aurlanis. You are permitted to come to us for kalinerre, but we are never permitted to go to you. That is by the pacts."

Nuela shook her head impatiently. "No one has told me yet just what the pacts are."

"You have seen Neptilis? He has declared himself to you?" When Nuela nodded, she hurried on. "There are three voices: Neptilis, the First Voice, who tells us what we must do, and the Deep Voice. If you are to stay you must hear them all, and if the Deep Voice tells you differently from the First Voice, then you must obey the Deep Voice. But the Deep Voice doesn't speak with words. And sometimes . . ." She hesitated, momentarily troubled. "It is the First Voice who instructs us to negotiate pacts instead of making war when we disagree. Anamirre says we brought the oldest pacts with us from the world of the silver moon. We made others after we were born to Pahla.

"They tell us where we may go and what we may do. They tell us when we may hold Pelosis and when we must go back to the sea. They tell us what we must do for candidates who come to us from Aurlanis." She shrugged.

So it was that simple. "And the lucticetes?" As long as Evanne was inclined to flush fish into her net . . .

Evanne met Nuela's eyes uneasily, then bowed her head. "They will come for us."

"You've seen them?" And if she had, why was her tone unconvincing, almost apologetic?

Evanne evaded her questioning gaze. "We have all seen them. In the dreams. Neptilis made them to carry us. He changed them, just as he changed us. But that was when we lived under the silver moon. Then we were born here and—they were not." The statement was doubtful, questioning. "But they will find us. Or Neptilis will send them to us when we are ready." Her fingers fluttered at Nuela's hand. "If you stay, we can watch for them together."

So the lucticetes swam only in the dreams. Disappointed, touched, regretful, she pressed Evanne's fingers and released them. "I can't stay, Evanne. I've only come to find my sister."

Evanne glanced quickly down. "Then we will watch together as long as you are here. And before you go, you will tell me about the room where you live and the work you do. And your friends. I want to know your friends. Then sometimes I can visit you when I think of Aurlanis. And sometimes you can visit me when you think of the Ra-meki. If you want—'' Her eyes flickered past Nuela. She stiffened and jumped up.

Nuela turned. Cela approached with a deliberate clatter of shells. Her eyes narrowed as Nuela took her feet, the fine lines at their corners marking her displeasure. ''You used the sticks?''

''I chewed the sticks you left for me last night,'' Nuela said, instinctively guarded.

The keeper's lips tightened. She peered at Evanne. ''And I see you have a friend. Evanne, surely Anamirre needs you.''

''No, Cela. She told me I could spend the day with Nuela. She—''

''Surely Anamirre needs you.''

''Then I'll go with Evanne to Anamirre's float,'' Nuela said, irritated by the keeper's manner. ''We can spend the day there if you have nothing here for me to do.''

Cela's pale eyes flashed. ''Until you are better bonded to the Ra-meki, you will not go into the water with anyone other than a caller. Swim without Tirin or Filien, and I bear none of the responsibility. None. Evanne?''

The girl bowed her head, evading the imperious gaze. ''I'll go when I've combed Nuela's hair, Cela.''

''Do it then.'' Cela turned away. Shells rattled in angry retreat.

Evanne sighed. ''She hoped to find you swollen with water.''

''What?''

''Neptilis made us so that if we are fit for the schools, we can chew the parching sticks without drinking too much and bloating. Sometimes candidates drink so much after they chew the sticks that they make themselves sick. Tirin says most of his friends on Aurlanis could drink only spring water.''

Nuela nodded. She could drink whatever she wanted, as could Sinjanne, but many of the people she knew could not. "She doesn't want me here."

Evanne shrugged. "Cela doesn't like the land-bred. Some people don't. And since Anamirre spoke—" She licked her lips uneasily, frowning. "Cela thinks Tirin has too much influence with Anamirre. She thinks he brought her to her wisdom."

"Anamirre hasn't always been your—your wisdom?" Nuela asked, surprised.

"Oh no. She found her daughterhood in the Year of the Haspipi—three years ago. Cela spoke against her when she found it. She challenged her wisdom. But Rotsin recognized that what Anamirre said came from Neptilis—Rotsin was our true son then—and he yielded to Anamirre. So Cela must heed the wisdom. But she doesn't like it, and she blames Tirin."

"But if Tirin tells Anamirre what to say . . ." Why wasn't he the wisdom?

"No, no, Tirin doesn't tell her what to say. But he talks with her a lot. He always has, since he came. And Cela thinks it was things Tirin said to Anamirre, ideas he shared with her, that brought her to her daughterhood. She—" She glanced over Nuela's shoulder and her pupils flared. "Filien!"

Nuela turned. A long formation of swimmers blazed through the water, making the lone mela-mela whistle with excitement. The first swimmer detached himself from the group and, with a quick thrust of brightly patterned arms, swung himself to the platform.

Filien was younger than Tirin, long-limbed and lithe. The markings of the Ra-meki glowed vividly upon his bare flesh. The seven other swimmers disposed themselves along the edge of the platform, their eyes keen, unsmiling. The mela-mela dived beneath the platform and emerged on the other side, leaping into the air.

Evanne took Filien's hands eagerly, her arms flushing with color. "Here, Filien. Here is Nuela—my friend."

Filien drew his hands from Evanne's. "Nuela." His eyes drew to narrow focus upon her, a blaze of blue. "Tirin told me to take you into my wake."

"Filien, we want to go to pod five, but Nuela can only go if you will call the stroke for us."

Nuela hardly heard the request, certainly did not have the opportunity to ratify or withdraw it. Because before she could guard herself, Filien had taken her hands. Quick syllables moved across his lips, and the beat of his blood was suddenly alive in Nuela's chest. Scarlet stripes burned upon her arms and spread swiftly beneath the fabric of the swimshift.

She drew a single helpless breath, and the world narrowed. Sea, platform, Evanne—vanished. Filien's thumbs pressed the tender flesh of her wrists, and his heartbeat throbbed in her every blood vessel. She felt his mark upon every part of her flesh.

He smiled broadly, pleased with his ability to rouse her, playful. "Let us go then."

And then they were in the water, the scarlet of limbs cutting the silver, the blue, the green of the morning sea. Nuela swam without being directed at Filien's side, Evanne close beside her. The others completed the formation. They swam as a single body, possessed by the same heart, beating the water with the same limbs.

Nuela did not notice at first what course they took across the sea. They swam sometimes at the surface, sometimes deep among beds of weed and pod. The mela-mela swam with them, paralleling their course without attempting to join their formation. Once, swimming in sunlit shadows, they slipped through a rocky arch. The swift rush of their shadows across the rocky surface flushed tiny orange fish from fissures in the stone. The mela-mela hurtled forward, but the tiny fish vanished back into the stone before it could scoop them up.

Nuela found she could swim longer and longer without surfacing. After a while, she found too that she could look around without losing the stroke. They passed another raft, and people waved at them from the joined platforms, the pattern of the Ra-meki brightening on their arms. Filien led them in a broad circuit of the raft and then into the cool, shadowed water beneath it.

Thick ropes extended from the underside of the platform deep into the water. A pair of children darted at them and sheered away, grinning with mischief. The mela-mela plunged playfully after them. Far below, Nuela thought she saw a pale human form hanging in the water, arms spread, hair streaming. Before she could wonder, they rose again and sped away into the open sea.

Their odyssey had the quality of dream. They passed a second raft. Again people raised scarlet-marked arms, and Nuela felt she had slipped into the time of the dreams, felt that she swam in review past the islands of the Chahera. She peered into the distance and filmy clouds briefly became shining white palaces. Children waved to her from another time, sounding shells.

And then, abruptly, Filien caught her wrists and drew her beneath the water. He held her there, his face so near hers that the black of his pupils absorbed her. His eyes were wide, confident, pleased—with himself, with her.

They rose together. "You swim well," he said when they broke the surface.

Nuela shrank from the strange, stirring intimacy of the remark and tried to study him objectively: tawny hair, cleft chin, humorous mouth. Seawater glinted on his shoulders, and for one jarring moment she imagined the taste of his lips, the pressure of his arms.

She freed herself with a convulsive jerk. Although the pattern had already faded from her arms, from her legs, her flesh remembered its heat.

Filien laughed aloud, pleased with the power of his touch, with her response to it. "I'll come for you this evening." And then he vanished beneath the surface, his entourage a swiftly fading stream of scarlet.

Shaken, Nuela turned toward the silhouette of a raft on the near horizon. Evanne bobbed beside her, hugging herself as if she clung to the scarlet markings that slowly ebbed from her flesh.

"Evanne?"

Evanne sighed happily, her eyes wide, unfocused. Then, without a word, she turned and swam toward the raft.

She did not speak until they pulled themselves over the edge of the raft. She stood, clasping Nuela's hands impulsively. "He will come for you alone this evening, Nuela." She spoke the words like a gift. Then, laughing, she shook her hair. Water sparkled and flew. "It's almost midday. Anamirre will want us to sit with her while she eats." She danced away across the platform.

Nuela stared after her, licking her lips. *He would come for her alone in the evening.* Tall, laughing, tawny, he would take her hands . . .

No one had asked her if she wanted that. No one had asked if she wanted to go with him, and certainly no one had asked if she wanted to respond to him in the way that she did. She gazed briefly across the water, alarmed, aroused, afraid at once. Finally she turned back. With a troubled frown, she followed Evanne across the gently rocking platform.

# Chapter Eight

Sunlight, laughter, turmoil . . .

Nuela and Evanne sat with Anamirre while she ate. Pleased, the old woman stroked Nuela's hand and quizzed her about people she remembered, people who had failed their tests and returned to Aurlanis. Nuela knew some of them. Others were the grandparents and great-grandparents of people she knew.

When finally the old woman grew too tired to talk more, Evanne settled her for her nap. Then she led Nuela to the edge of the platform and they swam.

Again as they passed through the cool, shadowed water beneath the float, Nuela saw thick mooring ropes disappearing deep into the water. Again she saw a human form suspended far below, arms upraised. "Evanne—"

But before she could question the Ra-meki girl, half a dozen mela-mela took possession of them. Antic, competitive, the mela-mela jousted for the right to bear them on their backs, and it was midafternoon before Evanne and Nuela climbed aboard the raft again.

Laughter, sunlight . . .

They dried their hair, and Evanne led Nuela to a sun-washed platform and introduced her to her friends. Sun-browned, laughing, the Ra-meki girls sat amid baskets of shells and coils of cord. They made room for Evanne and Nuela, but Evanne soon jumped up and led Nuela away. "They're too young, Nuela. They'll bore you. They can't talk about anything but boys and head-dresses."

They were young, little older than Sinjanne.

Turmoil . . .

It was easy to imagine Sinjanne sitting somewhere with a like group, chattering happily of boys and ornaments. Or slipping through the water with brightly patterned flesh, the restlessness that had driven her for the past year appeased. It was easy, this afternoon, to imagine Sinjanne safe and happy.

It was easy to imagine that she could renounce her search and return to Aurlanis before the sea—and the Ra-meki—seduced her entirely.

The hammer of her pulse when she thought of evening—*He will come for you alone this evening, Nuela*—told her it would not be so easy to return to the person she had been. She had met Filien that morning. He had spoken ten words to her, one of them her name. But she had only to think of him, and scarlet striae spread from her wrists to her elbows.

And each time it happened, Evanne saw and laughed softly.

Did she have no right to decide for herself what her responses would be?

Apparently she did not.

She shared a late afternoon meal with Anamirre and Evanne. Afterward she promenaded the raft with Evanne, stepping from platform to platform, shrinking from Evanne's laughing glance, trying to control a skittishness that might have been appropriate in a girl Evanne's age.

And then he slipped from the water and stood before them, as tall, as tawny as she remembered. Nuela drew back, fumbling for Evanne's hand, her breath catching sharply in her throat. The sun had set. Families had withdrawn to their shelters. The three of them stood alone on the gently rocking platform. Filien bore no marking beyond the pattern of stripes at his wrists. His swimpants were white against sun-browned skin.

Nuela's arms immediately burned and colored. She turned desperately to Evanne. "I must—I must go say good-bye to Anamirre." Her voice broke, embarrassing her as much as the color that burned on her arms

"But she has already gone to bed." Evanne cocked her head, her smile quizzical, surprised.

"Then she won't mind if you come along with us, Evanne. To pod two. We can return in the morning before she wakes. We—" She shook her head, annoyed at her own discomposure. But she had never been a girl sitting in the sun laughing with her friends about boys, flirtations, ornaments. Her work, Sinjanne, some deep-seated discomfort she could not fully define had always urged her to her feet when the exchange of confidences began. And this was no flirtation. This—

Evanne's delicate black brows rose. She stared at Nuela for a moment, open-mouthed, then laughed with delight. "Nuela, of course I will come with you if it is your first time. Is that why you have been so funny all day? She has been funny, Filien, watching the water for you, taking pattern when you weren't even there. And frowning at me. You've frowned at me so much this afternoon, Nuela. I knew you had never taken kerinchata. How could you take kerinchata on Aurlanis? But you haven't taken inchata either. Have you?"

Nuela stared at her. "I don't know what you mean."

"To take kerinchata is to mate while you bear the pattern upon your flesh," Filien said, studying her with fresh, smiling interest. "You may take kerinchata with the caller—" he tapped his bare chest "—or with someone in the string that follows the caller. To take inchata is to mate without pattern, outside the string. You have taken neither?''

''No. I haven't.'' Nor had she ever felt foolish about it before. She had only complied with the standards of behavior.

Without ever being tempted to do otherwise. Without ever thinking of doing otherwise.

Filien cocked his head, as quizzical as Evanne. ''Do you prefer to wait for Tirin?''

Color stained her face. ''I prefer—I prefer to return to Aurlanis as I came. I've come to find my sister. I haven't come— Is this a test? Must I take—kerinchata as part of my candidacy?''

Filien laughed. ''It's true what they say. You think about these things too much.''

''I hardly think about them at all. I—''

''No, I mean I've always heard that the land-bred think too much about these things. I never understood. But now I see. I came to swim with you, but instead we're standing talking about it. If you want to wait for Tirin, we will call mela-mela to take us to pod two. Have you ever ridden by moonlight?''

''I— No. No, I haven't.'' Was it to be so easy? Could he really accept her refusal so cheerfully? She still clutched Evanne's hand. She slanted an embarrassed glance at the girl.

Evanne squeezed her hand lightly before releasing it.

''I'll go call the mela-mela. You will enjoy riding by moonlight. If you don't look up at Lomaire, you can almost believe you're crossing the sea of the silver moon.'' Turning, Filien ran lightly across the platform and vanished into a maze of shelters.

Nuela frowned uncertainly after him. ''Have I— haven't I hurt his feelings, Evanne?''

''No, of course not. Why should it matter so much to Filien?''

''I don't know.'' Could a transaction that loomed so

large to her really be of so little consequence to him? And if so, why couldn't she be equally casual? "You must—you must think the land-bred are strange."

"Oh yes," Evanne agreed with artless candor. "Even Tirin was strange at first, I've heard."

Filien returned and the mela-mela appeared, subdued by moonlight. When Nuela, Evanne, and Filien had selected steeds, the other mela-mela coursed quietly behind them, occasionally vanishing beneath the water and surfacing with a quick expulsion of vapor from their nostrils. Once a pair whistled and bounded away. Gazing across the dark water, Nuela saw faint lights in the distance.

"Pod three," Filien said. "On a night like this, I can hear the First Voice speaking across the water. Listen, Nuela."

Nuela peered across the water and saw that he was right. If she did not look up, if she disregarded the faint bronze sheen Lomaire cast upon the water, she rode upon another world. And if she closed her eyes, surely she would hear a familiar bodiless voice. She lay forward against the mela-mela, her cheek pressed to its fine-grained flesh.

Abruptly Evanne hissed, "Black blood! Nuela—black blood!"

Nuela's eyes flew open as Filien drove his mela-mela near hers and pulled her into the water. He caught her wrists and spoke quick syllables. Startled, Nuela saw them on his lips by moonlight.

The mela-mela vanished in a burst of turbulent water. Nuela stared around in momentary confusion, scarlet blazing to life upon her arms. Evanne bobbed in the water before her, as if to shield her. But from—

And then she saw. White eyes flashed from the water. A swift-moving phalanx of swimmers, their flesh shadow black, raced forward, their stroke so precise, so relentless they seemed hardly human. Nuela stared at them, too stunned to retain the beat of Filien's chant, to follow as he and Evanne vanished beneath the surface.

An arm grasped her waist and pulled her under. She stared at the indistinct blur of Filien's face as he pressed her wrists to the throbbing blood vessels at his throat. Swiftly the scarlet pattern of the Ra-meki heated across her flesh again. The beat of the chant took belated possession of her pulse. Filien released her and darted away, Nuela close at his side, Evanne at her heels.

Nuela did not see the dark shapes that drove among them. She saw only the flash of eyes and the sudden thrashing turbulence of the water. For a moment, the beat of the chant grew louder, thundering in her ears. Then it faltered. Confused, she collided with Filien. Disentangling herself, she had the frightening sense that his limbs beat ineffectually at the water.

Water boiled around her again. She reached out—and this time could not find Filien at all. She felt a sharp sting at one ankle.

She had lost the stroke. The pattern cooled from her flesh as the sting at her ankle quickly became a throbbing pain that consumed half her leg. Her arms, her legs had grown suddenly heavy. Confused, helpless, she drifted to the surface.

Briefly she saw Filien. He was splayed across the water's surface. He stared at her dully, emptily, his shrunken pupils all but lost in the glassy irises. She tried to look around for Evanne, but the numbness that had invaded her limbs touched her neck now, her facial muscles, her eyelids. Staring helplessly at Lomaire, struggling—without success—simply to blink her eyes, Nuela fell into a cold void, her only companions confusion and anger.

Thready, impotent, her anger sustained her nevertheless through the boilings and rumblings of the world around her. Sustained her through turbulences she could

not identify. Through all the indignities of being helpless in strange hands.

She was moving through the water, drawn along on
her back. Sometimes her vision cleared and she
glimpsed the night sky. Each time that happened, she
saw that the moons, the stars had shifted from their
previous positions. Occasionally she stared down into
the sea instead, her lungs heavy with water. But although she listened, the First Voice did not speak.

Once, opening her eyes beneath the water, she saw
distant shinings and thought the lucticetes had come for
her. Instead a school of luminous fish darted toward
her and winked nervously away. Sometime later she
glimpsed Evanne, clutched unconscious against the
chest of one of their captors. But each time Nuela tried
to free herself, tried to reach Evanne, there was another
stinging wound and the heaviness, the numbness
claimed her again.

After a long while she realized two things: the sun
had risen, and the people who towed her through the
water were white, milky white, shadows violet upon
their abdomens and pooling darkly around their eyes.

Their black, cold eyes.

Eyes like the eyes of fish.

She didn't know who they were, but anger burned in
her, a frail thread that stitched the long, chaotic hours
of the journey into a whole.

It was midmorning when she felt the final stinging
wound. She arched involuntarily against her captor and
quivered stiffly until, abruptly, her eyelids fell. For a
time even anger was quenched.

She woke in darkness, although far above she saw
light. Her feet were secured. Her arms floated above
her, upstretched toward the distant surface. Her hair
spread in a cloud around her, moving with the current.

Her mind worked slowly, but she knew without looking that she was secured to the mooring rope that

stretched from the underside of the shadowy float she saw far above. She knew that to anyone swimming above she would be no more than a wavering paleness. She had seen such a wavering paleness twice herself.

Water had found its way into her mouth, her throat, her ear canals, into her lungs, her stomach and intestines. Her blood had given up its heat. It ran as slowly as her thoughts. The echo of her heart was distant, laggard.

She listened to it anyway, her eyes open and staring. Fish nibbled at her face and swam through her hair. A milminesa floated past her, its organs delicately violet within the translucent white of its body sac. It trailed gelatinous tendrils across her face, studying her with cold black eyes rimmed with violet. An inin-nana whipped through the water, its scarlet eyes burning brightly against its yellow flesh. Strangely, Nuela saw the colors true despite the depth. Once she saw a solitary ra-meki and cried silently after it as it flickered away.

Far overhead the light faded. Nuela hung alone in the dark and wondered, distantly, how long she could remain anchored to the mooring rope and live. Wondered why she felt no compulsion to reach down and fret at the bindings that secured her ankles. Wondered why she did not dream.

For a while diffuse light drifted on the surface of the water: Tuanne and Lomaire. Shortly after the moons passed, the water of the sea began to throb and to hum, as if somewhere a giant throat vibrated. The sound was jarring, penetrating. Occasionally it rose to a brief focused grumble, as if the throat tightened, then fell again.

At first Nuela simply let the sound pass through her— pass through her cold, slow blood and through the seawater that had collected in the channels and cavities of ..er body. Later, in the last and darkest hour of night, she found herself listening as the voice uttered syllables so elongated she could not follow them from beginning to end. Then, sometime near dawn the sea sighed, and the voice stilled. Without thinking, Nuela groped downward for the bindings at her ankles.

Her fingers were numb. She could not be certain what they did, but after a while she drifted free.

She rose with the sun. They lay together on the water, the sun golden pink, Nuela grey and without substance. She had neither inclination nor strength to swim toward the platform that floated a short distance away.

The sun edged slowly up the sky. A form appeared from the shelter that topped the platform and dived into the water. Reaching Nuela, the woman caught her beneath the chin and towed her to the platform. Climbing aboard, she knelt and pulled Nuela after her. Staring numbly, Nuela met smoky yellow eyes rimmed with brown. Although she was strongly built, the woman's close-cropped hair was sprinkled with grey, the flesh at the corners of her eyes deeply creased.

Her features drawn with barely leashed anger, she carried Nuela into the shelter and deposited her on a narrow mat. Kneeling, she wrung the water from Nuela's hair, then untied the candidate's girdle and threw it aside. Her movements were brisk, not at all gentle. Nuela knew she should protest, however ineffectually. But when the woman drew back, Nuela's eyelids dropped and she slept.

It was dusk when the woman shook her awake. "Come. We will go now."

Nuela sat, passing a confused hand across her face, and stared into the woman's smoky eyes. "Who are you?" The first question of many. Her voice was weak, but the gritty anger that had sustained her earlier returned as she spoke.

"I am Ria. We will go now. Come."

"No. My friends. I want to know—"

"We will go." The woman's hand came forward. She raked a thin black spine across Nuela's forearm. The pain was sharp, stinging, familiar.

Nuela gasped, struggling to take her feet. But the heaviness, the numbness were upon her again. She stared up at the woman, trapped in a body that suddenly refused again to obey.

She held fast to her anger as the woman pulled her back into the water, as she towed her away again. It was all she had.

The sun had set. Lomaire rose. Later the woman stung her again. Nuela convulsed and knew a moment's clawing fear as consciousness twisted from her grasp.

She woke in another shelter upon another platform, lying on a bedmat beneath a rough-woven blanket. Her arm throbbed violently. Her hair, her swimshift were damp. Her skin prickled with salt.

A lamp flickered in the corner. Beyond the uncurtained door, it was still night. Myriad small sounds—the creak of lashings, a distant voice—told her that she did not lie this time on an isolated platform. Pushing herself to her feet, Nuela stepped weakly, warily to the door.

Ria appeared immediately in the aperture, chin raised. She wore a coarse-woven shift and a braided arm band. "It is night. Return to your bed."

Nuela stared at her, trying to draw upon the strength, the courage of her anger. "Who—who are you?"

"I told you that. I am Ria."

"Then—what school are you? My friends—"

"I am of the Greater Milminesa. Return to bed and I will call for food and dry clothing."

Nuela released a slow breath. "My friends—Evanne—"

"The girl is as well as you are. And the other has returned to his pod by now."

"No. You hurt him." Shivering, Nuela remembered Filien's glassy stare, his slack limbs. "You—"

"I drove chiana venom under his skin. He was no more hurt than you were. He has long since returned to his pod. And by now the Ra-meki know that their disregard of the First Voice will no longer be tolerated."

Could Filien really be safe? And Evanne? "My girdle—" Ria had removed it, had cast it aside. "I am a candidate. I want my candidate's girdle."

Ria shook her cropped head, eyes glinting with angry pleasure. "You don't need it any longer. You have passed the tests."

Nuela's head snapped erect. "What do you mean?" Her mouth was suddenly dry. Blood sang a dizzy rhythm in her ears, although she did not understand why.

"I mean that you have passed the tests." Again the anger, the pleasure.

Her ordeal secured to the mooring rope—a test? "No," she said. "Evanne told me I must hear three voices. Neptilis, the First Voice—" The blood whined now. Three voices. Neptilis had declared himself when Tirin pulled her under—had it been six days before? The First Voice had instructed her upon several occasions.

*And in the dark hours of morning she had heard the wordless hum and drone—of the Deep Voice?*

A cold finger scratched at her spine, raising hard chills. "No. I've heard only two voices." No sane person would call that growling, inhuman drone a voice.

Ria shook her head. "No one releases herself from the Deep Listening until she has heard what she went to hear. You have heard the Deep Voice. So you have passed the last test, the test no one can pass if she has not first passed the others. You are no longer a candidate."

"Then—I am a Ra-meki. And you cannot hold me here. The pacts—" Surely there was something in the pacts to protect her.

"By the pacts, there is only the formality of our keeper's certification and you will be a pre-pledge Ra-meki. And we have brought you here as a Ra-meki under the clause of the black blood. You will remain in our custody until we have washed ourselves clean of grievance."

Nuela stared at her, drew a long breath. "I don't know what you mean. Black blood?"

"When a school, a pod, an individual offends, the blood of the offended runs black—and it becomes the right of the offended to do that which will wash the black away. This is by the First Voice, and this is by the pacts."

"I don't—" How had they offended the Greater Milminesa? *By riding the mela-mela?*

"You will understand when you need to. Your name?"

"I don't think you need to know that."

"Then I will call you Scarlet Fish. Why don't you sit down, Scarlet Fish, while you have the strength to do it gracefully. I will call for your meal. Then, when you have made yourself presentable, you will meet our keeper." With a last smoky yellow glance, she withdrew.

Nuela sat, weakly, and let her head drop into her hands. She had been brought here as a Ra-meki? The pacts permitted them to sting her with venom, to tie her to the mooring rope, to hold her against her will? Because she had ridden the mela-mela?

She took an austere meal, served from unpolished shellware. Ria watched with close-lipped disapproval as she set aside most of the meal uneaten. "If our fare isn't good enough for you, then make yourself presentable.'' She nodded to the comb and the unbleached garment she had brought and withdrew again.

Bleakly Nuela exchanged her damp swimshift for the gown and drew the comb through her hair. Taking the discarded swimshift, she wiped salt crystals from her face and arms.

Somewhere a shell wailed. Another answered. Nuela looked up at the sound of footsteps.

Looked up and slowly stood, facing the slight, golden-haired woman who entered the shelter. Stunned, she stared at the familiar lines of the face, at the eyes that were—she had forgotten—so like Sinjanne's. Her breath ebbed away.

She stared at the woman who had vanished into the sea one night so many years before.

Stared at the woman her father had gone to find.

Stared at the woman who had been entered in the keeper's log as drowned.

She was unable to give the woman who faced her by lamplight her proper title. It had been too long. Her shock was too great. ''Tuleja,'' Nuela said hoarsely when she could speak.

# Chapter Nine

STARING AT THE WOMAN WHO STOOD BEFORE HER, Nuela slowly recognized half-forgotten nuances: the unbending set of her shoulders, the lift of her chin, the utter, unbetraying stillness of every tiny facial muscle. Tuleja wore a shift of coarse-woven fabric, a wide band of the same fabric at her thigh. She had cropped her hair to lie close to her scalp, and the years had etched deep lines at the corners of her eyes. Otherwise she seemed little different.

"You have not changed," she said when Nuela did not speak. The observation was flat, unwelcoming.

Nuela drew a deep breath, remembering now why it was her father's place, never her mother's, she had tried to take in rearing Sinjanne. "Nor have you." Tuleja had always been just this unbending, just this contained—just this unreachable. "What—what are you doing here?"

"I am keeper of this pod. I have come to evaluate you."

Nuela shook her head. "No, what— You were entered in the log as drowned. Both of you were written as drowned."

Tuleja's eyes flickered, but her voice remained without expression or inflection. "In Altin's case truly. In my case not. Obviously."

So her father would not step next into the lamp-lit shelter.

Had she really thought he would? Confused, Nuela blinked sudden moisture from her eyes. "But—he went to find you. We waited on the beach. It got dark. We were cold. Sinjanne fell asleep. He—he went into the water to find you." She drew a tremulous breath, remembering. Evenchant had faded from the courtyard. Lamps had first flickered alive in palace windows, then been extinguished. They had waited, the only people remaining on the beach—perhaps the only people still awake on all the island. And finally her father had gone into the water, leaving her to a night as long, as cold as any she had known.

He had gone—and drowned seeking the woman who stood safe before her?

Something flashed deep in Tuleja's eyes. Bitterness? Pain? "Yes. He knew better—but he came."

"Knew better? When he thought you were lost? Or in trouble? When—"

"No. I told him before I went that I might be gone the night. If he had returned to our room, if he had gone to bed . . .

"But he never slept when I was in the water. I pulled myself early from the dreams a hundred times and found him watching for me on the beach. As if he thought I would drown if he slept while I was in the water."

*The dreams.* "You didn't go into the water to swim," Nuela said with sudden, devastating comprehension. Tuleja had gone to hide herself in the garden wall. She had passed the night rocking in the lucticete's sac— while her family sat cold and frightened on the shore.

"And he knew it. *Altin knew it.* But he came looking for me anyway. When I returned the next morning, they were searching for him." Her voice took a high edge. "They wanted me to help. He had been gone for hours, but they searched anyway. And when they came back, when they walked up the beach past me . . .

"And what did they expect of me after that? After they gave him up? That I would go back to the palace and raise you and your sister alone? Never knowing which of you would follow me into the water next? Never knowing what would happen if you did?

"*No.* I went to Polamaire. That morning. I told her I wanted to test you both. Then. That day. So I would know at least that much: whether you would drown too if some night you came to the garden wall to find me." Tuleja's lips quivered. "But no. She told me I could remain on Aurlanis on the terms she set me—or I could go. I was to take work in the palace rooms and never again go for more than an hour into the sea. I was never to take you or Sinjanne into the water with me. You would be tested as provided by the pacts, at kalinerre.

"I must go that long without even knowing what might happen if I went to the garden wall again.

"She forced the choice on me. But it was no choice at all. You were better without me. Your sister was better with you than with me. I didn't even stay for the last chants. I went to our quarters. You were sleeping. I watched over you for a few minutes. And then I came to the Greater Milminesa, to the pod where I had passed my kalinerre. They prescribed penalties for me, and they took me in."

"Penalties?"

"Penalties for returning to Aurlanis at the end of my kalinerre, when I knew I should not. Because that's how I killed him. By taking him for my lover before I made my kalinerre. By going back to him at its end. Because I knew he would be waiting.

"But I didn't go back to him just once. I want you

to know that. I went back a hundred times. I tore myself early from the dreams, I left the garden wall, I went back.

"But blame me if you want. Blame me because that one time I went back too late." Her eyes held a hard sparkle. "And what about you? Who have you left on Aurlanis? Do you have a lover there?"

"I—*no*. I came—" It jarred her to think of it. She had come because—like her father—she could not bear to watch the water and wait.

"Then you have observed the standards. And you didn't even know the reason for them, did you?"

Nuela gazed at her. A moment before, Tuleja had seemed distant, self-possessed. Now pain and anger sat clearly on her features. "I know now." So that just this sort of thing would not happen. So that a woman who was sea-called would not return to a man suited only for the land. And lead him, one day, to his death. "But Polamaire—" Polamaire had dreamed the dreams, had heard the voices—had returned nevertheless from kalinerre.

"Will took Polamaire back to Aurlanis, the will to succeed Kertin as keeper. But she'll return to the Rameki one day, just as Aliapara has returned to the Haspipi. Polamaire brought her son from school waters just as my mother brought me."

Aliapara, second keeper to Polamaire, had not drowned? And her own grandmother had brought Tuleja from her candidacy? "But I thought—"

"You thought that when you named your grandparents, you named the people who gave you flesh. Three of them did. Porsin did not.

"But of course even I never knew that until I went to my own kalinerre. I never knew there was a father I might want to search out. I never knew I had brothers and sisters among the Isawohna. I never knew anything of the schools before I took the sea trail.

"For good reason. The pacts exist for good reason, every term, every clause." The small muscles of her face contracted, drawing her lips tight, narrowing her eyes. She stepped back, once again distant, armored. "Once the Chahera rode with the moon-beasts. We obeyed Neptilis' teachings, and the world was good. We lived well both upon land and upon sea. But the schools grew slack. They turned a deaf ear to Neptilis' teachings. Perhaps they even made war again. And the moon broke and became two and we were exiled here at the center of the sea.

"Oh, I know the Ra-meki have told you differently. They have told you that we were simply born out of the world of our dreams into this one." She shrugged. "They're welcome to their own tales, even if they make no sense to anyone else.

"But even the Ra-meki will tell you that the three voices come from the time of grace, from the time before our exile. And so we must heed them. Just as we must obey the pacts we have made in response to them. We must obey the pacts to the least clause, to the finest point. To do otherwise—"

Tuleja's hands closed tight. The knuckles whitened. "To do otherwise is to bring every kind of wrong upon our people—and to drive back the day when the lucticetes will come to carry us out of exile." She drew a deep breath. "So I have come as keeper of pod four of the school of the Greater Milminesa to certify you. I come under the clause of the black blood. Display the scarlet of the Ra-meki for me."

Nuela hesitated. "I don't see that it was so wrong. The mela-mela wanted to carry us." When Tuleja only arched questioning brows, Nuela insisted, "If we hadn't ridden them, they would have followed us. They would have tried to take us on their backs anyway."

Tuleja's brows rose fractionally. She nodded once, tersely. "And yet the First Voice tells us we were never made to be masters of land or sea. We were made to be a part of the web of life, one form of life among many, each with its own reason for being, each with its own particular grace.''

''But if they come to us, if they want to carry us—''

''No. It is wrong. Every child knows it is wrong. The mela-mela will not come to carry you unless they have been taught to come. It is not their nature. They must be trained, and that is mastery.

''Show me the scarlet if you can.''

Nuela frowned. How could Tuleja be so certain what the First Voice intended? And so convinced of the true nature of the mela-mela? She turned her wrists—and caught her breath as scarlet blazed darkly alive against pale flesh.

''So you are a Ra-meki,'' Tuleja said without inflection. ''You have not been formally pledged, but the mark is upon you, and I certify you so.''

She was a Ra-meki? Wasn't she permitted to decide that for herself? ''No. Tirin told me I had the right to make the decision with my feet on soil. He told me that even if I passed the tests, I could return to Aurlanis.''

''Of course you have that right. But you cannot exercise it here. The Ra-meki themselves must offer you the formal choice. I can only certify your current status. You have passed the tests. You bear the mark of the Ra-meki, but you have not yet been offered the opportunity to pledge yourself. So by the pacts you are a pre-pledge Ra-meki.''

Nuela licked her lips. ''And does it make any difference at all that you are my mother?''

Tuleja's fingers strayed to the band at her thigh. ''The sea is your mother.'' The words were brittle, unyielding.

Nuela's shoulders stiffened. ''Then who are you?''

"In order, I am Tuleja, daughter to Neptilis and the sea. I am keeper of pod four of my school. And I am the bearer of a debt of pain. Here—if you must see." She untied the fabric band and whipped it from her thigh.

Nuela frowned, not understanding at first what she saw. Small sharp-pointed shells were sewn into the fabric of the band. Her mother's bare thigh was girdled with a dense, white layer of scar tissue where the shells had bitten into her flesh. "You—you don't wear this all the time?" she said, disbelieving.

"I wear it during daylight hours upon the raft. I do not wear it into the water."

"But—why?"

"This is one of the penalties set me when I returned to the Greater Milminesa. Upon certain dates, I lace the shells tight, and I bleed for what I did. I take pain from other shoulders, other backs, and I carry it myself." Her voice was bleak. "This is not one of those dates."

"But he wouldn't want it," Nuela said. "My father would never have wanted you to hurt yourself. He would have understood. He—surely he *did* understand."

"Of course he did, as well as any man who isn't sea-called can understand. Is that an excuse? The lessons were laid before me. I refused to learn them. I refused to choose between land and sea. I tried to have both. And Altin paid with his life. This—this is small enough penance for that." Her eyes narrowed, and her voice stung with bitterness. "We are a tale among the schools. You didn't know that, did you? Altin and Tuleja. When candidates come to the time of choice, keepers tell them our story. Every candidate who chooses to return to Aurlanis hears what I did and the result of it—so that she will understand exactly why she, why he must make the correct choice. Or pay the penalty in grief and blood.

"And just so do we all pay for the misdeeds of our ancestors. But we won't pay forever, Nuela. One day it will be enough. And when the lucticetes come back for us, no person will have to choose again. There will be land for us all—in the islands, on the mainland. Each school will have its own beach, its own palace. And the few who have lost the sea-gifts can travel safely upon the sea with those who love them. They can travel in the lucticetes' sacs.

"But that day will not come until Neptilis sees that we are prepared to be true sons and true daughters to him again. Only then will the great beasts return.

"So no, I am not your mother, and you are not my daughter. Before I listen to your voice, I must listen to Neptilis and to the First Voice. I must consider the pacts. And I must think of my pod, my school, and the Chahera people."

Nuela shook her head, understanding with aching clarity what Tuleja said. She had been orphaned once. Now she had been orphaned again, far more profoundly. The blood she shared with Tuleja meant less than seawater. "I'm tired," she said, her voice thick. "My friend, Evanne—"

"She is sleeping. You will see her tomorrow when everything is ready." She stepped back, slight, controlled, brittle. "Do not try to leave. There will be someone at the door."

Nuela stared at the empty doorway. Escape? Where would she go if she did? She had no better idea how to navigate from place to place than when she had first come looking for Sinjanne.

Sinjanne— Tuleja had gone without even asking about her.

But of course Sinjanne was no longer Tuleja's daughter either.

Did she remain Nuela's sister? Or had she already formed new allegiances? Had the blood they shared turned to water too?

Nuela sat on the bedmat, her head in her hands. Her eyes, her throat ached with tears. After a while she blew out the lamp, and the dark hid her tears.

# Chapter Ten

THE FLOAT ROCKED IN LONG, LAGGARD WAVES. NUELA woke from dreams as grey, as poorly defined as the dawn. Her lashes were stiff with dried tears, her muscles tender, as if she had abused them. A lean, barelimbed youth sat in the uncurtained doorway. He turned when she sat and fish-cold eyes met hers, black in a milky-pale face. His shaven skull was as smooth, as white as his face. The grey light painted violet shadows beneath his eyes. Nuela lay back and closed her eyes, wishing him away.

When she woke again, the sun had risen. A different youth sat on the matting beyond the doorway, the shadows beneath his eyes sharply defined violet crescents. She studied him briefly, then wished him away too.

Eventually the sun nagged her awake again. A tray of food waited beside the bedmat, the fish pungent, the polipods sliced to reveal dry, stringy flesh. Sitting, Nuela pushed the tray away with a queasy turn of her stomach. Children called in the distance, their voices high, accusing. Nearer, a string of shells chattered briefly and was still.

A third white-fleshed youth crouched beyond the uncurtained doorway. Nuela met his gaze, and the scarlet pattern blazed reflexively at her wrists. She stood, choosing her words, their tone deliberately. "I want my swimshift. And I want to see my friend."

The youth rose, faint violet veins pulsing into prominence at his temples. "I know nothing about your clothing. You are to wait here until Garin comes for you."

"Then tell him I'm ready." For what she didn't know. Perhaps only to bolster herself with an open display of defiance.

He shook his head, his eyes glinting. "Garin will come when he is ready," he said, obviously pleased to deny her.

Nuela bristled. "Then I'll wait outside until he comes." Before he could bar her way, she brushed past him through the doorway.

The sun was bright, the sky vivid. The shelter faced an open square of water bounded by floats. A second lean youth sat cross-legged at an uncurtained doorway nearby. Jumping up, he shot a startled question at the first youth. Before the first youth could respond, Nuela stepped past him into the shelter he guarded.

Evanne rose from the corner, her slight features pale. "Nuela?" Startled, concerned, afraid.

Alarmed, Nuela caught the girl's hands and pressed small, cold fingers between her own. "Are you all right? They wouldn't let me see you last night." Behind them, the two guards argued in low, vehement tones.

"I'm all right. They brought me food and water. I slept. I—" Evanne's eyes widened. "Oh, Nuela, you saw her. You met her. Your mother."

Nuela stiffened. "I saw the pod keeper." It surprised her that she could speak so evenly of Tuleja. "You—knew?"

"We've heard the stories. When you said you were from Altin and Tuleja, I knew. What—what did she tell you?"

"That I am a pre-pledge Ra-meki. And that it was

wrong to ride the mela-mela." *And that blood is less than seawater.* Nuela glanced around and the two guards, suddenly silent, peered at her. "What will they do to us? What is the penalty for riding the mela-mela?"

Evanne's eyes widened, then became guarded. She drew Nuela down beside her. "I—I don't know what penalty they might name for that. The Greater Milminesa and the Shihona have made formal charges at pact-call, but we've never been censured."

"Pact-call?"

"When the keepers and the true sons and daughters meet to form the Greater School. The Greater Milminesa and the Shihona have charged us several times with attempting to exercise mastery, but the Greater School has never found against us." Her eyes swept Nuela's face, wide and anxious. Her tongue darted at her lips. "Did—did Tuleja tell you anything else?"

"Nothing important." Only that if she wanted her mother, she must look to the sea. "Cela will send someone for us, won't she? Or Anamirre? Tirin—" He was somewhere in school waters, carrying Polamaire's message. "If the Greater Milminesa have brought charges, but the Greater School has never found against you—"

"They have not found against us for riding the mela-mela. But—" She drew a trembling breath and clutched at Nuela's hands. "Oh, Nuela, I've wished so hard for the lucticetes. I dream of them night and night again. Not water dreams. The other kind. I think about them. I watch for them every year when we meet on the beach at Pelosis. I call to them from my heart.

"But we've been wishing for so long—for the lucti-cetes and for land. What if there *is* no land? What if the 'cetes can't hear us? They haven't come, have they?"

"No," Nuela agreed, startled by the abrupt change of topic, by the girl's sudden, trembling vehemence.

"They haven't come, but we weren't meant to cry. I believe that, Nuela. I *feel* it. Even if we did something wrong, even if that's why we were sent away from the silver moon, Neptilis made us to be good to one another. He made us to give each other happiness, not pain. I believe in Anamirre's wisdom even if Cela doesn't, even if some of the others don't.

"But we will cry just as much if we follow Anamirre's wisdom and raise the black blood in the others. How can it be right to do that?"

"I—I don't know, Evanne," Nuela said, not understanding. What had Anamirre's wisdom to do with riding the mela-mela? Surely no one had cried simply because the other schools objected?

Nuela frowned. What had Anamirre said the day they met? *I cried every year when I was young, Nuela. I cried when we sent the floats on the current to the Great Land.*

The Great Land. The land at the end of the current.

"Evanne—" But Evanne's slight features had grown rigid. She stared over Nuela's shoulder. Nuela turned.

A man in loose trousers and tight-belted tunic stood at the shelter door. He was heavy and well muscled, his silver hair close trimmed. A gridwork of white scars pulled one side of his face taut. A long jagged scar crawled up his left arm and disappeared beneath his tunic. He studied Nuela and Evanne, silver brows bristling. "Your quarters are ready. Come with me and make no more trouble. I am Garin." He turned away.

Evanne clutched Nuela's arm, suddenly ashen. Startled, Nuela slipped a supporting arm around her and felt a long tremor run through the girl's body. "Evanne, if you want to stay here . . ."

"No. No, Nuela. I'm all right. We must go."

But clearly Evanne was not all right as they followed

Garin across the raft. She bit at her lips, the dark hair that fell across her face only half hiding the tears that spilled down her cheeks.

The two young guards had become four. They stalked after the party in grim-lipped silence, shaven heads glinting in the sun. Each time Nuela glanced back, the youth who had barred her door squared his shoulders, the veins at his temples darkening. Occasionally one of the four dived into the water and vanished beneath the floats, pulling himself out ahead of the party a few minutes later.

Women wrapped in loosely woven garments carried baskets and bundles from float to float, their hair cropped to their scalps. Children sat silent and unsmiling over small tasks. Older men turned scarred faces after them. Nuela had the impression of a people grimly absorbed in some communal task—a people who paused in their work nevertheless and stared, eyes turning fish black in the sun. Her forearms darkened in reflexive response, and her heart beat faster in a constricting chest.

"They are different from us, Neula," Evanne said softly, clutching her hand. "If we were the ones going to take our year on Pelosis, we would be laughing and calling chants."

"The Greater Milminesa will live on Pelosis next year?"

"Next year is the Year of the Greater Milminesa," Evanne reminded her. "But look at them. The women have cut off their hair and thrown it to Pahla. Do you think she wants their hair? And the boys—if you could see—are cutting themselves. Beneath their briefs— because they aren't permitted to scar themselves where it shows until they are older."

"But—why? Why scar themselves at all?"

"They do it to mark the year, just like the men.

When they are older—'' She halted, drawing a sharp breath.

Passing between ranks of shelters, they had reached the outer perimeter of the raft. A narrow walkway stretched in either direction, the shelters that lined it presenting blank rear walls to the sea. Ahead a pier covered with woven mats reached out into the water. A solitary float topped with an austere, windowless shelter was tethered at the end of the pier. The float rose and fell with the slow swell of the waves.

Evanne's nails drove into the palm of Nuela's hand. "Nuela—you came looking for your sister. Please—be a sister to me now.''

Nuela looked down at her in surprise. The girl's face was grey, her lips trembling.

Garin halted at the foot of the pier. "Your quarters.'' He stood aside. The pier stretched before them.

"Be a sister to me,'' Evanne said again, her voice little more than a breath. *"Please*, Nuela.''

Nuela slid a supportive arm around her and felt the shudder of her slight body. "I don't understand.'' She bit the words apart coldly, addressing them to Garin.

"There is little enough to understand. We have prepared your float. Everything is arranged. It is time now for you to go aboard.''

Unwillingly Nuela glanced across the open sea, across its boundless expanse. *I cried every year . . .*

Why recall those words now? "No,'' she said. "Take me to Tuleja.'' There was something here she did not understand. She had a right to hear the explanation directly from her mother's lips.

*I cried every year when we sent the floats on the current.*

*The Great Land. The land at the end of the current.*

But where did the current end? And why did she feel a numbing cold at the bottom of her stomach as four older men joined the youthful escort? The older men drew black quills from sheaths cinched at their waists and plunged into the water, surfacing at either side of the pier.

"Tuleja will see you later, as will Taric, our true son. Everything will be done with the proper ceremony. Neparra waits for you now." He gestured toward the solitary float. It rocked idly on the swell.

Nuela gazed at black quills in milk-pale hands, every instinct rebelling against compliance. "Evanne—"

Evanne pulled herself upright. "I'm—I'm all right, Nuela. I'm strong. But I asked you— I asked you, Nuela—" She peered up at Nuela, her eyes beseeching.

She had asked twice. "I will be your sister," Nuela said, "if you will be mine." Whatever was to happen next, surely she needed support as badly as the Rameki girl did.

They walked together across the pier, Garin a pace behind them, men in the water at either side. The sun shone brightly. Beyond the float, the sea broke into reflective sheets: silver, violet, green.

The shelter stood at the center of the float, a broad apron of matting surrounding it. Its double-paneled walls excluded all but a few stray slivers of sunlight. Nuela followed Evanne through the narrow, uncurtained doorway into the shadowy interior.

Compact as it was, the shelter had been partitioned into two small cubicles and a larger space. The cubicles were packed with chests and baskets, stacked one atop another. Household articles, implements, garments, toys hung on the walls of the larger area, as if on display.

A young woman in an enveloping white gown sat on the floor in the larger area, a tray and serving ware spread before her, a single small lamp at her right hand. Her cropped head was erect, delicately made, the bones standing prominently against the white flesh. Her eyes were luminous, her face glowing and pale, not with the opaque pallor of the Greater Milminesa school pattern but with some fragile inner brightness. The only sign of pattern was the smudgy violet stain beneath her eyes and a milky-pale patch at the inside of either wrist. She extended a narrow hand. "Sit down, please."

Nuela hesitated. Garin had not boarded the float. He remained on the pier, his back to the doorway.

"Please sit down. I am Neparra. I serve Taric and through him all our school. I am to give you your boarding meal. I've brought everything, surely, that will please you." Her voice was light, floating. "Please, I have prepared myself to serve you."

Prepared herself? How? Nuela glanced at Evanne and saw that the Ra-meki girl gazed at Neparra with wide, unfocused eyes. Slowly, as if caught up by some distant chant, she lowered herself to the mat.

Neparra inclined her head formally, then peered up again at Nuela. "Please?"

Warily Nuela sat, legs crossed. "Why have we been brought here?" And was Neparra ally or enemy? Evanne had been frightened and trembling a moment before. Now she sat as if overawed, breathing shallowly through her open mouth.

"You have been brought to take your boarding meal." Neparra's face was like the afterimage of a dream: pale, faintly luminous, enigmatic. Bending her slender neck, she poured amber liquid into a shell. "I prepared both food and drink with my own hands, the hands that serve Taric and through him our school." She extended a shell to Evanne and inclined her head gravely when Evanne accepted. Evanne sipped at the liquid, her eyes huge upon Neparra's face.

Neparra bent again to pour amber liquid. Nuela accepted the shell vessel reluctantly, sipped from it still more reluctantly under Neparra's watching eyes. Nuela frowned at the liquid's faintly familiar musk.

"It is not satisfactory?"

"It is—very good," Nuela said with little conviction. "But I want to know—" She hesitated at Evanne's quickly indrawn breath.

The Ra-meki girl laid a light hand on Nuela's thigh. "We must not ask questions now, Nuela. Neparra is serving us."

"But we need not be silent," Neparra interjected in a quick, light voice. "We can speak of the beauty of the sky on a quiet morning. We can speak of the gloss of moonlight on midnight water. We can speak of the day when the great pale moon-beasts will return to carry us all back to land. There are many things we can speak of while we take our meal."

But they could not speak of why they had been so brusquely escorted to this loosely tethered float. They could not speak of the fact that men with chiana quills waited to stop them if they tried to leave. They could not speak of what might happen when the meal was done.

*I cried every year . . .* The float rocked with each rise and fall of the sea, tugging impatiently at its moorings.

Nor, Nuela guessed, were they to speak of the pattern of scored flesh she saw on the underside of Neparra's upper arm when the wide sleeve of her gown fell briefly back. Nor of the faint dew of perspiration that came to her upper lip as she continued the slow ceremony of the meal, as if she were slowly devolving from some quiet, glowing ecstasy to pain.

She served them delicate slivers of puschis marinated in filii juice.

She served them strands of pispis meat, carefully teased from the spiny legs and artfully arranged upon a translucent silver shell.

She served them grasses Nuela could not identify, steamed to wilted tenderness and flavored with oils.

She served them tiny white pods that burst against the tongue, filling the mouth with prickling sweetness.

She served them morsels and tidbits, the flesh and organs of a dozen rare fish.

And with each course, Neparra poured amber liquid into their drinking shells and Nuela tried to identify its faint musk.

Neparra did not eat or drink. Occasionally she spoke, but after a while Nuela realized with distant perplexity that she no longer understood what she said. Neparra's voice came like a thin breeze, wisping through the small chamber to sparse effect. Her inward brightness had ebbed, leaving her face grey, drawn. She hesitated over the serving pieces, groping her way through the ritual of the meal with increasing debilitation.

Later still Nuela turned and found that Evanne lay upon the mat, one arm outflung. Her hair fell across her face, partially concealing her lax features.

When had she fallen asleep? Nuela gazed at her in confusion, her own thoughts retreating to a distance. She called to them, and they echoed back to her from far away. Strangers. Remote.

*Narsa-pika.* She recognized the musk now. Neparra had served them dilute liquor of narsa-pika.

Narsa-pika: pale flower of the depths, shy recluse within garlands of its own heavy black foliage. It would not grow in the sea gardens, and no one had ever gone into the deepwaters and plucked it fresh. No one, in fact, had ever seen it in its growing state. Instead, on Aurlanis, they waited for the occasional storm to sweep long strands of it ashore. Then they harvested the blossoms and brewed and bottled their liquor, to be applied to abrasions and skin lesions.

*Never to be taken by mouth.* Every bottle was labeled with that stern instruction. And no bottle was permitted to leave the pharmacy. The pharmacist applied narsa-pika herself, in the consulting room.

Never . . .

How much had she taken?

Now Nuela lay upon the mat too. Had she been able to formulate her thoughts more clearly, she might have wondered when that had happened. And she might have been afraid. Instead she lay nerveless and still and watched as Neparra returned the serving pieces to their original configuration and stood.

The single lamp glowed. Slowly, ceremonially, Neparra opened her gown and stepped free of it, raising her arms high above her head. Her body was cruelly emaciated, even more cruelly marked. She had patterned the flesh of her upper arms and her rib cage with wounds. As she stretched, new-crusted lacerations opened and bled. Her thin buttocks, her starveling thighs were blue with bruises. She had tied a broad band of fabric at her waist. It was dark with half-dried blood. Only her slight breasts were untouched.

Now it was no longer the lamp that glowed. It was Neparra, her face, drawn a moment before, was bright again from within as she began to chant. Nuela lay silent witness to the ecstasy of her celebration.

Lay silent witness until Neparra's tortured body disintegrated into particles and was swept aside by the vivid colors of a rising vision.

Nuela had seen the land before. Now she saw it again: hillsides tangled with green growth, great crystal rushes of channeled water, bands of tall-striving vegetation, inland expanses of sand where no sea washed.

Jagged shores with palaces rising in dark spires.

Other, less grandiloquent palaces set along gentler shores.

And finally, leaving the body of the land itself, her vision swept across green and lavender shallows to islands where low, pale palaces gleamed and bright-patterned folk swam. A single silver-white moon floated in a noonday sky.

Sea surfaces glittered and tossed, casting up froth. A gleaming white palace appeared, rambling along the crest of a white-sand island. Vegetation stood around it, stiff fronds casting black shadows. Nuela fixed the vision in place, holding it, listening for the First Voice.

She heard only the rush of her own blood as the vision abruptly disintegrated, flying apart into bright particles. Suddenly she was caught, bodiless, at the center of a storm of color. Light entered her, penetrated her, rushed through and around her. Charged particles of energy impinged upon her every nerve ending, striking effects upon them.

*Never to be taken by mouth.*

For a while she was lost in the stinging assault. Then, from somewhere near, she heard a voice. It brought with it a rush of heat, and the cooler colors—the blues, greens, violets—no longer struck their light in her brain. Even the reds, the oranges, the yellows impinged upon her with less force.

The voice spoke again, husky, male, and intimate, and the oranges and the yellows melted into a torpid, near-liquid flow of scarlet.

The heat grew more intense, and Nuela recognized that it came not from some external source but from the rise of blood to the surface of her skin—from the sudden manifestation of the Ra-meki pattern.

The pattern seared her in every tender place, a swift-engulfing agony. She groaned, the sound of her own voice anchoring her tentatively to reality. She groaned again, more loudly, and a cool hand glided over her fevered skin, turning agony to shuddering pleasure. Gasping, Nuela found her way back to the place where she had left her body and dragged reluctant eyelids open.

He half lay, half crouched upon her, his milky skin cooling her where it touched her even as the chant he whispered drove her to greater fever. A caller. He had to be a caller. Who else could bring her to such burning arousal with his touch, with a few murmured words?

Looking up, she saw that she clutched the pale flesh of his upper arms with bold scarlet fingers, drawing him nearer. Her lips burned, and she arched upward to cool them upon his. The fish black of his eyes was oddly compelling. A single thin scar bisected one cheek.

The very cold of him drew her.

She found his lips with hers. She pressed herself greedily to them, crushing them between his teeth and hers. Crushing her own lips as well. Tasting their mingled blood, the hot of it, the salt of it. Reaching then with one hand to guide him to the place where the fire burned most intensely, where the pleasure would be sharpest, keenest.

But he forgot, when he drew back from her pressing lips, to resume his whispered chant. He forgot to web her freshly around with the soft syllables of seduction. He forgot.

She remembered.

She remembered that she did not want him. She had not chosen him. She had neither invited nor assented to this experience.

Suddenly coherent, she rolled her head and stared around the dimly lit shelter. Evanne lay where Nuela had seen her last. Neparra had gathered the remnants of their meal and gone, leaving only the lamp. Its flame cast scare shapes on the shelter wall.

From the corner of one eye, Nuela saw the doorway, saw darkness beyond. She expelled a sharp breath. How long had she been lost in the charged storm? It had seemed little more than minutes.

Outside hours had passed.

Weakly she raised one arm, pushed. Black eyes frowned down at her, for a moment not comprehending her resistance. Purple veins pulsed at his temples. His eyes shimmered, then came to sharp focus.

He resumed his husky chant.

Too late.

Nuela's foot found the lamp even as her body arched involuntarily against his. Hot oil spilled across the matted floor. The scare shapes on the wall subsided for a moment, then leaped high. Nuela stared at them, breathless, waiting for them to disintegrate into charged particles.

Instead flame leaped up the wall, bounded across the mat, and suddenly the fire that licked at Nuela's flesh was real.

# Chapter Eleven

NUELA HARDLY REMEMBERED HOW SHE REACHED THE
water. Had she plunged through the burning wall? Fled
by the doorway? She remembered only an orifice
rimmed in flame, herself momentarily framed within
it. Glancing back, she saw the caller bend over Evanne's
limp body, and she felt a moment's sharp compunction.
She could not leave Evanne.

Then she was in the water, stunned, breathless—but
not so disoriented that she did not see the pale shape
that loomed quickly before her, black quill in hand.

He slashed, but she was already beneath the water,
kicking herself downward. Her escape, her descent were
a series of desperate thrusts and lunges. The gown
wrapped itself heavily around her. Pausing, she wriggled free of it. It hung briefly before her, a cast-off
skin, then vanished.

Her eyes remained wide upon the dark water, but she
saw nothing more as she drove toward the depths. Roll-
ing over in the water, she peered back toward the surface. The faint orange glow of the burning float lay
almost directly above. If she could surface far enough
from the raft—

Cold fingers slithered across her back. She spun, uttering a silent scream, closing her mouth on inrushing

water when she realized she had only drifted into a bed of weed. Reflexively she kicked free.

Water had already found her lungs. She hung for a moment, stricken, confused, as crushing pressure rose in her skull. Her chest was heavy. White light blazed behind her eyes, intensifying quickly to the level of pain. Blood pulsed heavily in her ears. Her heart jumped once, angrily, at her chest wall.

And she stood upon a beach of fine white sand. It was night. The moon silvered sand and sea. Warm air mantled her in fragrance. She turned slowly, little willing it, and gazed at the shining white palace that rambled across the raised crest of the island. She had seen it not so very long before, standing within its girdle of stiff green vegetation. She had seen it. . . .

*She could not lose herself to the dream now. She would bob back to the surface. They would find her.*

*She had abandoned Evanne. She had promised to be a sister to the Ra-meki girl—and then she had left her helpless in the burning shelter.*

She had seen the white palace; she had seen the black shadows leaves and fronds cast upon white sand not so very long before. She watched the slow dance of shadows again as she moved forward.

Moved forward against her will. Moved forward because it was already too late to escape the slow, deliberate thrust of the dream.

Neptilis stepped from the shadows, his brow high and vaulted, cut by a single deep vertical crease. Black hair swept back from his forehead; the black cloak swept back from his shoulders. Beneath it he wore some silver garment that hugged torso and limbs. At his waist was a narrow band of black caught by a silver object of some substance Nuela did not—

But Nuela did recognize the substance. She knew, looking at it, how smooth, how hard, how light her fingers would find it.

Like Polamaire's device.

Neptilis came steadily nearer, setting glossy dark footwear to white sand. His brows arched to steep points. His lips were full, dark. His pupils, brightly reflective by moonlight, caught an image of her face and cast it back changed.

Polamaire's device, then, came from the world of the silver moon. She had held in her hand an artifact of that world.

But was her own world that one, the one moon torn into two? Or was it some other?

What force could tear one moon into two?

Neptilis stopped before her, his voice full and dark. ONCE AT THE BEGINNING OF TIME, WHEN WE WERE A SINGLE RACE LIVING UPON A SINGLE WORLD, NAMED EARTH, THERE WAS A MAN WHO CALLED HIMSELF MOSHITILIS. IT HAPPENED DURING HIS TIME THAT HIS PEOPLE BECAME NEGLECTFUL OF THE ENTITY THEY HAD CREATED AS THEIR GOD AND FATHER, AND SO MOSHITILIS WENT TO THE MOUNTAIN AND RETURNED WITH A STONE GRAVEN WITH COMMANDMENTS. BY THESE COMMANDMENTS MOSHITILIS' PEOPLE WERE TO TURN THEMSELVES BACK TO THE WAYS OF GOOD AND TO RECLAIM THEIR LIVES. FOR MOSHITILIS KNEW THAT ONLY AS A PEOPLE LIVE IN THE WAYS OF GOOD CAN THEY AVOID DESTRUCTION.

SO IT WAS WHEN WE WERE ONE RACE UPON ONE WORLD. AND SO IT IS NOW UPON OUR OWN BELOVED WORLD, CHAHERAS. THERE MUST BE ORDER AND THERE MUST BE GOOD. OTHERWISE THERE ARE ONLY THE TWIN DESTROYERS, CHAOS AND EVIL.

THE PEOPLE OF MOSHITILIS' TIME CREATED THE ENTITY THEY CALLED YAHVELIS AND DESIGNATED HIM THEIR GOD AND FATHER. IF YOU WISH TO REGARD ME AS YOUR GOD, DO—BUT REMEMBER AS YOU STUDY THE COMMANDMENTS I GIVE YOU THAT I AM TRULY HE WHO MADE THE CHAHERA PEOPLE. YOU HAVE NOT MADE ME,

AND IF YOU DISOBEY MY COMMANDMENTS, IT IS NOT I WHO WILL CEASE TO EXIST BUT THE CHAHERA.

THE COMMANDMENTS I GIVE YOU ARE THESE:

HEED YOU THE VOICE OF NEPTILIS ABOVE ALL OTHERS, FOR I AM TRULY FATHER OF YOUR RACE. HONOR THE FIRST VOICE, WHO SPEAKS FOR ME, AS YOU WOULD HONOR ME. OURS ARE THE VOICES OF ORDER AND GOOD.

AS I AM YOUR FATHER, SO IS THE SEA YOUR MOTHER, THE LAND THAT RISES FROM HER ANCIENT BEDS HER EARTHEN LIMBS. HONOR LAND AND SEA AND PROTECT THEM FROM ALL HARM, FOR THEY MUST SERVE AS MOTHER TO YOUR OWN CHILDREN TO MANY GENERATIONS.

DO NEVER STRIVE TO TAME YOUR MOTHER, TO MASTER HER, TO OWN HER. SHE IS NOT YOURS. INSTEAD YOU ARE HERS.

ACCEPT THE PLACE OF THE CHAHERA IN THIS UNIVERSE AND HONOR THE PLACE OF ALL OTHER FORMS OF LIFE. REMEMBER THAT YOU WERE NEVER MADE TO BE MASTERS OF ANYONE OR ANYTHING BUT YOURSELVES.

CHERISH YOUR BROTHERS AND SISTERS IN ME. DO NOT MAKE WAR UPON THEM. DO NOT DESTROY THEIR CHILDREN OR THEIR POSSESSIONS. I AM THEIR FATHER AS I AM YOURS, AND I CARE EQUALLY FOR ALL.

INSTEAD SPEAK WITH EACH OTHER WHEN THERE ARE DIFFERENCES. MAKE UP TERMS AMONG YOURSELVES AND ABIDE BY THEM IN ALL THINGS.

CHERISH GOOD. CHERISH ORDER. TAKE HARM UPON YOURSELVES BEFORE PERMITTING IT TO BE INFLICTED UPON OTHERS. LISTEN FOR MY VOICE AND FOR THE FIRST VOICE. WE ARE EVER DEEP WITHIN YOU.

LIVE IN THE WAYS I HAVE GIVEN YOU AND YOU WILL BE STRONG.

SO DO I COMMAND YOU.

He lingered for a moment, stark in his black cloak. Then he closed his eyes, hooding the reflective pupils, and was gone.

Nuela turned slowly, shaken, and looked upon the silvered sea.

The First Voice came in a whisper, bodiless but compelling. *In our lives, there is a time to walk upon the land and a time to go upon the sea . . .*

And now, Nuela knew, was her time to go again upon the water. She moved down the beach and entered the surf. Silver, cool, it slipped around her knees, tasted at her thighs. A brightness waited for her, like a moonlet lying upon the surface of the sea. She swam toward it. She met its ancient eyes, depthless and black, and slipped into its half-inflated sac.

The air within was heavy with moisture, fragrant with oils. The lucticete folded Nuela against its side, its heartbeat jarring at her breastbone. Her own heartbeat slowed to meet it. They moved away together.

Nuela heard the First Voice as if from far away, the words blending into a susurrus as calming as the beat of the lucticete's heart. Later the voice died away, and they glided in mammoth silence.

After a while, Nuela saw a second brightness in the water and realized that her lucticete traveled in company with another. They swam deep, weed beds parting for them, tiny fish appearing in luminous schools, winking out as swiftly as they appeared. The lucticetes' glowing membranes cast a pallid light upon the ocean floor.

The beat of the great heart changed, grew deeper, more reverberant, and soon Nuela heard something else. The lucticetes crooned to each other, their elastic voices reaching out through the dark water in a series of rising calls. She listened for a long time as the lucticetes haunted the ocean bottom with their song. Finally she slept.

When she woke, the lulling heartbeat, the moist warmth of the sac were gone. She lay upon a mat. Daylight shone against her closed eyelids. She heard the sounds she had heard upon waking the morning before: the creak of bindings, the rattle of shells, the voices of children. A bitter taste flooded her mouth.

She opened her eyes. She lay in a large, airy shelter. The door was wide and uncurtained, the walls loosely woven. Ria sat watching her, her spine rigid, her cropped hair finger-combed into spikes. Her brown-rimmed eyes flickered and narrowed. Deliberately she hunched her muscular shoulders. She wore trousers and a sleeveless tunic. "So you are awake, Scarlet Fish."

Nuela sat, brushing salt crystals from her face. "My friend— What have you done with my friend?" There was no sign of Evanne in the shelter. No second bed-mat. No discarded clothing or dirtied serving pieces.

"You set the float afire and left your friend to burn. Now you demand to know what *we* have done with her?"

"But she didn't burn. Did she? What have you done with her? What—"

"Better to speak of what you have done. The First Voice tells us to let the black blood rise only upon severe provocation. She tells us too that we are not to raise the black blood frivolously in others." She extended her hands. Darkness pooled in the open palms and ran to the fingertips, dyeing them black. "Your school, the Ra-meki, has offended mine. Now you have offended me—and every other Greater Milminesa of my pod."

Nuela stared at the blackened fingertips, then shook her head impatiently, drawing a rebellious breath. "I have offended you? You *took* me. You tied me to your mooring ropes and left me there." In the dark. In the cold. "Then Neparra drugged me—drugged us. Your caller came—your caller came and tried to force himself upon me."

Ria's brows rose steeply. "Kzien came to force you? No, Neparra brewed the ovulant and served you with all proper ceremony. Then Kzien came to give you a child to carry to the Great Land. That is according to the custom of every school in the sea, the Ra-meki included—until Rotsin yielded to Anamirre.''

A child? To carry to the Great Land? "What do you mean?''

"Three times now—each year since Anamirre spoke—the Ra-meki float has carried nothing more than straw dolls to the Great Land. Effigies. The Malin-ji permitted it. The Maku-hiki tolerated it. The Sia-kepi ignored it entirely when their year came.

"But now we come to the beginning of *our* year, and our blood runs black. What kind of wisdom is this? Why should the Ra-meki send straw dolls while we send living flesh? Who has excused the Ra-meki from Neptilis' teachings? Who has excused them from obedience to the First Voice? Who—'' She glanced toward the doorway and pushed herself abruptly to her feet. "Stand. You are in the presence of our wisdom.''

Nuela turned. Sunlight struck through the long, pale hair of the man who preceded Evanne and Tuleja into the shelter. He was tall but sparsely made, the scars that marked his cheeks little more than silvery stripes. Although he had passed his middle years, his face was devoid of lines, as if he had never frowned, had never smiled, had never squinted into the sun—as if he had never permitted himself the display of emotion.

He studied Nuela, black pupils narrowed in eyes as pale as shallow water. "I am Taric. Let me see your hands.''

Nuela stood, caught by the still, penetrating quality of his gaze. Slowly she extended her hands—and drew a startled breath. The creases of the palms were black lined. She stared for a moment, uncomprehending, then scrubbed at the stain with a fingertip. It did not rub away.

"So in attempting to dispell the stain from our own

blood, we have raised it in you.'' His voice was dry, devoid of emphasis. He sat, motioning Nuela down opposite him. ''That means we must negotiate, because your right is the same as ours: to do that which will wash the black from your blood.''

Nuela stared again at her hands, then darted a glance at Evanne. The Ra-meki girl's eyes were wide in an ashen face. ''I don't understand,'' Nuela said. ''You—you planned to send us away on the float.''

Taric inclined his head. ''You have come from Aurlanis. You are new to the dreams and new to school ways. And you are new to the very things that are ingrained in us: attentiveness, discipline, obedience.

''The First Voice tells us that we must go now upon the land, now upon the sea. And so we do. We live the year upon the sea, and at the change of years, the schools send their floats to the Great Land. We send them in obedience to the First Voice.''

''But—where is it? Where is the Great Land?''

''The Great Land rises where the current ends. It may be the land we see in our dreams. It may be some other. We will know when the lucticetes return for us— when we have proven to Neptilis that we are fit to be taken back into their sacs.''

Nuela shook her head, confused. ''No—where *is* it? How did you expect us to find it? What did you expect us to do when we got there?'' She drew a long, angry breath. ''You attacked us. You brought us here, you drugged us—''

''We followed custom and the pacts.'' Ria squatted beside Taric, her smoky eyes fierce. ''As your school should have done for itself.''

''The Ra-meki should have set us loose themselves?'' To drift alone on the sea until—

Until what? Nuela glanced up at Tuleja, then turned back to Taric and Ria—and realized with sudden clarity that they no more knew where the Great Land lay than she did. For a moment she was too stunned to speak. Then her voice hardened to grit. "The Ra-meki should have set us loose to die?" What else did it amount to? How long could she and Evanne have survived, drifting alone at the center of sea and sky, bound for a land that might not even exist?

She shuddered. They might have survived for years.

Evanne knelt beside her, touching her arm. "We have always done what the other schools did, Nuela. We sent a float every year until Anamirre found her wisdom."

Until Anamirre told them that Neptilis wanted good for them. That tears and pain were not good. And what could be more painful than setting daughters, sisters, friends adrift on the sea?

"How do you even know it's possible to reach the Great Land—any land—on a float? If we were born here from another world . . ." Perhaps there was no land. Perhaps the world was just as she had always envisioned it, a few spill cones breaking the surface of an endless sea.

Ria's shoulders snapped taut. *"There*—there is the seed of the heresy. The Ra-meki do not even admit that we did wrong. The moon broke and we were cast out into the sea—but the Ra-meki will not admit it.

"Oh yes, they sent floats before Anamirre spoke, but not because Neptilis tells us to go upon the land. They sent them because every other school sent them. Because they knew it would raise the stain in us if they did not." She turned back to Nuela, the black stain rising along the backs of her hands. "Ask your friend. Now that we've brought her here, now that we've prepared the float, she will go. She will drink the ovulant again. She will let Kzien pass his seed to her. And she will go. But only because she respects the stain."

"As we must respect the black blood we have raised in Nuela," Taric interjected. The reminder was dry, without apparent bias or sympathy.

Ria's breath hissed from between her teeth. "Then tell us what will settle your blood, Scarlet Fish? Shall we turn you loose? Take you back to the Ra-meki?"

Nuela glanced up at Tuleja, saw her frowning tension. As if she cared how Nuela answered. As if she cared. "Take us back. Take us both back."

"I don't see the stain on your friend's hands."

Nuela turned to meet Evanne's eyes, and for a moment her heart did not beat. "Evanne—"

Evanne shook her head. "You are wrong, Ria. We sent the floats because we hoped it would help. We hoped Neptilis would see that we were trying to obey his word—even here." Her lips trembled. "But why— why would he want that from us? We were so unhappy as we built the floats. We had nightmares every night. We knew someone had to go, and we woke up crying. My friends did. I did.

"Why would Neptilis want that? He found us living in the warlands, and even after all the bad we had done, he made us so that we could go into the sea. Because he wanted good for us. He didn't want us to be sick and afraid, even then. Why would he want it for us now?"

Nuela caught the Ra-meki girl's hand. "Evanne—"

Gently Evanne withdrew the hand and extended it beside the other. The exposed palms were pale. She addressed herself again to Ria, her voice husky. "I can't believe Neptilis wants me to go to the Great Land. But neither—neither does he want me to show disrespect for the stain we have raised in you. And I have no stain of my own." She turned, pleading. "You can see that, Nuela. I have none of my own."

She intended to go. *"No.* Evanne, they have no right to send you. To send either of us. They—"

"But they do, Nuela. They have the right to do whatever they must to wash their blood clean. Anamirre is not their true daughter. She is ours. The Greater Milminesa have the right to demand respect for their own wisdom."

They had the right to demand respect for their own interpretation of the pacts. They had the right to insist upon the observance of custom.

They had the right to loose a float on the current, bound for a land no one had seen, a land that might not even exist. And to send Evanne aboard the float if she could not display refusal on the palms of her hands.

Anger flooded Nuela's fingertips, painting the nails black. It overflowed her palms and rose to meet the scarlet pattern that flared at her wrists. She suddenly felt very much a Ra-meki, very much a disciple of Anamirre's wisdom. "This is your wisdom?" she demanded of Taric. "This is the wisdom you feel?" She pressed knotted fists to her chest. "You can't even tell me that there is a land at the end of the current, that there is any end to the current at all. But you expect us to go there. You've sent people of your own there." Girls like Evanne, cast away with their own frightened consent.

Taric's pale eyes deepened and became intent again. He seemed for a moment to hold his breath. "I have sent both a daughter and a granddaughter."

"He sent Misenne—his granddaughter, my child."

Startled, Nuela recoiled from the angry pain in Ria's eyes.

"The Ra-meki think that because they cry when their daughters go, they can send an effigy—a woman who was never alive except as a weed growing on the seafloor. And her child—a thing with shells for eyes, woven into her belly.

"The Ra-meki think that because they cry, they can send a token.

"Do you think I didn't cry when my baby went? Do you think I didn't bleed? Do you want to see the scars

I drew across my ribs, trying to take the harm of the journey onto myself?

"And do you think I didn't wake after she went—night after night—and stare across the water with my heart churning in the pit of my stomach? We cut the mooring ropes and the float drifted away—where? Where did the current take it? I don't know any better than you do, any better than the Ra-meki do, where land lies. Perhaps the current travels wide of the land. Perhaps it never touches shore. There are currents out here that will set you ashore on Pelosis—and others that will carry you so far wide that you will never see the torches in the tower.

"But Neptilis tells us that we must go now upon the land, now upon the sea. And how can we go but by float? And so Misenne went." Her fingers curled, nails biting black palms. "Why do the Ra-meki have the right to send an effigy, a token, when I sent my living daughter? Why do the Ra-meki have the right to hold back the day for us all?"

Nuela licked her lips, her heart jarring to Ria's pain. Evading the accusing eyes, she glanced up and saw tears glistening at the corners of Tuleja's eyes.

Tears for Ria and Misenne? Or tears for herself and her own daughters, lost on a different current?

Nuela turned back to Taric. He sat straight, still, his pale-water eyes intent upon her face—waiting, watching. If he thought she would say that she understood, that she would go . . .

She *had* begun to understand. The Greater Milminesa were caught in a web of custom and pact. It bound them tight—had bound them for so long that they accepted the stricture and the pain.

But she would not be bound. She felt her anger fully now, but remotely, coldly. She was angry for all the girls and for all the women who had gone on floats, for all the people who had cried—and sent them anyway.

For all the mothers who had punished themselves and hoped it would spare their daughters. And she was angry for the children who woke crying from nightmares of a desolate sea.

She met Taric's eyes. "Why do you think Evanne will be any less a symbol than a doll made of sea grass? If Neptilis tells you to go now upon the land, now upon the sea—why don't you go? Why don't all of you go?"

There was a soft intake of breath in the shelter, as if everyone inhaled at once. The three Greater Milminesa grew suddenly still, eyes fixed upon Nuela as if in shock.

"If you're so certain that's what Neptilis wants, why don't you all go? Once you find the Great Land, you can come back into the sea whenever you want."

No one moved. Ria was frozen in a half crouch, her eyes wide and fixed. Tuleja stood as if paralyzed. Even the tears at the corners of her eyes clung, caught in place.

Finally Taric released a long, sighing breath. Deliberately he lidded his eyes. When he opened them again, his voice was frail, constrained—commanding. "Bring me an implement, Ria."

*"No."* Stunned. Eyes still wide upon Nuela.

"Bring me an implement."

Ria stood, hesitated, withdrew from the shelter.

Taric leaned toward Nuela. The muscles of his face had grown rigid, but his eyes were bright, ardent, the pupils suddenly wide and glistening. "My father told me once—and I have always remembered this—that sometimes wisdom wears such a commonplace face that we do not recognize it for what it is. It requires a stranger to show us its true nature."

Nuela frowned, confused by the sharply changed atmosphere in the shelter. Evanne clutched her arm, nails biting sharply at the flesh. Tuleja remained motionless, frozen.

Returning, Ria crouched beside Taric, the honed spine ridge of a chakapis in one hand. "True Son—"

Taric shook his head, extending one hand. After a long moment, Ria placed the implement upon the palm. Quickly, before Nuela understood what he intended, Taric drew the cutting edge across his forearm. A line of scarlet erupted.

Taric stared down at the wound. When he raised his eyes to Nuela, they were brilliant. "So it is ended. I have served as the wisdom of my school for twenty-seven years. Now I am the first to draw blood for you as you begin your term." He took his feet. "We will leave you now. You will want to be alone for a while with your thoughts. Tell us when you are ready, when you think it is best that we go. We will cut our moorings at the time you name."

Slowly Nuela stood. "Please. I don't understand." They would cut their moorings? At the time she named?

"But of course you understand. Wisdom always understands, even when it wishes it did not."

"No. I don't understand," Nuela repeated. But he was right. Dazed, unwilling, she did understand.

She understood what she had said. She understood how he had heard it. She understood what he thought must come of it—and she wished fervently that she did not as the three Greater Milminesa turned to withdraw from the shelter. Tuleja turned back briefly and gazed at her, her tongue caught between her teeth. Bending, she tightened the band at her thigh. When the first scarlet drops stained the coarse fabric, she followed the others.

# Chapter Twelve

TIME PAUSED. THE FLOAT ROCKED. BINDINGS RASPED and creaked. Sunlight forced its way through loosely woven walls and shattered on the floor. "I didn't mean it," Nuela said finally, testing her voice. "It was only—" A challenge. Words tossed out in anger. Words she hadn't even considered before speaking.

*If you're so certain that's what Neptilis wants, why don't you all go?* Why, of all the things she might have said, had she said that?

And how could she have guessed anyone would listen? They hadn't listened to anything else she had said. Nuela sighed. Evanne hunched at her feet, her arms wrapped tightly around her updrawn knees. Nuela knelt, touching her bowed head. "Evanne, come back with me to the Ra-meki. Don't let them send you away. There is no reason for you to go."

Evanne raised her head, peering at Nuela in astonishment. "But they won't send the float now, Nuela. You spoke for them. Taric recognized what you said. You are their wisdom. You must go with them. And I am you sister, so I must go too." Tears broke from her eyes and flooded her cheeks. "I must go to the Great Land with you, and I don't even like these people."

Nor did Nuela, although she was finding a certain

strained sympathy for them. Nuela slipped an arm around the Ra-meki girl. *"No,* Evanne. I am no one's wisdom. I hadn't even heard of these people ten days ago. They can't cut their moorings just because of me."

"But they will. You spoke, and they heard. They will set themselves on the current, every pod, every raft—"

"Then let them," Nuela said with sharp impatience. What was it to her? She had not asked to be abducted, drugged, assaulted. "We will go back to the Ra-meki. And once I know Sinjanne is safe—"

Could she return to Aurlanis? She settled back on her heels, listening for some compelling voice to tell her she could not.

She heard none. And Aurlanis—safe, solid, sanely ordered—called very loudly at that moment. She brushed quick tears from her own eyes. "You will go back to the Ra-meki, and I will go back to my own people."

Evanne sobbed in frustration. "But Nuela  Taric has yielded to you. He has *yielded.* "

"Then I will yield back to him."

"But you can't, Nuela. Your term extends until someone speaks to you. Until someone says something that you feel in the same way Taric felt what you said. Or—until you die. And then the wisest of your children will come into your wisdom. Until Anamirre spoke, our true sons and daughters came from the same line for five generations.

"You can't refuse your term, Nucla. To be true son or daughter—" She shook her head, groping helplessly for words. "No one matters the way a true daughter matters. Everything you say, everything you do—the Greater Milminesa will do whatever you tell them, Nuela."

"Then I will tell them to let us go."

*"No!"*

Nuela turned at the single, stricken syllable. Neparra hovered in the doorway, frail in a gown that enveloped her to her toes. Her features were tight-drawn, the flesh standing white against sharp bones. "You can't leave us! You just came. You just spoke, and what you said has touched everyone who has heard it." She laid one thin hand to her chest, as if she cupped a painfully beating heart. "You cannot speak of leaving us. We have already begun to take harm for you, those of us who have heard. Don't you see? I bleed for you, as do the others."

"You—" Unwillingly Nuela stood, staring at the slash of color that appeared at the breast of Neparra's gown where she pressed the fabric to her flesh. The stain widened quickly into a bloody crescent. Nuela shook her head, suddenly unable to catch her breath.

"I saved my breasts for you. I knew that one day we would have a new wisdom, and I saved my breasts so that I could offer virgin blood." Her voice was high, thin, breathless. Her face had begun to glow. She fumbled at the fasteners that secured the gown. "There will be so much danger as we go upon the current. There will be so much peril to you, to all the school. But I will serve you, just as I have served Taric and through him all the school. I will—"

"No!" Her breasts—the one part of her body she had not already disfigured. Nuela jumped up, struggling against nausea and swift-rising hysteria. "Taric—get Taric. Tell him—"

But Neparra did not respond to her demand. She seemed not to hear. And suddenly Nuela could not remain a moment longer in the shelter. Her heart was leaping too fiercely at her chest. She plunged to the door. "Where is he? Where is Taric?" She would give him back his *wisdom* before any of this went farther.

Neparra clutched her stained gown, her face bright and pale, her eyes focused upon some inner brilliance only she could see. Evanne jumped to her feet, staring at the Greater Milminesa woman with distended eyes.

Nuela turned wildly. A child watched wide-eyed from the shadows of an adjacent shelter. "Take me to Taric."

"Nuela—"

Nuela shook off Evanne's entreating hand. "I won't have this. I won't have any of this. Take me to him!"

The child stood undecided for a moment. Then, ducking her head, she ran across the floats, glancing back to see that Nuela followed.

People sat and stood in clusters, obviously drawn together by news of Taric's abdication. They stared uncomprehendingly after Nuela as she passed. Once Nuela brushed against a woman, and the woman cried out, a startled yelp that made Nuela's heart slam harder still against her breastbone. Children bobbed up from the water, wet hair streaming down astonished faces.

From somewhere behind her, a wail rose and wavered in the air. Ghostly, protracted, it drew people who had not yet heard the news from the water, from their shelters, from their tasks. They stood rigid, slack jawed, as if snapped taut by cords. The child hesitated, glancing back at Nuela, then pounded desperately along the passageways.

"Here! Here!" the child gasped, directing Nuela into the uncurtained door of an enclosure built to cover three adjoining floats.

Nuela did not have to search for Taric. He emerged from an inner room as she fought to catch her breath and stared past her, his attention fixed by the rising notes of the wail. His pupils widened, swiftly consuming the pale irises.

Nuela licked dry lips, started to turn back—and from the corner of one eye glimpsed Tirin poised just within the doorway from which Taric had emerged. Tears of relief rushed to her eyes. She pushed past the older man, throwing herself at Tirin as if he were harbor against sea and storm.

He closed his arms around her, but the gesture was more reflexive than protective. His chest and back were damp, his swimpants wet with seawater. His shoulders knotted tight as the cry quivered, broke, and abruptly died.

Nuela drew back, but not before she felt a long shudder pass through his body. "What—what is it?"

He shook his head, pulling her near again, holding her against his beating heart.

He knew. He knew what that high keening meant. She pushed free, turning back to the door.

This time it was Taric who caught her. He pressed her to his thin chest, his arms unyielding. She did not understand the words he whispered into her hair. Oddly, they seemed benedictory.

More oddly still, they calmed her. She yielded to sudden weakness and let her head rest on his shoulder. Tuleja appeared briefly at the door of the enclosure, her features taut, masklike, then vanished at a nod from Taric.

Nuela raised her head and met Taric's eyes. The irises were pale water again, the pupils no more than points. "Please—"

Taric released her, studying her with a distant frown. "Come and sit down with us. Neparra left a meal."

Neparra—the vivid stain growing on her gown. Nuela stifled a quick surge of nausea and glanced at Tirin, expecting—what? What *did* she expect from him? He only nodded, turning back toward the inner room. Reluctantly Nuela permitted Taric to guide her there.

The inner room was spacious and plain, furnished only with floormats. Taric eased himself down, still frowning, and gestured toward an artfully arranged tray of fish and pods. "If you are hungry?" His voice was detached, as if he had carefully set all emotion aside. The slash on his arm had been washed but not bound.

"No." Had Neparra cut herself before delivering his meal? Or after? And the cry— "Please tell me—what happened? Neparra—" Because clearly something had happened. And she was the only one who did not understand.

"Nothing—unexpected." Taric bowed his head, briefly resting it against steepled fingertips. He seemed for a moment old and bowed. When he looked up again, he said, "It appears we must release you briefly to your school."

Nuela's heart bounced against her breastbone again, this time in fierce relief. "Evanne too," she said quickly. "You must send Evanne back to the Ra-meki too. And Neparra— Is there someone who can treat her? She—she's—" But Taric knew, surely, that she had harmed herself again.

No, that she had taken harm *to* herself. Wasn't that how she served him and, through him, the school?

Taric bowed his head again, a long quiver passing through his sparely made body. "No one can treat Neparra now."

"You don't have a physician? You don't have anyone who can close up the wound? Or anyone—anyone who can make her stop hurting herself? You just let her . . ." The rush of words dwindled. Taric's silence, Tirin's, had a special quality. So did the expression in their watching eyes.

She drew a trembling breath, and what Taric and Tirin had to say, they told her without speaking. Neparra had taken herself beyond help. Nuela shuddered, a wave of intense cold moving up her spine, snapping the vertebrae rigid. Her mouth was suddenly dry. "I left Evanne with her. I left her there." To witness whatever thing Neparra had done to herself when she had finished her wailing call. To witness whatever final horror she had inflicted upon her disfigured body.

"You knew she would do it," she said, her voice harsh.

"These things follow a course. She was drawing near the end of her course."

A course? How could he speak so dryly, so dispassionately when they both had heard the long, keening wail? Nuela shook her head angrily, taking to her feet. "Take me back to Evanne." She should never have left her. "Take me back."

People were gathered in every passageway, upon every float, hushed, wide-eyed. Nuela did not recognize the route they took across the raft. But when there were no more people, when there was only a long, empty passageway ahead, she knew they approached the enclosure where she had left Evanne.

She ran then, her courage failing her only at the final moment. She stopped short of the uncurtained door, sickness rising hot and sour in her throat. "Evanne!"

She turned at a slight sound. Evanne stood small, rigid, dry-eyed against a nearby panel, her teeth chattering violently. Her hands were red with blood. She had smeared it on one cheek. "Nuela— She had a blade."

Nuela caught her. "I'm sorry. I'm sorry, Evanne. I didn't know." She clutched the Ra-meki girl. "Sister. My sister." The kinship was suddenly real; she felt it without reservation. She ached with it and with her own failure. Evanne had given herself as a sister, and Nuela had left her. Last night. Again today.

No more. "Tirin has come for us. We're going back to your school. You're going back to Anamirre." And when Evanne was safely there . . .

But Nuela could not return to Aurlanis yet—unless Tirin had brought news of Sinjanne. "Tirin—" But Evanne shuddered then and began to sob in large gulping spasms, burrowing against her shoulder. Nuela held her tight, rocking her.

Tuleja emerged from the enclosure, a frown deep-bitten between her pale brows. "The family will prepare the body. When it is done, I will call for the required ceremony." The statement was carefully without emotion.

It took Nuela a moment to realize that Tuleja expected some response—not from Taric, but from Nuela. "What do you mean?"

"I mean that when an ecstatic offers herself against our harm, her remains are given over to her mother by flame, with proper ceremony."

"Her mother?" Did she have to ask?

"The sea.'"

And Tuleja expected assent from her? As the Greater Milminesa's new wisdom?

Wasn't it for her that Neparra had offered herself? "Do whatever you consider suitable," she said with tautly held anger. "I won't be here."

Tuleja's brows rose in sharp question.

"Nuela has not yet completed her kalinerre," Taric interjected, his voice as carefully dispassionate as Tuleja's. "By the pacts, she has a candidate's right to speak her choice with land beneath her feet. And by the pacts, we must respect Tirin's right to judge when she has completed her kalinerre. He has come displaying a stain to match hers."

Nuela drew a long breath. So that was why Taric seemed prepared to release her. Tirin had demanded it. Had cared enough to demand it with blackened palms. Still clutching Evanne, she said, "Tirin—my sister? Sinjanne?"

Tirin shook his head. "I found two candidates with the Shihona and another with the Oso. They will be given their rights. Then I reached the Maku-hiki and I heard you had been taken. So I sent Polamaire's device

ahead with her message and came. I must have arrived
at almost the moment when you—spoke your wisdom."
His sand-gold eyes flickered, questioning.

It must seem as incredible to him as to her: what she
had said, Taric's response to it. "I want—I want to go
now." Her voice shook, rising again toward hysteria.
She wanted to leave these people, this place with a
force, an urgency she had seldom felt before.

"No. You will go when you have taken a meal,"
Taric said firmly.

"No. I can't eat."

The pale eyes met hers with silent authority. "The
meal will not be served until you are ready to eat." He
raised a silencing hand to her protest. "There is a manner suitable to every undertaking. You will see that
yourself if you stop to reflect. You cannot undertake the
final stages of your kalinerre until you are rested and
calm."

Nuela sighed, recognizing reluctantly that he was
right. She had not eaten since the bizarre meal Neparra
had served them the morning before. She had passed
the day drugged, the night in the water. Little wonder
she was sick and half hysterical. "If there is a place
where we can be quiet?"

Tuleja conducted them to a shelter at the outer verge
of the raft. The uncurtained doorway faced the open
sea. The water offered freely of its seductions, shatter-
ing sunlight to bright fragments, taking colors from the
sky, buoying the float to a gentle rhythm. All of it was
lost on Nuela. Sickness and anger weighed heavily at
the pit of her stomach.

She helped Evanne to a mat and sat beside her, one
arm around her shoulders, as the Ra-meki girl yielded
to another spasm of tears. Tuleja brought a damp cloth
and Tirin knelt at Evanne's other side, cleansing her of
Neparra's blood. When Evanne was quiet again, they
tucked her beneath a blanket.

"You too," Tirin said, touching Nuela's hand. "I'll stay with you."

Relieved, Nuela yielded to his ministrations, letting him draw a second blanket over her and smooth the hair from her forehead. For a moment, as she drifted toward sleep, she thought that she looked up at Rinarde. "You are like him."

"Like who?"

"Rinarde." Tall, calm, protective.

He smiled. "Perhaps he was like me. Sleep."

Some commands were made to be obeyed. Nuela slept.

In the late afternoon, she pulled up the blanket to protect her eyes against intruding sunlight. Later, when the sun set and the shelter was lit only by lamplight, she entered into a long, restless dream of somberly rising chants, of ceremonial cries and calls. She turned and from one drowsy eye saw the sun again, sitting large and fiery on the dark water.

It paused for a while, blazing more brightly as she watched, then began to recede. Knots tightened in Nuela's stomach. She sat. Tirin and Evanne sat together just beyond the doorway.

She pressed her eyes shut. When she opened them again, the fire still blazed. Forcing herself from her bed, she joined Tirin and Evanne, shivering as Neparra's pyre drifted away on the current.

"I always thought it would be beautiful to serve that way," Evanne said finally, when the cries and chants had died, when the light of the pyre had been quenched by distance and night. "I thought—" She shuddered, bowing her head.

"The Ra-meki don't permit—ecstatics?" She had slept, but the heaviness, the sickness remained. Only the anger had dulled.

"We have none," Evanne said. "But I've heard the stories. When Anamirre found her wisdom, I pressed a sharpened bone under my thumbnail and squeezed out blood for her. I caught it on a piece of bleached fabric, and I kept it. I was so happy that she spoke. We were all so happy that no one else would go to the Great Land. I loved her so much. I never wanted any harm to come to her.'' She peered up at Nuela, her dark eyes questioning. ''And it never has, Nuela. I've kept the blood, and she has never been sick or hurt or even unhappy, not for more than a few minutes.''

''But not because you hurt yourself, Evanne,'' Tirin said gently.

Evanne bowed her head, frowning down at the mat that covered the surface of the float. ''Are you sure?''

''Yes. I am certain.''

Evanne sighed. ''But you're land-bred, Tirin. Nuela, I would kill myself for you. I would do it to keep you safe. But I wouldn't make myself ugly first. I—''

*''No!* I don't ever want to be safe that way, Evanne,'' Nuela said in quick revulsion. She caught both the Rameki girl's hands. ''We are sisters, and I want my sisters safe. I don't want harm done them, not even if it would make me safe. And it wouldn't, Evanne. I don't believe that. I want you to promise me—''

''But Nuela, Neptilis says—''

''Neptilis says that we are to take harm upon ourselves before permitting it to be inflicted upon others,'' Taric said, stepping from the shadows. He carried a laden tray. He bent, setting it carefully to the matting, and eased himself down before it. Night and moonlight silvered his hair and turned his eyes to pale wafers. ''He does not promise us that by taking harm to ourselves, we can divert it from others.''

''Then you don't believe—''

''I don't believe that harm can be diverted. Not absolutely. Certainly not infallibly. Neptilis does not promise us that at all. His promise is that we will make ourselves strong by living according to his word. And his word tells us to take harm upon ourselves before permitting it to be inflicted upon others.''

Nuela glanced down at the wound on his arm. ''But you cut yourself for me.''

''Yes, and I am stronger because I did it. That—and the scar—may be the only result of it.''

It was Nuela's turn to frown down at the coarse matting. The tray held four delicately arranged platters. The sight, the smell of food brought nausea surging to her throat again. Her stomach contracted sharply. ''And Neparra?'' she demanded. ''Is she stronger now?''

A faint frown settled around Taric's eyes. ''She is stronger because she fulfilled her nature than if she had denied it.''

''She would be alive tonight if she had denied it. She would be eating her dinner, looking at the stars, listening to the sea . . .'' And Neparra had loved those things. She had woven poetry of them the day before, her voice high and floating, as she served their meal.

''But Neptilis made her, and he made her as she was. Perhaps it was a mistake. Neptilis is a man, and men make mistakes. Perhaps in the making of the Chahera, he committed this one particular error and the ecstatics were born among us. There are not so many of them, but they come from his hand, just as we do. And neither our disapproval nor our reverence will change their nature. Are you calm enough yet to eat?''

Nuela recoiled from the platter he set before her. ''No.'' Sickness sat like a rock in her belly.

''Nuela—'' Tirin and Evanne touched her at the same moment, one clasping her shoulder, the other pressing her arm.

Taric shook his head at them both and took her hands in his. ''She did not do it because of you. You can put that fear from your heart, Nuela. She fulfilled her nature. She was born to it, and she followed the course it prescribed. Faithfully and without flinching. You did not endow her with that nature, and you could not have changed the course it took.''

Nuela choked, recognizing then the source of the nausea, the continuing heaviness. ''I could have stopped her. If I had known—'' Why hadn't she guessed? She had seen the wounds on Neparra's body the day before. She had seen her rekindling excitement when the blood stained through her gown. ''If I had stayed instead of running for you, if I had talked with her—''

''How long could you have stayed with her? And how many words do you have?''

''Surely I could have made her see—'' What? That she must deny the strange excitement, the strange pleasure Nuela had seen in her luminous features? That she must turn back from a course she had already followed so far?

''Yes, you might have persuaded her that she followed the wrong course. You might have kept her from harm until the middle of the night or the moment before dawn, when her own voices outspoke yours. Listen to me.'' He clutched her hands, his grip cool, dry, unyielding. ''Her aunt came to me not so very long after my father's wisdom passed to me. Quina was fourteen, and she wanted to serve me—in the way her nature told her to serve.

''It hurt me to look at her. She had only come into the—the first blossom of her nature a year before, but she had already starved herself to stems and her arms were striped with a hundred wounds. I could not bear what I saw. So I took her from her family and brought her into my shelter.

''My wives were not happy that I did it, but I kept her with me, night and day. I made her eat. I threw her—implements—into the sea. I caught her once burning her hand over the lamp, and I scolded my wives for leaving the lamp unguarded. They were even less happy.

''Finally one night, I took inchata with her. She had

grown so plump, so pretty. Her wounds were healed, the scars were fading. I held her in my arms and brought pleasure to her eyes. I brought excitement, and I did it without exercising my caller's touch. I made love to her as an ordinary Chahera makes love to his mate. I made her face glow in the way an ecstatic's face will glow. Afterward I congratulated myself for everything I had done. I had restored her, and I had shown her a new, better ecstasy.

"Or so I thought. Until I woke the next morning drenched in her blood, her dead body beside me."

Nuela caught a sharp breath.

"Wisdom is truth, Nuela. Wisdom is not what you wish to be true. It is truth itself. You can't wish the nature of the world different. You cannot even wish yourself different. You can impose will upon yourself as I tried to impose my will upon Quina. But the truth changes only in response to its own evolutionary nature.

"There is comfort in that, once you accept it. Because then you can turn your will against its proper targets and listen more serenely for the voice of your wisdom. It doesn't always speak loudly, and it doesn't always speak when you need to hear. Sometimes it waits and whispers to you in the deep hours of night. Sometimes it makes you wait years for an answer to your question. Wisdom, true wisdom, is one of the quieter, one of the subtler, one of the more elusive of Neptilis' gifts to us." He pressed her hands tight, then freed them.

She released a long breath, rigid muscles loosening in her shoulders and back. She measured out the words of her response carefully. "Then you will understand when I tell you that I won't return here from my kalinerre. I—I said something to you, but it wasn't wisdom. It was only—" Anger. Defiance. Fear for herself, more especially for Evanne. "I didn't think before I spoke. You should never have listened, not in the way you did.

"I have just enough wisdom to know one thing: I am land-bred. I came to find my sister. When I know she is safe, I will return to Aurlanis."

Taric drew back, a shadow hooding his eyes. "Perhaps you will," he said, his voice dry again, dispassionate.

Was it to be so simple then? Did he intend to accept her refusal so easily, without argument? "So you are still true son of the Greater Milminesa," she said gently, as if she gave him a great gift. "The wisdom is yours." There was no need for the pods to cut the mooring ropes that held their rafts in place. "Nothing has changed."

Taric bowed his head. The sea washed gently at the side of the float. When Taric looked up again, the warmth, the grace of his smile was transforming. His face, normally so dispassionate, was gentle and pleased. "No, Nuela, everything has changed. My term has passed. I haven't become witless, and I will never be impulsive or driven by will. But you have brought my time to an end, although that was not at all what I expected when Ria went to Ra-meki waters."

"What did you expect?" Nuela said when he did not go on. When he waited, still smiling, for her to ask.

"I expected," he said, stringing the words together deliberately, reflectively, "that when Ria returned, something would move me—finally—to the very wisdom that Anamirre found. And then I would go to my people and tell them what Anamirre told the Ra-meki. That we have misunderstood what Neptilis wanted. That we have heeded his words to the detriment of his intent. He wants good for us, and sending our young women alone on the current surely is not the good he wants."

"You never intended to send us to the Great Land,"

Nuela said, shaken. Evanne's hand crept into hers, and she pressed it against her thigh.

"I did not think it would be necessary. Instinct told me there was to be a change. I've felt that since I heard of Anamirre's wisdom. I was convinced when Ria went that at some point there would be words, there would be tears, there would be *something*—and Anamirre's wisdom would finally strike me in the way I required. Here, like pleasure and agony at once, knocking my breath away." He pressed a fisted hand to his diaphragm. "It would strike me in a way I would recognize at once, unmistakably. In a way I could never question or doubt."

Instead her own words had struck him: *why don't you all go?* "But your people—" How would the Greater Milmincsa accept this particular blow to the solar plexus? Ria had been stunned, Tuleja paralyzed.

"My people accede to the wisdom of their true son or true daughter. Even when they don't feel its force, they respect its authenticity. And its necessity. They have bowed to my word for twenty-seven years. Today I spoke to them for the last time as their true son when I told them the wisdom had passed to you.

"We think, Nuela, living as we do in this moment, in this day, that things are as they have always been. It isn't true. We have no reliable word of the events that led to the breaking of the moon. We don't know what we did to cause it. But our way of life has undergone a continuing evolution since the time when we first found ourselves cast out at the center of the sea. We have built palaces on Pelosis and Aurlanis, where there was nothing. We have divided into schools and constructed rafts. We have negotiated the pacts. We have grown in numbers, and our customs and practices have grown with us.

"We have a history of change, but most changes are so small, so gradually made, that we are hardly aware of them. I knew it was time for a change, but I did not see its direction or its magnitude. Only you saw that.''

''No,'' Nuela protested. ''I didn't see anything. I—''

''You saw it,'' he said. ''Otherwise how did you speak it? When no one has spoken it before?''

''But you can't cut your ropes,'' she said. ''I'm going back to Aurlanis. Evanne is going back to the Ra-meki. I—I unspeak what I said, Taric. I unsay it. I never said it. I—''

He laughed softly, and the sea chuckled back at him. ''No, no. You spoke, I heard, and every Greater Milminesa knows by now what we must do. If you don't come back to us from kalinerre, that is simply because it wasn't intended that you come with us to the Great Land. Your wisdom will pass to someone new.''

''No. It's yours. I give it back to you.''

''No, no. There is a designated line of succession. I don't stand in the line.''

''Then who does?'' When he only shook his head, still smiling, she scowled down at her feet. ''But you said—you said you would cut the mooring ropes when I told you to. If I tell you not to cut them, never to cut them—'' For the first time she saw clearly what she had set so carelessly into motion. Thousands of people set adrift on the sea. An entire school following the current into the emptiness that lay beyond the horizon. What would happen when storms came? What would happen if the rafts were separated? Was all the sea like this part of it? Or did the water wear other faces, other moods in other places?

What would happen if the current never passed near land?

What if there was no land?

''You speak now out of fear of your own wisdom,'' he said gently. ''But the person who will succeed you if you don't return has already heard what you said and has been touched by it. If you fail to return, then that person will reiterate your wisdom, and we will go.''

*"No.* Evanne told me the Greater Milminesa would do whatever I told them. Did she lie to me?''

Sighing, Taric passed one hand over his face, wiping away the remnant of his smile. "If you come back, we will do whatever you say.''

"You will leave your ropes intact? You will stay in school waters?''

Taric turned, for a moment catching the rising moons in his eyes. "Yes,'' he said with patent reluctance, turning back. "If you come back to us, if you tell us not to cut the ropes, then we will not. And the change will be less than I thought, and many of our people will think that you act from a failure of courage. And when your term is done, the idea will still be loose among us. Your years will be finite in number, you know, just as mine have been.

"In fact, if you return, your term will surely end over just this very issue. Because someday someone will come to you and say boldly, 'It is time.' And you will recognize the words.'' His fist struck again at his diaphragm. "But they will be from another mouth. They will be from the mouth of your successor.''

Starlight gilded the water's surface. Nuela's shoulders sagged. Closing her eyes, she let the sea touch her through her other senses. The rush of it, the laugh of it, the damp tang of it— She felt its power beneath her and knew it held the raft upon its back without even feeling it there. If Pahla was their mother, she was a mother of limitless expanse and force, but she was as oblivious as she was powerful.

If Nuela did not return to the Greater Milminesa, they would release themselves to the water. They would entrust themselves to a mother who cared as little for them as—

She opened her eyes with a shuddering sigh, aware

of Tuleja before she saw her. Tuleja stood at the corner of the shelter, a child of perhaps seven peering from behind her. The two of them were made to a common scale, slight, their features and limbs delicate, their eyes large and unsmiling above steeply sloping cheekbones. Nuela drew a long, reluctant breath, and the child's eyes widened and she vanished entirely behind—

—her mother.

For a moment, Nuela was stunned. Then the pain began, digging tight fingers into her temples. If she did not return to the Greater Milminesa, they would release themselves to the current. If she did return, they would release themselves anyway one day.

And she had a sister among them. She had another sister. She had come seeking Sinjanne. Instead she had found first Evanne and now this awe-struck child.

*She would return to Aurlanis when she knew her sister was safe.* Her own pledge, uttered only minutes before. Could she return to Aurlanis knowing that the current would bear this child away?

"Please," she said, leaning forward, catching the child's eyes again. "What is your name?"

The child stepped briefly free of Tuleja's shadow and studied Nuela, this time with a firm, direct gaze. "I am Sumirre," she said when she was ready. "My mother has promised me that I can cut the first rope, the smallest one." The declaration was soft, prideful. Abruptly the child flushed and vanished again.

Nuela slumped back, pressing her fingers to her temples, to her brows. The pain had already moved firmly into place behind her eyes and anchored itself there, fierce and cramping. She shook her head helplessly.

"Your best wisdom now," Taric said quietly, "is to eat, to sleep, and to go tomorrow to complete your kalinerre. There is no need tonight to think beyond that."

Nuela was embarrassed by her own jagged bark of

laughter. What good *ever* to try to think beyond that? She had been seven days at sea now, and beyond each dilemma all she found was another. "Yes," she said. "You're right." She glanced at Tirin. "Can we go tomorrow? Polamaire's message—"

"I have sent it with a reliable swimmer. He carries her device to authenticate the message. We can go."

"How long will it take? I've heard the three voices. I've had the dreams." And she had passed the test of the parching sticks.

"It will take until it's finished. And when it is finished, you will know. Not all the tests are—imposed upon you. The most important ones you must impose upon yourself."

More decisions to be reached. More doubtful wisdom to be dredged from her reluctant viscera. Nuela bowed her head and gave herself briefly to the rocking of the float. It soothed her little. When she looked up, Sumirre studied her again.

"Come," Nuela said, patting the mat beside her. "Let's take our meal together. There's enough for both." Perhaps it was unwise. Perhaps she should reserve herself from this child as Tuleja had always reserved herself from her. But in a night full of perplexity and pain, the touch, the smell of a child—her sister—would be welcome comfort.

# Chapter Thirteen

THEY SLIPPED AWAY THE NEXT MORNING INTO A SEA stained gold with dawn. Clouds trailed tenuous grey fingers along the horizon. Only Tuleja came to witness their departure, and she did not appear until they had already entered the dawn-misted water. She stood at the edge of the float, her posture, her expression unbetraying, but when Nuela raised one arm, Tuleja returned the salute. And when Nuela glanced back later, Tuleja remained poised at the edge of the platform, the rigid line of her shoulders softened by mist and distance.

Tirin called the stroke for Evanne, leading her an easy pace through the water, and permitted Nuela to lag, the marks at her wrists little more than pale stripes. Evanne gave herself to the sea as to healing hands, matching Tirin's stroke with eyes closed, face intent upon some inner voice. Nuela hoped it offered comfort. The Ra-meki girl's face was thinner, paler, bones that had been invisible just a few days before standing against the flesh.

Soon after the sun rose, hundreds of silver-grey bodies came surging from behind them, bound with cheerful purpose toward some destination of their own. A long, thick-bodied animal with a scarred head quickly claimed Nuela. None of the others challenged him, although eager animals bobbed at his flank and nudged Nuela's bare leg, demanding that she rub their smooth-fleshed heads. Others slapped their tails playfully against the water, splashing her with crystal droplets. After a while, Nuela realized that each animal that approached called the three-note whistle she had identified herself by days before. She laughed, letting go of some of the pain, some of the perplexity she had brought with her into the water.

Later, as sunlight brightened across the water, the mela-mela launched into an acrobatic display, scores of animals leaping and plunging in concert. Nuela's steed surged sturdily forward among his companions, occasionally dipping below the surface of the water, never flying above it.

Once their pod met another swimming with just as much exuberance, just as much purpose toward a different point on the horizon. The two groups briefly intermingled, glistening bodies flying in every direction. Animals shrilled and whistled in noisy exhilaration. Then the second group was gone, boiling away in a surge of foam.

The sea wore its most enchanting face. Nuela looked into it and listened for some voice like the one that had called Sinjanne to her candidacy, like the one that had told Tirin he could never return to Aurlanis. She heard only the splash of water and the three-tone whistle of her name.

Because she had not wakened to the sea, despite passing the first tests? Or because Aurlanis called so much more plaintively to her than the sea ever could?

They parted ways with the mela-mela at midmorning. This time Nuela let Tirin touch her wrists and impose the beat of his heart upon hers. Her forearms flushed with color. Her flesh burned. Her feet kicked her eagerly forward.

She swam at his right heel, Evanne at his left, the

three of them darting and gliding through the water like a single organism. Sometimes Tirin led them beneath the surface, and they swam for long periods in filtered sunlight, small fishes flickering like bits of rainbow as they passed. He took them back to the surface for breath at longer and longer intervals, until finally Nuela realized from the position of the sun that they had passed most of an hour without surfacing for breath.

Then it was midafternoon. Glancing down, Nuela saw a long ripple of scarlet in the water beneath them. Her heart clutched, losing the beat—finding it again as Filien led a string of six vividly colored swimmers from the shadowy depths. He arched his back, his tawny hair sweeping back from his brilliantly patterned face, and led his swimmers around them in a wide circle. By the time Tirin guided Nuela and Evanne into place between the two wings of Filien's string, the pattern of the Rameki blazed with fresh fire upon Nuela's chest and arms.

They swam with a hard beat, coming soon within sight of a raft. Distant figures moved upon a gently rocking platform. Tirin and Filien swung around in the water. Tirin caught Evanne's wrists, releasing her from the stroke, then drew Nuela under. Deft fingers stroked leaping pulses, and heat ebbed swiftly from Nuela's body. They rose together, breaking the surface of the water in a spatter of bright droplets.

The swimmers of Filien's string already stroked toward the raft. Evanne clung to Filien, hugging him so tightly he winced. "You're all right?" he demanded over her shoulder, pushing wet black hair from the Rameki girl's cheek with a hand both awkward and tender.

"We're all right," Nuela assured him. "You weren't hurt?" The grimness at his jaw, the hardness in his eyes were like a shadow on the sun.

He shook wet hair from his forehead. "I woke with black blood pooling in my palms, but Anamirre told me I must let Tirin negotiate it for me." A frown deepened between his tawny brows. "I wanted to come myself. If Anamirre had not spoken . . ."

"I understand," Nuela said gently. He had sustained more than the bite of a quill. The Greater Milminesa had mounted an assault against his pride, and he had not been permitted to dress the wound. "But it was best this way, Filien. You were right to respect Anamirre's instructions."

"And the matter is negotiated, if not in any orderly manner," Tirin assured him. "Here—let me see." He caught Filien's hand, turning it palm upward.

The palm was veined with black. Instead of clearing under Tirin's stroking fingertips, the stain darkened. "It does not fade so quickly," Filien said with a stubborn shake of his head. He looked down at Evanne. "There was an injury done you both. It was done when I led the string, and I did nothing to make it right. I only waited to see if you would come back."

"But an injury was done you too, Filien, and neither of us could help you. And we wanted to." Evanne caught his hands, kissing each palm in turn, then clasping the hands between hers. "But we've come back. We're safe. So you must let it go. If we return to the Greater Milminesa—"

"Return?" Filien pulled his hands free, staring at Tirin. "What terms are these?"

"There are— There are no terms, Filien," Evanne interposed hastily. "Not with the Greater Milminesa. If we go back—" She glanced anxiously at Nuela. "We aren't required to send a float to the Great Land, Filien. The Greater Milminesa are going instead. Unless—" She drew a long, quivering breath. "Unless Nuela goes back and tells them they must not, the Greater Milminesa intend to cut their mooring ropes. They intend to send their entire school on the current."

"To the Great Land?" Filien said with flat disbelief. "The Greater Milminesa intend to do that?"

"Unless Nuela tells them not to do it, they will."

Filien's eyes widened. He stared hard at Nuela. "Then—"

Evanne caught a tremulous breath. "Taric yielded to her. And if she goes back to them after she finishes her kalinerre, then I must go too. We are sisters. We—"

"No," Nuela said sharply. "Whatever I do, Evanne, you will remain with your school."

"But how can I do that? I won't leave you alone with the Greater Milminesa, Nuela. I won't—"

"No." Nuela spoke more gently. "No, Evanne. Sisters can't always be together. Sometimes they must separate. Whether I go back to Aurlanis or to the Greater Milminesa, I want to remember that I left you here safe and happy. With your family. With your friends."

"Anamirre needs you, Evanne," Tirin reminded the Ra-meki girl.

"Because I'm the one whose name she can remember?" The girl's laugh was shaky.

"She remembers your name because you are important to her. She isn't as strong as she was a few years ago. She gets tired. She needs someone who knows how she likes her meals prepared. She needs someone to braid her hair, to listen to her stories, to rub her back when she's ready to sleep. Lienne doesn't have the patience you do."

"Anamirre needs you more than I do, Evanne," Nuela said softly.

Evanne ducked her head, tears joining the seawater that still wet her face. "But you will come back to us before you return to the Greater Milminesa. Won't you, Nuela?"

"If I decide to return to them, yes. And even if I don't see you again, Evanne, we are sisters."

"Then—be safe, my sister," Evanne said, holding Nuela tight, releasing her reluctantly.

They parted then, Evanne and Filien swimming toward the float, Nuela and Tirin watching until they climbed aboard and turned to wave. Then Tirin touched Nuela's wrists, a light, fluttering caress, and spoke a few soft words.

Heat took her. The beat of his heart became hers. They darted beneath the water and swam swiftly toward the point where the sun would set with evening—swam so swiftly she soon forgot everything but the rush of water, the stroke of limbs, the flash of scarlet flesh, Tirin's and her own.

They reached the platform shortly before the sun set. Nuela thought at first it must be the platform the fantasy beast had escorted her to the night after she left Aurlanis. But when she followed Tirin aboard, she saw that this float was wider, the three-walled shelter larger and more sturdily made. She stood for a moment shivering and dripping. They had spent all the day in the water, pausing only once in the late afternoon to harvest pods. She turned toward the shelter, her knees so weak she staggered. "Are there blankets?"

Tirin padded into the shelter. "And food too, unless someone has visited since I came last."

She followed him and let him wrap her in a blanket from one of two wiregrass chests. She hugged the rough fabric close, her teeth chattering. "Where are we?"

"In the water beyond the seventh pod of the Torahon."

"Near Aurlanis?"

"No. Here, sit down before you fall down." When she crumpled to the mat, he sat beside her, wrapping himself in a second blanket. "We are as far from Aurlanis as we can go without leaving school waters. And you must eat before you fall asleep. You swam long today."

She laughed unsteadily. "You swam just as long."

"And I'm starved. Let me see—" He crouched over the nearer chest. "No, first this." He drew out a long, seven-string shell chime. He rose, still wrapped in his blanket, and hung it from a projecting pole at the corner of the shelter. "Now anyone who approaches will see that we are in residence. We won't be bothered."

Nuela listened to the gentle chatter of shells, wondering who might approach them in this remote reach of the sea.

She ate the dried fare he laid out, hardly noticing what she ate. Her eyes prickled from long hours of submersion. At some point, she closed them for a moment. When she opened them again, she lay on the matted floor. It was dark beyond the shelter, and Tirin slept beside her. Nuela stared briefly into the field of stars, then slept again.

She woke to bright sunlight and the chatter of shells. Tirin was not to be seen, but his blanket hung from a cord strung across one corner of the shelter. Nuela hung her own blanket beside it, then searched the chests for pilchis grains or plainwater. She found neither. Running one hand through her hair, she bent and shook it vigorously, then tossed it back over her shoulders. She rubbed at her forearms, at her face, grimacing at the faint grit of salt.

She stepped from the shelter to see a ripple of scarlet in the water. Tirin pulled himself over the edge of the float, flipping wet hair back from his forehead, laughing. "Did you sleep well?" He wore a carrybag on his back, one strap looped over each shoulder. "I've brought us a feast."

She was hungry again, sharply. "Let me help you." She eased the bag from his back. It dripped with good things, some of them still squirming. She pulled out a wriggling grippie and dropped it to the mat. Its gaudy scales glinted in the sun. ''How did you catch this without a net?''

''I had a net.''

''I don't see one now.'' There were pale popo pods, long fat streamers of whitegrass, several kinds of crustaceans she did not recognize. And there were a dozen bulging crespi pods. The grippie flopped on the matted floor, trying to heave its away back to the water. Nuela did not notice as she tore open the fattest crespi pod and splashed her face with cool plainwater.

''I tore my net apart after I made my catch. It wasn't worth keeping. I only made it when I saw I needed it.'' Stepping into the shelter, Tirin emerged with a bone blade and swiftly thrust it into the wriggling grippie. ''This will be better cooked, don't you think? We have a firepot and fuel. It won't take much to coax a spark out of the stems. And when we've eaten, do you know what we're going to do?''

''No,'' Nuela said, suddenly guarded.

He laughed again. His eyes glinted, as if grains of sand caught the sun. The scarlet markings were vivid at his wrists. ''Nothing. We're going to do nothing all day, Nuela.''

No tests? No decisions? No challenges to her courage or her equilibrium? ''That sounds good,'' she said cautiously.

''It will be.''

He brought the pot and rubbed and twirled a spark from two thin, rigid stems Nuela could not identify. It ignited the bed of dried grass at the bottom of the firepot and sent up a thin curl of smoke. ''You've never seen that done,'' he said, pleased with himself.

''No.'' On Aurlanis fire lived in the kitchen and in pots on every floor of the palace. It was fed regularly, and at night lamps were lit and carried along the corridors to light other lamps. She had never seen flame born, leaping up in a spark, as if a bit of the sun had flown loose.

Tirin said, as if he read her thoughts, "Neptilis tells us that the sun is a ball of flame and the stars are suns that burn far in the sky."

"I haven't heard him say that." But it explained why sunlight burned against her back on hot days. And why the stars, distant, immaterial, not even visible by day, glittered so fiercely at night.

"You will one day. But not today."

Today they would do nothing.

They did it lazily and with relish. They burned stems and grasses in the firepot, skewered the grippie and cooked it. They ate the flesh hot from the bones. They ate the crustaceans raw and crunched happily at popo pods and whitegrass. Then they let the fire burn itself to powdery ashes while they stretched out replete. The sun beat down. The float rocked. The shell chime sang its brittle song.

Occasionally Nuela dozed. Occasionally Tirin went into the water and returned to shake wet jewels from his hair, from his fingertips. Cold droplets spattered Nuela, and they both laughed. Later, when the sun stood directly overhead, Nuela retreated to the shelter and sat with her knees drawn up, watching light sparkle and shiver on the surface of the water.

They feasted again late in the afternoon, and Nuela celebrated the first day in many when she had not gone into the water. But she celebrated silently because she knew that Tirin watched her, waiting to see if she wouldn't soon be drawn in.

She was not. She watched the sun set, and no voice called her to the sea. Tirin slipped over the side again, glancing back in question, but she shook her head.

If he had touched her wrists, if he had spoken the soft words of his chant . . . For a moment, the markings at her wrists grew hot. But he did not touch her.

He did not chant. And so she let him swim away without her.

Quickly light fled the sky. Retreating to the shelter again, Nuela worked at the sparking stems, trying to ignite a wad of grass so that she could light the tiny oil lamp she had found in one of the chests. The sticks were futile in her hands. The sun refused to leap into the pot.

"Let me."

Nuela started. "I didn't hear you. I thought you were in the water."

Tirin shook his head, his smile a streak of white in the dark shelter. "I met a stray toothfish. I didn't stay to see if he was hungry."

Nuela shivered. She had never seen a living toothfish, but occasionally one of the long, whip-thin bodies had washed up on the sand and she had gone with her friends to shudder over the blade-sharp teeth that lined the mouth—a mouth which in turn accounted for almost half the predator's length. "Your pattern—" Wasn't that why the Chahera bore school patterns? Because the large predators of the sea did not prey upon the twelve consort breeds?

"Not much protection from a toothfish once the sun sets. Their night vision is poor. Let the dark catch a toother away from his grotto, and he'll strike at anything that moves." Tirin bent over the sticks, chafing them. He grunted with satisfaction as a spark jumped from the sticks and fire flared. "Do you have the lamp?"

Starlight, moonlight—lamplight was more comforting than either. They sat on the gently rocking platform, night cooling softly around them, Tuanne and Lomaire staining the water with light. Occasionally a roiling globe of phosphorescence welled from the deep and broke the surface of the water. Schools of luminescent fish winked past. Once a small pod of mela-

mela appeared. The creatures lifted questioning beaks over the edge of the platform. Nuela knelt to rub their heads, whistling to them. They repeated the notes of her whistle before sliding back into the water.

However comforting, lamplight created a disturbing sense of intimacy, as if the light held them within a contained globe, separate from the world. Nuela was much aware of Tirin's presence, of the flicker of shadows across his face, of the rhythm of his breath. Surges of heat at her wrists spread, heating her forearms and upper arms, extending exploratory fingers across her chest and abdomen.

"Tell me—about your family," she said finally, anxious to place him within some other context than this one. "I met Lienne. Do you have other children?"

"Oh yes." He raised his head to gaze briefly at the sky directly overhead. "I'm a caller. I have a mate in every pod—seven altogether. I have children with four of them, children from five women I have called the stroke for, and I've sent two sons back to Aurlanis." He smiled at her startled expression. "One mate, two children, three at most— That's the way on Aurlanis. Here, for a caller, that would be selfish. And none of my mates are exclusive to me. None of them holds me as her primary mate."

"You share them? But—isn't there one you really care for?"

"I care for them all. I take inchata with no one but my declared mates. I never have."

To take inchata: to mate outside the string, without pattern. "But the other—"

"Kerinchata? Do you think Neptilis gave me a caller's touch if he didn't intend me to use it? And do you think he made the touch, the gift, so important to us all if he didn't intend it to be passed on to succeeding generations? I mate as freely as any caller with the people who swim with me."

"Then the sea must be full of callers." Seven wives. Eleven children. And he was young.

"No. If Lienne finds her touch, she will be the first of my children to do so. But they're young, most of them too young to hold the pattern yet."

She shook her head. "Don't you ever regret that you didn't return to Aurlanis?"

"Do I have to say simply yes? Or no?"

"Say whatever you want."

Shadows wavered across his face. He frowned down at the mat. "I think of the gardens, of the palace, of people I knew. Sometimes at night, I walk along the beaches or through the corridors, visiting places I remember." He drew his knees up, hugged them to his chest. "But I leave no prints on the tile. I make these visits from my bed." He glanced at her, frowning. "And sometimes I go to Pahla's Nipple, or to one of the other nipples, just to feel land under my feet for a few hours.

"There is hardly any person in the schools who isn't land-called. There is hardly any person who doesn't want to live at least part of his life on a surface that grows right out of the bottom of the sea, a surface thrown up from mother rock and welded solidly into place. The weather is quiet now. When storms come, we all wish for land.

"Every year, at the change of years, one school yields Pelosis to the next. And I look at the palace—so solid, so firm—and I marvel. If Neptilis hadn't left his words living in us, do you think we could share this one thing we all want so badly? Without war?"

"I don't know," Nuela said. The very concept of war was strange to her. But children on Aurlanis sometimes fought for pieces of the beach or for positions behind the courtyard wall. And the game didn't always remain a game. "So you regret leaving Aurlanis."

"Of course. But I would have regretted returning

more. Could you go back to Aurlanis tonight without regrets?''

It was Nuela's turn to bow her head, to frown down at the mat. "I would regret not seeing you and Evanne and Sumirre again. And Anamirre. I would regret not riding the mela-mela. And I would be frightened for the Greater Milminesa every time I thought of them. But Sinjanne told me, the night she left, that she heard a voice calling her to the sea. I don't hear a voice calling me here, Tirin. I don't think that Neptilis truly made me for the sea.''

He raised challenging brows. "Maybe he made you for the sea but you are reluctant to hear the call.''

Reluctant? Or afraid? " I came to find my sister,'' she said stiffly. "Polamaire withheld my tile from the basket for four years. My friends went to Pahla's Nipple without me. And I never felt—restless. I never felt called. I have my work. I have friends. I have—I had Sinjanne. I've never needed more.''

Tirin shook his head. "I'm not satisfied, Nuela. I've guided candidates who obviously had no place in the sea. I've guided others who could not have remained on Aurlanis if they had returned. Who could only have caused grief.''

"Like my mother.''

"Like Tuleja. I've guided just one who was awake to Pahla but strong enough to return to Aurlanis. Polamaire is like that. Will binds her to the palace—but not easily. It has never been easy for her.

"I've never guided a candidate who passed the tests but refused to waken to Pahla. I don't think you have opened yourself in the way you must.'' He caught the tip of his tongue between his teeth, compressing it. "I'll take you down tomorrow. I want you to listen again to the Deep Voice before you make your decision.''

Nuela's voice snapped rigid. Let herself be tied again to the mooring rope? "No. I listened for the Deep Voice once, and it said nothing." Nothing helpful. Nothing instructive. "I—I passed that test. And why—why do I need to test myself at all? All I want is to know that Sinjanne is safe before I go back to Aurlanis."

If indeed she could leave Sumirre and return to Aurlanis. If she could really let the Greater Milminesa cut their moorings.

And what did tests have to do with either of those things?

Tirin clasped her wrists. She jerked, startled, her face flushing, but he pressed firmly at the pulse points. "If you are so certain that you don't need to listen again for the Deep Voice, why is your heart leaping?" he demanded, releasing her. "You're afraid to listen again. And why be afraid?"

Why be afraid of being tied to the mooring rope and left until the very thoughts had chilled from her mind? Why be afraid to let vibrations from some unseen throat jar her to the marrow? Why— "Are you going to sting me with a quill? That's how Ria tested me. She stung me with chiana venom and tied me to the mooring rope. I woke that way, tied to the rope."

He drew a long breath. "No, I won't sting you with chiana. I won't force you. I have never forced any person to anything. But let me tell you the same thing Taric told you. Truth is what is, not what you wish it to be. And wisdom should tell you it is better to turn your will to finding the truth than to hiding it.

"I won't force you, and I won't coerce you. But I am within my rights to insist that you spend two more days here. When you have done that—" He shrugged. "Then I will take you to the pledging rock."

"The pledging rock? Not Pahla's Nipple?"

"Candidates pronounce their decision on the rock. Then they gather on the Nipple for conduct back to Aurlanis. If you choose to go back, I will escort you myself.'' His eyes narrowed. "But if you choose incorrectly, you will regret it. For all your life.''

Shivering, Nuela remembered the band Tuleja wore at her thigh, remembered the tiny, sharp-pointed shells that lined it. "What if there is no right choice, Tirin?''

"There is always a best choice. And if you fail to make it, the responsibility is not mine.'' He held her gaze, his eyes neither angry nor judging. Then he stood. "I'm tired. I'll leave the lamp for you.''

He withdrew into the shelter and briefly she heard him moving around. After a while, she knew that he slept.

And then the lamp held only her within its hemisphere of light. She stared over the restless water. She listened to the chatter of the shells. Once she briefly stroked a pair of mela-mela who approached the edge of the platform. They whistled softly, as if they knew Tirin slept.

Was she willfully failing to wake to the sea? Or was there something lacking in her, something Tirin had every reason to expect to find there?

Courage?

But if she chose the sea, she must go back to the Greater Milminesa. She must try to live wisely among people she did not understand. She must try to dissuade them from the very course she herself had suggested to them. No, urged upon them.

Mustn't she?

The moons described their bright courses. Stars that had stood high in the sky set. Finally Nuela entered the shelter and knelt beside Tirin's mat. When she touched his shoulder, he woke with a single sharply drawn breath. "Tirin, if I choose the sea, must I go to the Greater Milminesa? Can I come to the Ra-meki?''

He stared at her through the dark. "Either,'' he said finally, the word distinct although his eyelids had already shut again.

Either.

And how did it help to know that? If she did not return to the Greater Milminesa, if she went to the Rameki instead, apparently the Greater Milminesa would accept her decision. And, accepting it, they would go without her. Sumirre, Tuleja, Taric—they would cut the mooring ropes and vanish on the current.

And what hollow place would open up in her then, where once courage had lived?

# Chapter Fourteen

AGAIN NUELA WOKE AT MIDMORNING TO THE CHATter of shells and found Tirin gone. Again he came through the bright water like a swift-moving ray of scarlet when she stepped to the platform. Glancing up at the sun, Nuela shivered. Her thoughts of the night before ached in her head. She did not meet the day with anticipation.

Nor did Tirin offer her a feast, although his carrybag held many of the same things they had eaten the day before. His unsmiling demeanor as he boarded the float declared that this was not a day for lazy pleasures.

Silently he made the sun jump into the firepot, and again they ate grippie hot from the bone. It had little savor. When Nuela finished, she rinsed her face and hands with plainwater and met Tirin's eyes for the first time since the night before. "What will we do now?"

Setting the firepot aside, he splashed his own hands and face. "How many ways have you dreamed?"

"What do you mean?"

"How many times have you dreamed? Did you dream when you were with the Greater Milminesa?"

"For a few minutes after Neparra drugged us. And later in the water, when I escaped."

"Before that?"

She shrugged. "I dreamed when the drowning wave came in. I dreamed again when you pulled me under. I dreamed . . ." She frowned. "I dreamed the night you came for me with the others." She had drifted away in the belly of the fantasy beast and dreamed to the beat of his chant.

"So you have dreamed three times by water, once by a caller's spell, once under narsa-pika. Not in any other way?"

"I don't know what you mean." Other ways? "Why did I dream when you chanted? I never dreamed when Polamaire chanted. I never dreamed during even-chant." At most, Polamaire's evocation of Pahla had been ephemeral, as much a product of stories heard at bedtime as of the syllables Polamaire spoke.

"Polamaire has only the slightest touch of the caller's gift—enough to earn her the keeper's gowns on Aur-lanis, not enough to permit her to lead a string of swimmers."

"But when Ria tied me to the mooring rope—I didn't dream then either."

"If you had been conscious when she took you down, you would have dreamed. There is normally a period of dreams before the Deep Voice speaks."

"So the dreams lead to the Deep Voice?"

He hesitated, frowning down at the mat. "Not exactly. Not every episode of water dreams opens the throat. And the Deep Voice doesn't always require that you let the sea in before it speaks. Sometimes . . ." His frown deepened. Abruptly he turned his head and stared narrowly across the sea, calculation in his gaze. "The more we learn about the gifts Neptilis bred into us, the less simple they become." He stood, extending a hand. "Come. I can show you a way into the dreams that will only cost you a swim in the sun."

Nuela rose reluctantly, reluctantly let him draw the

pattern to her flesh. He released her wrists quickly, plunging into the water.

She followed. She swam. And she wished as she did so that she did not feel the pleasure of it. But water rushed through her hair like a hundred stroking fingers. Scarlet striae glowed upon her bare arms. Her legs beat the water as if released from restraints: with eager, joyous power.

Tirin glanced back and there was laughter in his eyes again. Sunlight glittered there, as if on dry sand. He arched briefly into the air, a leap of celebration, and then led Nuela beneath the surface.

They sped through the sunlit layer that extended beneath the surface of the water. They flashed past startled sea creatures. Once they propelled themselves through a school of haspipi. Startled, the tiny fish winked every color of the rainbow in swift succession, then fluttered in a body toward the depths. Yellow, orange, blue—and they were gone.

As before, Nuela found she had the capacity to swim for long periods without surfacing for air. She surged forward at Tirin's heel and wondered how far she could follow him without rising to the top. Wondered how long he could swim without drawing breath. Wondered, involuntarily, what depths they might explore, what things she might find there.

The sun told her almost an hour had passed when they broke the surface again. Almost immediately a small pod of mela-mela bounded toward them, shrilling for attention. They converged on Tirin, whistling the notes of his name. Laughing, he first rubbed their heads and then, when they began to press too hard, slapped their beaks. "We don't want to ride today."

Rejected, the creatures converged on Nuela, bumping her with playful beaks. Three of them leaped in tandem over her head, raining cold droplets on her.

"Give them a good slap. We don't need to ride to-day."

But Nuela could not bring herself to discipline the mela-mela with any conviction. They trailed her as she swam after Tirin, nudging her, cajoling her. Finally she brought the flat of her hand smartly against the beak of the most insistent animal. It whistled shrilly, threw itself into the air, and landed with its tail already flailing at the water, propelling wet gouts into Nuela's face.

Its companions shrilled and darted at it, driving it away. But there was something clownish, unconvincing in their indignation. By the time Nuela shook the water from her eyes, the pod was gathering again. The animals bobbed in the water at either side of her, their broad features insolent and playful at once.

How could she not be charmed? How could she not be seduced?

Finally the creatures abandoned them, slipping beneath the surface in a body, not reappearing. Nuela peered around and caught no glimpse of them. Looking up, she caught a sharp breath. The sky was a featureless blue dome upended over an equally featureless sea, the sun at its center directly overhead. They were alone at the center of the sea. There was nothing to mark their place, nothing to lend perspective, to indicate distance or direction. Nuela spun in the water, disoriented.

Tirin touched her wrists, and the pattern that had faded with the approach of the mela-mela darkened again. He shaped a few syllables with his lips, and Nuela followed him gratefully beneath the water again. Her vision was limited there. She felt enclosed, directed by the very pressure of the water.

Tirin led her directly downward through the sunlit region and they swam in dark waters, swam in cool waters, swam where large fish lived in slow-moving silence. Occasionally lush stands of grasses or polipods streamed upward from the bottom, tangling loosely around them as they passed. At other times they saw nothing of either fish or vegetation. They swam in clear, empty solitude, the bottom lost in darkness below, the surface a sunlit glimmer far above.

Emerging from a gently swaying growth of pods and grasses, Nuela saw a milky glow in the water ahead— and stopped herself short of drawing a startled breath. Her heart momentarily broke step with Tirin's and made an eager lunge against her ribs.

But when they glided nearer, they approached not a lucticete but a greater milminesa. Its large, fragile, globelike body hung suspended in the dim water, glowing with some faint luminescence. A tangle of filaments whipped at the water, sweeping up an unseen harvest. As they drew nearer, Nuela could see the faint violet shadow of the creature's internal organs.

Tirin led her in a broad arc around the creature.

And suddenly they entered a system of straight, tall stems that reached like giants from the dark water below to the surface. Nuela stared up, briefly losing the stroke. She could no longer see the faraway shimmer of sunlight on the water's surface. The surface was shadowed, only occasional glints of light penetrating.

Tirin led her among the stems, then swung, baring his teeth in a broad smile. He touched her wrists, releasing her from the stroke, and caught the nearest stem between his knees. He pulled himself up hand over hand, the pattern fading from his limbs. Suddenly short of breath, Nuela scissored upward toward a narrow glint of light. She burst through the surface, gasping for breath.

Tirin bobbed up beside her, concerned. "Are you all right?"

"I—ran out of breath," she gasped, surprised. It had not happened before.

"I released you too soon. I should have brought you to the surface. You make better use of stored breath when you swim to the stroke. Here—" A wide green canopy lay on the water's surface. "Slip aboard." He slid over its rippled edge and drew her after him. "Stretch out."

She did as he instructed—and found herself lying beside him on a huge floating leaf, stiff, round, its edges crimped, a dimple at its center where it joined the stem. "But—what is it?" Gingerly she sat. The leaf rocked but did not dip. Its surface was tough and heavily veined.

"We call it monster-leaf. We've mapped seven patches like this one in school waters."

Mapped. Nuela stared across an entire broad raft of overlapping leaves. They had surfaced somewhere near its center. "But—how did you find it? How did you know how to get here?" How had he known how to reach the float, for that matter? And how would he find his way back to Ra-meki waters? She had been ten days at sea now without learning how to find her way from place to place.

He shrugged. "I know. Callers usually do know how to navigate from place to place."

"And other people?"

He shrugged again, smiling. "They learn. You know how to use the sun to find the four directions. Using those, you draw up a chart in your mind and you use the sun, the moons, the stars to guide you across the chart. Are you hungry?"

Nuela wrapped her arms around her updrawn legs, armoring herself within her own embrace. "Yes," she said doubtfully. It was midafternoon. Clouds stood tall upon the horizon, drifting like slow giants. The sea was as wide, as undemarcated as it had been earlier. And she perched at its center on the surface of a green leaf.

The scale was wrong. She felt dwarfed, frail, threatened.

"Then we don't have to look far." Tirin slid over

the side, vanishing into the water. A moment later he reappeared, a single large, knobby grey shell under each arm. He tossed the shells to the surface of the leaf and slid out of the water. "These cling to the undersides of the leaf, where it joins the stem. Let's see if we can wake them."

Nuela stared in consternation at his harvest, at the fat, glaucous appendage that emerged tentatively from the mouth of each shell and groped damply at the leaf's surface. "I don't think—"

"You don't think you can eat it?" Tirin took up one of the shells and teased the appendage farther from the shell. It was rubbery, rough textured, its underside lined with papillae. The entire appendage rippled and the papillae contracted. "You've eaten uglier things than this. I've seen you do it."

"Yes. But not this. We—we seldom eat that kind of thing in the palace." Things that left trails of sticky mucus. But he knew that. Why else the glint of laughter in his eyes?

"Nor on the rafts. Watch." He set the creature to the surface of the leaf.

The pair of them oozed across the leaf, shells rocking cumbersomely. When they reached the edge of the leaf, they paused, as if consulting. Then they extended their appendages, groping at the rippled surface. Their shells tilted as if they would overbalance, then slowly disappeared around the rim of the leaf into the water.

"This is our meal," Tirin said, carefully gathering the string of translucent white globules the creatures had left clinging to the rim of the leaf.

Nuela accepted a single pale globe cautiously, expecting it to cling to her fingers. Its surface was damp but not sticky. "An egg?"

"Yes. Nip it open with your teeth and squeeze out the material inside. Don't eat the membrane. It's bitter." He followed his own instructions, biting open a pale globe, draining it, tossing the sac itself into the water. "You are hungry, aren't you?"

Nuela continued to stare at the globule in her hand. "Is this—will this make me dream?"

"No, this will give you a full stomach. Don't worry about the dreams. They'll come later."

She would rather worry than eat. Still, forcing herself, she tore the sac with her teeth and put her lips to the opening.

The contents of the egg were thick, smooth, faintly tart. They slipped down her throat easily, neither coating her tongue nor leaving an aftertaste. Nuela laughed, shakily, and permitted herself to be hungry again.

They lounged together on their rocking green platform, draining eggs, watching the sun as it executed its deliberate plunge toward the horizon. The last of the tall clouds marched away after it, and soon the sky was full of stars.

Nuela sat with her head bowed, aware that Tirin watched her. Aware that he had brought her here for a purpose. But when did he intend to fulfill it—and how?

"Last night you asked me about my family, my feelings," he said finally. Although he lay several paces away, his fingers interlaced behind his head, the intimacy of his tone brought him near.

"Yes." Uneasily.

"Tonight I will ask you. Is there someone waiting for you on Aurlanis? Someone calling you back?"

*"No,"* she said, and realized she had spoken too emphatically. "There is no one," she said evenly. "There never was."

"Not even Rinarde? Polamaire told me last year that he was waiting for you."

Nuela's body grew taut, as if muscles suddenly strained against each other. "Rinarde was a friend. We grew up together. Sometimes . . ." Sometimes he had walked too near, his hand touching hers, and she had drawn away. Sometimes he had watched her face too intently when they talked. Sometimes he had frowned, had hesitated, had called back words he obviously wanted to speak.

More often he had maintained the careful balance of friendship with unruffled grace. "He never asked me to swim with him, and I never went to the men's beach to find him. I—I don't think I would have."

"Never?"

"I don't think I would have," she repeated, her throat tight.

Tirin grunted softly. "Then—why is that, Nuela?"

"I told you. Rinarde was a friend. We—"

"Why was there no one? Why did you never intend there to be anyone?"

Her throat grew tighter still. "It wasn't a matter of intention. I had my work. I had Sinjanne. There was no time for those things. And no point in thinking of them until my tile was chosen."

"But you did think of them—and rejected them."

Nuela bristled. "You think that because I refused you—" But she had not refused him, had she? He had seen her reluctance and he had been sensitive to it. Now, instead of challenging her with his touch when they swam, he fluttered his fingertips lightly at her wrists. She frowned down at the veined surface of the leaf, grateful for darkness. Color burned in her cheeks, at her wrists and forearms.

"I remember your parents, Nuela," he said quietly. "I remember how little happiness they gave each other. Tuleja wanted to stay and she wanted to go—and she was angry because there was no way she could have both land and sea. She tore herself into pieces, and she tore your father into pieces too. They never had a certain day together. She never knew when she might go into the water and not come back. He never knew either."

Nuela drew a painful breath, remembering cold nights, her father rigid and silent at her side. He laughed during the day. He talked. He played games. Never at night, while they waited on the beach. "Tirin—"

"And you felt it. You didn't know why she went into the water when everyone else was gathering for evenchant. You didn't know why she stayed long after everyone else had gone to bed. You didn't know why your father watched for her. I saw him there myself, sitting night after night on the beach, with you beside him. You were little more than a baby. But you felt it, didn't you? You felt his pain. You learned from it. You learned that it hurts to care too much for another person. You learned that the best way to avoid the pain is to avoid caring."

"*No.* I loved my father. And my sister. He told me to look after her, and I did. As well as I could. I—"

"But if Rinarde had asked you to care for him?"

"I cared for him as a friend. He never asked for more." But that was wrong too. He *had* asked for more—but so quietly, so cautiously, that she had refused him without a word spoken. She closed her eyes and felt the sudden heat of tears against the lids.

She had failed Rinarde as surely as she had failed Sinjanne. As surely as she had failed her father. "There's nothing I can do about it now," she said in a brittle voice. She had not been with him when the drowning wave came, and now his memory carried with it another accusation as well—an accusation far more justified.

And when she opened her eyes again, refusing to cry, starlight fell upon the familiar contours of his face, glinted from his familiar eyes. Tirin studied her silently.

"I thought—I thought we came here for a reason," she said sharply.

Tirin studied her a moment longer, then nodded. "We did. Let's be quiet now, and we will hear."

"I don't hear anything." Nothing but the accusing rush of her own thoughts.

"Why don't you lie down? You'll hear better if you lie down."

Nuela sighed, recognizing the same protective calm she had seen in him after Neparra's death. She stretched out on the leaf's gently rocking surface. If only Rinarde had spoken plainly what he wanted . . .

Then she would never have walked alone with him again. And he had known it. Tears welled in Nuela's eyes, turning bright pinpoints of starlight to shimmering abstractions.

A small, crisp detonation at the water's surface startled her upright. She stared around as the sound came again. "What was that?" The air had taken a faint, sharp edge, as if its composition had been subtly altered.

Tirin did not move. His smile was slow, anticipatory. "The nightbreath has begun."

"But—what is breathing?" Something large, surely. Several widely spaced bubbles burst. Then there was a long volley of small concussions, raising a faint mist in the starlit air.

Pinpricks of moisture peppered Nuela's bare arms. "Tirin—what is it? Is there something under us?" A sharpness that was not precisely an odor made her rub her nose. She blinked rapidly and realized, confused, that more than tears blurred her eyes. The world was losing focus.

"The monster-leaf is breathing. It breathes every night soon after the stars come out. It breathes from the nodules that lie along its anchor roots." Tirin's voice was distant, disengaged. "Lie down, Nuela. Listen."

For what? Resistant, confused, still rubbing her nose

and blinking, she lay down again. The water crackled and fizzed as bubbles broke all around the leaf. Her breath tickled huskily in her throat. She felt giddy, weightless—frightened.

"Listen."

She shook her head irritably. How could she help listening?

*Listen, and you will learn how the Chahera may best serve the lucticetes. For in certain seasons, these great beasts must leave our warm southern seas and feed in northern waters. This they did upon our cradle world Earth. This they do here as well. For in the pattern and distribution of land and water, Chaheras is much similar to Earth, as it is in the pattern and distribution of life. Even the moon in our sky is much like the moon that looked down upon Earth.*

*Here, as on Earth, the southern waters are a hospitable nursery to lucticete young. Cold waters steal warmth and energy from the body, while warm waters permit it to conserve its energies, turning them more fully to growth.*

*So each winter the pods stream south for the birth of the young. There, in quiet lagoons and watery byways, the newly born feed on the milk their mothers make from their great reserves of fat, and they grow and thrive.*

*But on Chaheras as on Earth, these great beasts find southern waters nutrient poor. The organisms the lucticetes must strain from the water in such great numbers if they are to maintain body mass and function are sparse. These warm waters, which seem so rich to the Chahera, are desolate barrens for the lucticetes.*

*So when the young have safely completed their first growth, the pods must leave and travel to the edges of the northern glaciers, where the waters are dense with*

*the species they feed upon. Only there can the lucticetes*
*replenish their stores of fat.*

When had she closed her eyes? When had she passed
into the dream? Nuela peered in confusion at the single
silver moon, at the unfamiliar configuration of the stars.
Slowly, reluctantly, she turned her gaze downward. Her
hands lay outspread upon an expanse of firm grey flesh.
They looked very small there, very pale.

She sat high on the creature's back, its glowing sac
hidden from her by the bulk of its body. But other
moons glowed upon the rocking waves. Hers was one
lucticete among several. There were two calves as well,
nestled at the sides of protecting adults. Looking more
closely, Nuela saw that each adult beast had its own
shadowy rider.

She turned. A palace stood tall and white upon
the crest of an island she did not know. Lamps
glowed from its broad windows. Vegetation cast stiff
shadows upon pale sands. Somewhere someone
chanted, and there was a sweetness in the warm air
Nuela could not identify. Strangely, it brought tears
to her eyes.

Turning back, she stirred with a tremor of—excitement?
anticipation?

*Through the winter months, the lucticetes bear you*
*cheerfully across the broad basins of the southern seas.*
*They carry you from island to island, permitting you to*
*meet with friends and kin in far palaces. They bear you*
*to places where you can test yourself in unknown wa-*
*ters, to places where you can study and harvest rare*
*plants and fishes, to other places where you can ex-*
*amine the very workings of the earth itself as it builds*
*itself upward from the sea floor.*

*The lucticetes offer you depths and breadths, and the*
*pleasure of the journey is both yours and theirs. So has*
*Neptilis fashioned you both, Chahera and lucticete.*
*Neither is master, neither is subject or object to the*

*other. Instead you serve, protect, and enrich each other, each sharing in the affection of the other, both beloved by him who made you.*

*But when summer approaches, the pods must return to the northern waters to feed. Some from among you will be chosen to make the journey with them. Your protection will be valuable to the lucticetes. And only by venturing from the warm seas of home can the Chahera learn the true nature and dimension of this world. Only by traveling from the hospitable and familiar into the unknown can you fully comprehend the size and complexity of the world and begin to guess at your place in it.*

*The lucticetes will carry you to places where huge sheets of ice come grumbling down to meet the sea. Taste the cold air that sweeps down from those broad, icy wastes. Ride with the lucticetes where the very stars are strewn in unfamiliar shapes across the sky.*

*Watch as you go for the ruins of the cities that once stood near the sea. See them and reflect. Consider how little is gained by conquering a world if, in the moment of ultimate mastery, you turn your very habitations to slag.*

*Do not touch shore near these cities. Not everyone who survived the wars came into Neptilis' saving hands. Some remain in the area of the ruins. If you must, protect the lucticetes against these feral humans as you would against any other predator. They are not your kind. They neither hear nor heed Neptilis.*

*Join me and journey in dream. Thus will you prepare yourself to travel later upon the waking sea.*

For a moment, Nuela was aware of her body, aware of the veined surface upon which she lay. Bubbles continued to burst at the rim of the leaf, throwing a fine mist into the air. The moons had risen, and Tirin had moved nearer. He lay with eyes closed, one hand outstretched.

Summoning all her will, Nuela moved her arm a bare fraction. Her fingertips touched Tirin's.

Then the two moons were one again. She sat upon the lucticete's back, as frightened, as exalted as if the journey she was about to undertake was real.

# Chapter Fifteen

AFTERWARD NUELA WAS ABLE TO RECALL ONLY ISO-
lated images from the journey: brief, bright flashes of
memory, like reflections caught and crystallized in
grains of ice. Only by calling up each discrete burst of
vision in succession could she reproduce the flow of the
journey.

The palaces of the southern islands, gleaming like
jewels as the lucticetes and their riders passed in parting.

Strings of swimmers racing to escort the pod, brightly
patterned limbs flashing at the water.

Later long stretches of uninterrupted sea, her gaze
probing restlessly in every direction, finding only an
unbroken horizon. Her unease, quickly communicated
to the animal she sat astride.

Then the tall bluffs and tilted coastal plains of the
northern coast. Dark palaces set at sparse intervals beside an increasingly chill sea. Here the swimmers who
came to greet them wore strange, dark patterns upon
their flesh.

Still farther to the north, enormous jagged palaces
stretching back from the sea like the stubs of huge,
ruined teeth: the cities of war. Again Nuela communi-

cated her misgivings to the beast. Its answering shudder told her it too knew of cities and war.

She began to wonder then at the depth of its mind, at the form and direction of its thoughts. They shared no language. Its huge face was incapable of expression. Yet the creature bore her gently and communicated the pleasure it found in her company.

Soon after they passed the third city, a great storm caught them. Nuela crawled into the lucticete's sac, and it plunged to calm depths, the slow, deep reverberation of its heart lulling her. Later, when they passed again into calm waters, she listened to the songs it exchanged with its companions and wondered why they so moved her.

Then the north waters announced themselves with cold breath. Chunks of broken ice bobbed drunkenly on the current. The calves darted ahead as if they knew the riches that waited.

Again memory was broken into swift, isolated crystals:

Water more like stew than seawater, rich as it was with countless tiny organisms and the larger organisms that fed upon them.

Herself laughing from the back of a calf as her own beast vanished into the water, tail wagging exuberantly, then reappeared with water, fish, vegetation, and mud streaming from between its straining plates.

Narrowed passages bounded by sheer walls of ice that cracked fiercely and spilled sheets of white crystal into the water.

A sky so vividly blue at midday that it hurt to look into it.

Sunsets that began but never seemed to end.

Later, farther to the north, nights that were only a little paler than days. Stars she had not seen before winking weakly from midnight skies.

The sharply etched moment when a pack of predators

darted among the feeding 'cetes, and she responded by lunging at them with spear in hand. She had not noticed before that she carried a weapon.

Times when she joined the shadowy figures of other Chahera on shore and slept beside a crackling fire. She learned then the musky perfume of wood smoke.

Things she ate: roasted fish, tiny fruits harvested from the vegetation that grew along the shore, brews of barks and leaves. Sometimes she moved so far into the trees that she lost sight of the water. After a while she grew accustomed to the haunting breeze-song of leaves and branches and sang with them.

Then it was time to travel south again. For the first time, Nuela resisted the dream. She had caught glimpses of land creatures moving among the trees. She wanted to become better acquainted with them. There were still a few varieties of fruit that had not ripened. She wanted to taste them. And one night, when the sky began to darken with the passing of summer, she saw faint curtains of green and blue light dancing above her. She wanted to stay and see how brightly the curtains might shimmer when the sky grew darker still.

But the dream carried her to the lucticete's back, and the lucticete bore her away.

And the images ceased. She remembered nothing of the return journey beyond a distant rumbling. After a while, she realized that she lay on the veined surface of the monster-leaf again. The rumbling continued— thunder.

But when she opened her eyes, it was to a clear morning sky. She sat, rocking the leaf, and Tirin stirred and gazed up at her. His smile was slow, sleepy, full of pleasure. ''Tell me. Tell me what you saw.''

She told him, calling up bright crystals of memory, letting them blaze and sparkle in her hands. Daylight did not dull or diminish them.

"Ah," he said, sitting. "And did you know, there are many more dreams as wonderful as that one?"

Then she wanted to dream them all. She wanted to taste and see everything. "And it isn't even real." She hungered for a series of figments.

Seductive figments.

His eyes narrowed. "If you feel the spray on your arms, if you hear the lucticete's heart—how can it be anything but real?"

Nuela drew a doubtful breath. "But those things aren't material like—like this is." She stroked the leaf. "Or this." Scooting to the edge of the leaf, she dipped water from the sea and splashed her face. It was salty, warm. She dipped again and drank thirstily.

"Oh? Is what lives outside you so much more real than what lives inside you? Must a world, a 'cete, a person exist in material form to be real? The beast you rode— I've ridden it too, more than once. The last time, it was carrying a calf. I lay in the sac and felt the beat of three hearts: mine, the 'cete's, the calf's. I don't know what eventually became of the 'cete and the calf, but they are as real for me as any mela-mela I've ridden."

And the fact that he had not put flesh upon flesh did not make them less so. Nuela crouched at the edge of the monster-leaf and pressed probing fingertips to her temples. She carried an entire world there, somewhere within her mind. It was emerging, becoming as real to her as Aurlanis—as real as beaches she had walked, gardens she had harvested, as real as her room in the palace.

She had walked upon that other world, hadn't she? In memory. What was her room to her today but a memory?

She didn't even know that the Chaheras where she rode with the 'cetes was separate from the world where she woke this morning. If the moon had broken—

But what could break a moon? She shook her head in confusion.

Tirin stood, laughing. "Come. Time to eat." He touched her wrists, lightly.

And color blazed instantly upon every fraction of her flesh. Nuela caught a sharp breath, wanting momentarily to call back the scarlet pattern. But she was on her feet, poised at the edge of the leaf. Tirin spoke the first words of the chant and arced into the water. She followed, the joyful leap of his heart in her chest, driving her.

He led her a swift and furious course through the morning water. They swam in bright sunlight, in shadowy depths, in the range between, where light pierced the water in long rays. They dodged among the straight, tall stems of the monster-plant, lost themselves in tangled grasses and polipods, darted through open water. When the first hot fury of the swim had passed, they made their harvest.

Finally they crawled together over the rim of a stiff-veined leaf, and Nuela spilled pods and grasses and a pair of wriggling fish from the bodice of her swimshift. She laughed aloud, then realized that Tirin crouched beside her, that he had not released her from the stroke.

She met his eyes, met all the brightness of sunlight there, and felt the renewed impact of his heart in her own chest. Pulses throbbed at her throat, leaped at her temples. Sunlight and seawater glinted upon his vividly patterned flesh.

She licked her lips. "Please." Please—what?

He leaned toward her. His fingertips found pulse points, pressed, and her heart stumbled momentarily as it regained its own rhythm. Relieved, disappointed, she traced the prickle and tingle of the pattern as it slowly cooled from her shoulders, from her arms.

Tirin ate briskly, with relish. When he had swept the

scraps of the meal into the water, he stretched out and extended one hand, brows raised in invitation.

Nuela frowned. The scarlet pattern, the heat were gone. The ache of an appetite aroused, then denied lingered. "I think—"

"You think too much, Scarlet Fish. Isn't that what the Greater Milminesa call you?" The rebuke was affectionate. Again he extended his hand. But when Nuela stretched out beside him, when she let the heat of his arm warm hers, he only squeezed her hand and sighed with satisfaction, closing his eyes. After a moment he slept.

Nuela squeezed her eyes shut. She thought too much. She refused to listen for the voices he wanted her to hear. She recoiled from his touch—and was sorry when he did not press her. If he were less patient, less confident—

But he was not.

Why? Because he knew she must wake to the sea eventually?

Perhaps the sum of small seductions was already too great. Perhaps she could never return happily to Aurlanis.

Tears stung her eyes. Pressing her eyelids tighter, she forced herself to breathe deeply, evenly. Eventually she escaped into sleep, linked to reality by the touch of Tirin's hand.

Then linked to a different reality by the husky chant he spoke over her. The sound brought her from sleep to a state where her senses were alert but her body unresponsive. Helpless, she listened from behind closed eyelids to long chanted verses that sometimes sank so low she had to strain to hear them. Listened until eventually it did not help to strain. Tirin's voice faded, and Nuela opened her eyes to a sun subtly different from the sun she had seen earlier.

Later she could not recall details of the dream, only

that there were rituals, ceremonies, celebrations, feasts. She was conducted to secret places. She swam in sacred waters and explored caverns where mythic things had happened. She moved among people innocent of the knowledge that they no longer lived. Sometimes the First Voice instructed her. Once she saw Neptilis standing alone beside a pool of silver water, lean and austere within his tightly furled cloak—his reflection lying just as lean, just as austere upon the water's surface.

At first, when she heard thunder growl, she thought a storm approached. But no one else noticed, and the sky remained clear. Drawn ahead through the dream, she listened more closely. Listened—

And then she was awake—sitting bolt upright, clutching Tirin's hands, staring beyond him at a sky as clear as the one she had left so abruptly behind. Her entire body shook, as if it knew something she refused to recognize.

"What is it?"

She drew a gasping breath. "I heard— I thought I heard thunder." *A grumbling, a rumbling, a deep, wordless growling* . . . She stood, rocking the leaf. "I want to go. Tirin, I don't want to stay here." It was late afternoon. Dark was coming. Soon the nightbreath would draw her back into the dreams. Back . . .

"Then we will go back to the float." He stood, unalarmed by her sudden agitation, and steadied her. "Do you want that?"

She did not. She wanted to go back to Aurlanis. To herself. To the person she had been before the drowning wave had caught her, before she had heard the First Voice, before Neptilis had spoken to her, before . . . She stared up at Tirin. "I can't go back. Can I? I can't go back to the palace."

"You can't return to the same palace. It isn't there any longer." Words at once gentle and implacable. "We move forward, Nuela. We don't move back."

She shuddered, understanding what he said. Reality was in a state of constant change, sloughing off the skin of its past, revealing the unfamiliar face of the future. The Aurlanis she remembered, the person she had been when she lived there, had as little substance now as the images of a dream. The sea was finding its way into her. Its voices spoke in her, slowly drowning the voices of her previous life.

She stared over the water, pain at the pit of her stomach, at her temples. "Take me back."

Tirin touched her wrists. Silent words moved on his lips.

They were in the water, joined by the beat of his heart, by the rhythm of their limbs. As if he knew her mood, Tirin led her to the dim layers far beneath the obliquely lit surface. The rush of cool water stroked heat from scarlet striae, yielding the fleeting illusion of control.

The sun had set. A passing pod of mela-mela whistled to them. Tirin whistled back, releasing Nuela from the stroke, and the animals rushed them, jostling for possession.

Nuela rode away on a sleek back, Tirin beside her. Glancing at him, seeing the glint of starlight on his wet skin, the flash of his teeth, she understood that he was truly made for the sea. Reluctantly she understood something she had not understood before: how much her mother had loved her father, to think that for him she could give up the sea.

Night spun the stars and drew the moons from below the horizon. After a while, by some witchery, they arrived at the float. Nuela drew a long breath, grateful to hold a solid surface beneath her feet again. Tirin stepped into the shelter for the lamp and firepot.

Nuela saw the narrow strip of scrip cloth fluttering from the end of the roofpole a moment before fire leaped alive in the pot. Startled, she reached to pull it free.

Tirin turned. "What is it?"

Nuela bent, holding the scrip to the fire that blazed up in the pot. "A message. *Sinjanne—*" Her heart pressed hard against her chest wall. For a moment she could not breathe. "Sinjanne is going to the pledging rock. I can meet her there." Nuela looked up, disbelieving. "She's safe. Sinjanne is safe. But— Who knew we were coming here?" How had a message found them at the center of the sea?

"There are only so many sea stations where we bring candidates." Tirin examined the scrip and frowned, firelight glowing against the planes of his face. "Don't you want to sleep before we go?"

"*No.* I want to go now. Tonight, Tirin."

Her excitement was slow to ignite him. He nodded, a faint frown trapped between his brows. He peered briefly over the water. Shrugged. "We will call the mela-mela back. We can reach the rock sometime after dawn."

His patent lack of enthusiasm did not dampen her. Kneeling at the edge of the platform, she whistled for the mela-mela and clapped her hands in the water. *Sinjanne was safe.*

The mela-mela came bounding back for them. Soon they coursed smoothly across a sea tipped with moonlight, troughed with shadow.

"How do you think she will choose?"

"She will choose the sea," Nuela said, with no hesitation. And she could accept that now. Sinjanne had not gone early to kalinerre because Nuela had failed her. She had gone because she had already begun to waken to Pahla. And she was safe.

Safe tonight. "Tirin—if you could not be a Ra-meki, which school would you choose?"

Tirin lay forward on his steed's back. "I would

choose the Malin-ji, because they think they can make life better by wearing bright colors and playing games. I take Anamirre to visit their rafts whenever she feels strong enough to ride.''

"You care very much for her."

"I love her better than anyone I know," he said, challenging her with a direct gaze.

But she had no argument for that. "If you could not be a Malin-ji?"

"I would be an Oso because they are gentle."

And he had little tolerance for hardness, for cruelty.

"And after that, I would be a Haspipi, because they dream the wheeled dreams."

"Wheeled dreams?"

"They lie on the water in wheels, holding hands, and enter the same dream at the same moment. Not the dreams the rest of us have. The Haspipi dream things—" He frowned. "They ride wheels of light. Voices sing to them that are more beautiful than human voices. They hear their own voices as more than human. And when they wake, they know things no one else knows. But they can never explain what it is they know."

Nuela nodded, only half understanding, and bent over the mela-mela, pressing her cheek to its cool flesh. Perhaps Sinjanne would be a bright-garbed Malin-ji, a gentle Oso, a Haspipi.

Perhaps she would not. Nuela clung to the mela-mela. If Sinjanne pledged herself to a school like the Greater Milminesa, if she chose to live among people who scarred themselves, who punished themselves . . .

The moons shone brightly. The water danced. The mela-mela seemed to divine their destination and took it as their own. Nuela clung to her animal's back, muscles suddenly taut and painful.

Sometime after the moons set, she slumped forward and slept.

She woke to a soft whistle, opened her eyes to mist

and jagged rock. Nuela drew a sharp breath, startled fully awake. The pod had shrunk to just four animals. The mela-mela threaded their way carefully among sharp spires of stone, rocky arches, blunt monoliths that jutted from the water. Morning mist lay in a thin layer, masking the water's surface.

Peering down through the mist, Nuela saw that the water was in places so shallow that it was little more than a series of interconnected pools. Tiny haspipi darted from the mela-mela's path, their colors flickering rapidly as they fled. "Where are we?"

"Near the pledging rock."

"But—what is *this?*"

"Land that has drowned—or land that is rising from the water. Who knows?"

Land, drowned. The concept struck an odd chord. Her steed quivered and faltered, then drove ahead again through the last rank of rocky formations. The sea stretched ahead again.

The mela-mela quivered once more, and abruptly the entire pod faltered, seeming to lose direction. Alarmed, Nuela glanced at Tirin. He turned to peer back in the direction they had come, then stared with sudden intensity at the sea ahead. Color fled his face, leaving it ashen.

Nuela followed the direction of his gaze.

She had not noticed the solitary rock before. Now it stood directly ahead of them, a black monolith much like those they had just left behind. With one difference. This monolith was rising up out of the sea. As she watched, breath held, it raised its blunt head above the water, bared a thick neck, broad rocky shoulders, outspread arms— It reared like a kneeling giant taking its feet.

Nuela caught a breath so sharp it stung. What she had thought was a rocky monolith was in fact an entire steep-flanked island. A moment before it had stood hidden beneath the water. Now—

She understood then what was happening. Understood far more quickly than she had understood the first time. She did not see a giant rearing to its feet, shaking off the sea. Instead the sea itself drew back, baring rocky flanks to view. And at the same time, the retreating sea drew the pod of mela-mela back with it, so that the giant seemed at once to rise and to recede.

A cry caught in Nuela's throat. The drowning wave had returned. The water was pulling back, and when it had retreated as far as it intended, it would rush forward again, picking them up as casually as if they were strands of sea grass, tossing them against jagged rocky flanks. Or dragging them apart, sweeping them deep into a featureless sea.

She turned. The arches, spires, monoliths behind them were rising from the sea too, their separate rocky foundations straining the retreating water into turbulent streams. Nuela stared at the boiling water behind her, at the rearing giant before her, and her mela-mela floundered, panicked.

Nuela leaned forward, reflexively digging her knees into the frightened creature's sides, clinging to it as if together they had some chance. The mela-mela tried to turn, tried to swim with the receding tide. But it was quickly drawn into heavy turbulence where the water was sucked away between irregular stony foundations.

Nuela saw Tirin vanish into the turbulence, his mela-mela's fluke flailing. Then she was thrown against an outcropping of jagged black rock, her steed torn from under her.

She clung at first by reflex, grappling at stems, at tangled grasses, at bare rock. Water, sand, and shattered fragments of vegetation swirled around her and tumbled away.

The level of the water fell rapidly, then ceased to fall,

its rush suddenly little louder than the fierce drumming of blood in Nuela's ears. Numbed, not certain if she was broken or whole, she peered over one shoulder. She clung to the upper wall of a deep natural basin of rock. The lower level of the basin held an agitated stew of water, sand, collapsed vegetation and stranded sea life. The newly bared island stood black-shouldered behind her in the grey morning light. Waiting.

For her. For the returning sea.

Instinct sent her eyes searching for a crevice, a cavity. She had only minutes.

Below and to her left, a suspension of sand and water rocking in its mouth, half flooding it—an aperture in the wall of the basin?

Her fingers had frozen to the rock. Biting her lips, she pried away muscles caught in hard spasm. Quivering, gulping for every breath, she picked her way diagonally down the exposed inner surface of the basin, trying to ignore torn, bleeding fingers, strained muscles, numbing fear. For Tirin. For herself.

For Sinjanne. Where was she?

One precious minute gone. Her foot slipped and she caught herself by little more than a fingernail. She sagged against the rock, permitting herself one long, steadying breath. Then she groped downward again.

There was no time to consider the odd regularity of the aperture. No time to think about the sense she had of some large, smoothly contoured shape lying half hidden by the thick suspension of water, sand, and torn vegetation. No time to wonder at the smooth surface she felt beneath her probing foot. The foot slipped. She snatched again at the rock. Her fingertips tore. She fell with a strangled cry into the liquid brew.

Breaking the surface, she propelled herself toward the aperture, through it. Inside she groped for rocky walls and met a cold smooth surface instead. Water thick with sand stood to her waist. Confused, half swimming, half staggering, she distanced herself from the aperture, fleeing the dim light it admitted to the interior of the—

Of the *what?* Nuela turned and stared briefly back the way she had come. Saw—a corridor? A door? She shook her head in confusion. Then the dim light showed her a second door—if it was a door—opening off the corridor. If it was a corridor. She threw herself through it, hoping the wave could not snatch her from so deep within the interior.

Something flopped at her feet. She drew a harsh, startled breath.

And then she heard the thunder roar of the returning wave. She pressed herself against a smooth surface, squeezed her eyes shut—and hoped desperately that she would wake again to the world.

# Chapter Sixteen

COME NOW TO THE DEEPWATERS, CHAHERA. COME with me to places where old lands lie drowned, where ancient palaces raise their towers into a dark sea. Explore great vessels that are host now to fishes. Think of the bones time has left there on the floor of the sea.

Rock, bone, and shell are the hard stuff of this world. Look closely and you will see that much of what you perceive to be rock is in reality bone and shell pressed hard by time.

Think of that. The nature of things is not always immediately apparent. You must look closely at this world if you are to see the truth of it.

Do that, Chahera. Study the truth of this world and resolve yourself to guard and preserve that truth. You have sentience, mobility, intelligence, but you are made up of the stuff of this our world, Chaheras—and so what are awareness, movement, and thought but temporary gifts from the world that formed you?

The stones of the earth neither feel nor move nor think. The plants of field and sea move in their limited way but have no thought and little awareness. Animals sense and move but cannot think in the special way that you can think. You alone are aware, moving, capable of abstraction.

*But you are of this world, not separate from and superior to it. And you were born bearing these three gifts so that you could employ them to the benefit of the entire sphere.*

*Come now to the deepwaters, Chahera. Come and consider the long history of the universe, the short history of the Chahera people—of human life. You are but one filament in a living web.*

*Consider these things and understand how little right you have to disrupt, to distort, to destroy that web.*

*Consider too that if you do so, you disrupt, you distort, you destroy the very living system that supports your own life.*

*Consider, Chahera . . .*

The beat of a great heart sounded deep in Nuela's bones. She lay furled snugly against the lucticete's belly, its oily scent comforting. It moved, casting pale light before and beneath it, and Nuela wondered briefly about the body she had left behind.

Then the lucticete carried her forward among towers and spires that pointed, as the First Voice had promised, upward into a dark sea. At first the lucticete's light showed her only near objects: eroded stonework, expanses of broken wall, dark cavities that once had been windows. Gradually darkness settled from the water, and the lucticete swam through the dim environs of a system of palaces that stood tilted and broken on the seafloor, their foundations lost in silt.

*Look closely, Chahera. Here is a city that was lost before your own cities ever were built. If you could see, you would find that this city was built upon the bones and stones of another city—a city ancient before the people who built this one ever came here.*

*This then is the scale of time. There were human habitations in this place for so many generations that no person could number them. And yet the human race is new—upon this world, upon our cradle world Earth, in the universe. Long before the first human walked, stars were born and died. Suns gave heat to living worlds and burned themselves out. Creatures like us and unlike us appeared, evolved, and vanished.*

*We are children. Yet upon many worlds, entire races of humans have already fallen to their own blindness and will. They have torn the web that supported them and died. Many are the webs that have reconstituted themselves with no human link.*

*So it very nearly happened here upon Chaheras. And so I tell you this: if you would survive, respect the web that sustains you. Use your three gifts for the preservation of the sphere into which you were born.*

*Dream the dreams.*

*Listen to the lessons.*

*Heed.*

*Live.*

Nuela listened, clasped securely against the lucticete's belly, and felt as the First Voice wanted her to feel.

Awed.

Humbled.

Touched with incomprehension and poorly focused yearning. Time was long, beyond her capacity to understand. Her own life was brief. She could extend her own years only by encompassing what had gone before, by incorporating what had been bred into her awareness.

She reached out. She caught at words, images, ideas. She held them glittering on the palm of her hand.

The lucticete carried her through the dim mazes of the drowned city. Nuela peopled its palaces from her imagination and from the First Voice's occasional whispered comment. She set men and women upon busy thoroughfares. They moved from place to place, intent upon activities Nuela did not fully understand. She drew children to their windows. They wriggled small fingers in greeting, and she saw that their hands were much like her own.

They were different as well, their proportions subtly alien.

She did not fully glimpse their faces. Perhaps that was as well.

Then the lucticete carried her from the city. The light of its sac dimmed. Peering into the sea, Nuela saw only an occasional shimmer of phosphorescence and once a pair of large yellow eyes that immediately winked out.

The First Voice continued to cast up images crafted of dark words and bright. Peoples, races, worlds, destinies . . .

The sac cast light again. They glided toward the seafloor and circled a sunken vessel—a palace made to travel the sea. It sat on the rocky bottom at a derelict angle, sea windows staring blankly, fish and sea creatures circulating lazily among its spires and towers.

Not so far from where it lay, they found a second sea palace, this one more modest.

Then, by some magic, they swam in a different sea. Sunlight struck through pale water and startled blue fish darted to hide beneath a sunken vessel at once sleek and cumbersome. Its long body was fat but smoothly contoured. Two wide, flat arms—smashed, broken—protruded from its sides, their tips vanishing into the sand.

*A flying vessel*, the First Voice said. *It carried almost three thousand people in its belly. It flew the sky like a metal bird.*

But what was metal? What was a bird? And how had a thing so heavy traveled in the air?

Not well, obviously, or it would not be lying broken in the water.

They visited other sea palaces, other flying vessels, another city. Instead of towers and spires, this city presented a series of long, low shelters made of rough-faced stone. Sand swept its thoroughfares and fish glided among its half-tumbled chambers. Peering down, Nuela saw that many of the interior walls had been patterned with scenes from life. Fragmentary faces peered at her. Eyes, noses, dark-lipped mouths wavered in the current.

The light dimmed, as if clouds covered the sun, and briefly Nuela was aware of nothing. Then she saw again, as through a darkened sea. They passed a place where mammoth shapes hid in the shadow of rocky formations. She could not identify the shapes, and the First Voice had faded to inaudibility. She saw ruins and remains too tumbled and eroded to identify. Saw another flying vessel, differently made.

*. . . flew once between stars, carrying people and materials among worlds that drew life from different suns. If you could go upon a journey in the belly of one of these great space vessels . . .* Wispy, fragmented, the First Voice faded again without telling her what she might see.

Once, where the water lay shallow and clear, Nuela saw massive flat stones laid upon the sea bottom in rays, spirals, and wheels. She glided above the meticulously placed stones in the lucticete's sac, shivering with awe, with bewilderment. She knew without being told that the stones had been moved, shaped, placed with enormous effort. By whom?

*. . . ancient peoples commending themselves to the sun,* the First Voice whispered.

And she knew without being told that the stones were not always visible.

*. . . the sand sweeps in, the sand sweeps out.*

The dream grew still dimmer, the First Voice's narration increasingly fragmentary. It spoke again of the scale of time, of the nurturing web, of human violence—sometimes swift and harsh, sometimes deliberate, often so subtle it was not recognized as such until too late.

Finally the First Voice fell to nothing. And in its place, Nuela heard a distant rumbling, a grumbling, heard thunder that came without storm. Heard syllables from some great throat, syllables that unfolded slowly, at a deep, growling pitch.

She knew what she heard, and panic touched her. Seawater had found the cavities and channels of her body. Her blood had grown cold, slow. She had dreamed her way to the realm of the Deep Voice.

She could not remain there. The wave had torn Tirin into the sea. If it washed him ashore again, hurt, she must find him. And Sinjanne was on her way to the pledging rock. If she had been injured—

Drawing herself to tight focus, Nuela found her scattered limbs. Arms, legs, hands, feet— They were so heavy, so cold they were almost without sensation. They refused at first to flex. She dispatched instructions— frantic, then angry—along reluctant nerve ways. She drew upon the memory of movement and tried to communicate it to cold, contracted fibers. Distantly she became aware of grudging response.

At the same time, she struggled to close the Deep Voice from her mind. And not just because of Tirin. Not just because of Sinjanne. Because of herself. She would not yield. She would not let this unbidden voice speak in her bones. She would not let its growling notes possess her.

With effort, with will, she roused her arms, her legs, and drove the Deep Voice grumbling back to silence. Reaching out with slow, fumbling effort, she touched a smooth, cold surface.

A wall. She pressed the palm of one hand to the wall and tried to open her eyes. Realized reluctantly that they were already open, that she stared wide-eyed into total darkness.

For a moment she panicked, her heart jumping at her chest wall. With will, she tamed it and patted her way along the wall. Finding the door, she bobbed into the corridor beyond, searching for the light that would guide her from—

The word came unbidden, and her heart jumped again.

She hovered in the dark corridor, searching for the light that would guide her from—*the ship.*

She tamed her heart once more and examined what sense and her senses told her. She had hidden herself in a ship. Perhaps it was a sea palace, made to bear passengers along the surface of the water. Perhaps it was a flying vessel. Perhaps it was a star vessel, built—

*Built to join worlds that lay beneath different moons.*

She examined that conclusion. It wasn't only the sun that would be different if a ship traveled from one world to another. The moons would be different too.

*Large silver moon, floating solitary against scattered stars.*

*Paired moons, smaller, darker, forever meeting, parting, pursuing each other across the sky.*

The Deep Voice growled again, deep in her bones. Anamirre and the Ra-meki were right. The moon had not broken. This world and the world of the silver moon were two different worlds. The Chahera *had* been born from that world to this one—not magically nor in some mystic fashion but by the simple fact of a space vessel, a kind of raft fashioned to pass between worlds.

Nuela shook with the force of understanding, and the Deep Voice spoke more loudly, grinding out long, slow syllables.

Their ancestors had not warred and broken the moon. Neither had they been cast from the land into the sea. Instead they had been hurled across the stars from Chaheras to an entirely different world.

Was this simply an even more drastic casting away?

At whose hand? Had Neptilis himself cast them out? And if he had, were they still bound by his commandments? And where were they? Was there land? Or had the ship brought them to a world entirely drowned in seawater?

Nuela groped along the corridor wall, dizzy with confusion, with the resurgent grumble of the Deep Voice. Her lungs had begun to hurt for air. Why didn't she see light from the door? If she had turned the wrong way—

The wall moved under her groping fingertips. She snatched her hand back, startled, then touched the smooth surface again, experimentally applied pressure to it. It moved to one side, yielding a narrow crack. She probed at the opening, pushed against some binding resistance, and created an opening large enough to slip through.

Confused—was this the door she had entered by?— she slid through the narrow aperture into cool, still water. She paused for a moment. Turning, peering, she saw no light. Hesitating again, she kicked her way upward.

She quickly collided with another flat, hard surface. A wall? No, a ceiling. She had turned the wrong direction down the corridor and entered some chamber sealed off from the remainder of the ship by a reluctantly sliding door. She bobbed against the ceiling, fighting the growing need to fill her lungs, then groped back toward the aperture.

Perhaps it was the beat of a heart that stayed her from slipping back into the corridor. If so, the sound was so slight, so muffled she did not consciously identify it. She simply became aware, as she groped along the wall, that she was not alone. There was another presence in the isolated chamber, something large, living, silent. If she kicked herself forward, if she extended exploring fingertips—

She found flesh: dense, cold, unresponding.

Startled, she propelled herself backward and hovered uncertainly in the water. A knowing coldness slowly took hold of her. She moved forward again, reluctantly.

Working with numbed fingers, she found a wall of flesh and traced a path the length of it. Sides, belly, fluke— Probing her way back along the contoured body, she pressed her ear to the rib cage. The throb of the heart was so weak, so laggard that she very nearly failed to detect it.

Nor did the creature that hung before her in the dark water stir as she continued to explore its great body. Oddly, she discovered, it wore a hard bubble over the spot where its nostrils should have been. A fat, flexible stem connected the bubble to the wall itself.

She found two more lucticetes in the chamber, each as cold, as emaciated, as unresponding as the first. Nuela counted their ribs, examined their dark, furled sacs, probed their gaping mouths. The material of their straining plates was surprisingly fine and pliable.

Had she not listened for the thready beat of each heart in turn, she would have thought the beasts dead. Instead they seemed caught in a cold, silent paralysis, stranded somewhere between life and death.

The Deep Voice growled, the syllables it spoke as incomprehensible as before. Nuela hardly heard. Lucticetes—hanging like dead things in the water. Cold, gaunt, still. Had they been cast from Chaheras with the Chahera?

But there had been Chahera on Aurlanis for more generations than anyone knew. Could the lucticetes have waited that long beneath the water, drifting sand obscuring the contours of the starship, choking its door?

How could anything live so long?

And how much longer could they survive? Their sacs were dark. She could trace their ribs with her hands. If they were not dying, then certainly they were no more than half alive.

Her lungs were suddenly afire, with lack of air, with shock, with panic. She had to find the surface. Turning, she blundered back to the wall. Found the aperture, slipped through it. Passed down the dark corridor, groping desperately at invisible walls. The lower half of the corridor was clogged with sand. It rose in gritty clouds as she passed.

A dim strip of light beckoned. Nuela groped toward it, her lungs shrieking now. The doorway was half choked with sand. She wriggled through it, kicked herself upward, broke the surface.

Air struck her like a blow. Startled, she gasped reflexively, choked, vomited—hugged herself against a series of spasms so profound they wracked her entire body. She fought to clear her throat and lungs, fought to draw air, fought alone in her own arms.

When she could breathe again, she shook tears and seawater from blurred eyes and peered weakly around. A rocky prominence rose from the moonstruck water— a prominence that had been the crest of a great, rearing mountain the last time she had seen it. Its top was tabled, its sides sheer.

Her arms, her legs were hanging weights. She forced them to motion and foundered toward the prominence. Torn fingers bled as she grappled her way up its rocky flank. Finally she lay on the tabled peak, struggling again for breath, the empty sea spreading in every direction around her.

No, the full sea. The living sea. The beckoning sea. It rocked in the light of the moons, a restless thing of dark troughs and froth-capped crests. It moved endlessly toward her from far places, moved ever and impatiently forward on its way to other far places. It drowned mountains and flatlands in its path. It covered them deep, hiding them from sunlight and human eyes.

It raised voices to her as it came, sweet, keening, hypnotic. It sang in her flesh, chanted in her blood, resounded in her most secret organs. It called to her from within and from without, singing to her of colors never glimpsed, of voices never heard, of mysteries and enigmas only it could reveal to her.

It was a failed seduction. Nuela lay upon the rock, her limbs spread around her, and other voices drowned the witcheries, the beguilements, the seductions of the sea.

The voices of fear. Of bewilderment. Of anger.

Fear for Tirin, for Sinjanne. The very sea that sang its siren song to her held them in its arms. Would it give them back? Or were they forever lost?

The sea held the lucticetes too. Had held them, had hidden them for—how long? And now that it had revealed them to her, what was she to do? They lay in a hidden chamber, their ribs standing in sharp relief against their sides, the beat of their hearts thready and unsure. Instinct told her she should free them, should turn them out into the sea where they belonged.

But when people saw those great, gaunt bodies—what then? What would the schools do when they recognized the bitter joke that had been played on them all? When they realized that they had been cast from beneath the silver moon entirely, the lucticetes with them? When they understood that their dreams instructed them in the ways of a world they would never see?

What would happen to the carefully drawn pacts? What would happen to the painstakingly evolved customs? To peace and negotiation? The Greater Milminesa were prepared to cut their mooring ropes at her word. What would happen when the spiritual mooring rope that anchored an entire people snapped?

Worse, what would happen if she freed the lucticetes and they never woke from their comatose state? If they simply continued their long dying—in open water, where everyone could see?

She could not guess. She had been among the Chahera for thirteen days. She understood them no better than on the night when she had left Pahla's Nipple in the belly of the fantasy beast. All she had really learned was that they were various, volatile, unpredictable.

Perhaps it was better that no one ever know what lay beneath the sand. Better that even she forget, if she could. Better that she return to Aurlanis and wipe the memory of cold, unresponsive flesh from her memory.

Fear. Bewilderment. And finally anger—because she was the one who must make the decision that would touch and affect everyone. The wave had caught her, and she had exchanged a difficult decision for a decision far more agonizing.

And she could not take long over it. She had found the luciticetes' chamber sealed. It was open now to sand and sea life, to predators, opportunists, to every organism that lived in the water. She must return to the vessel soon and close the door forever—or open it wide.

If the sea was her mother, it sang its seductive lullaby to a child too frightened, too confused, too angry to listen.

The stars followed their prescribed paths. Lomaire harried Tuanne to the horizon and vanished after her. Occasionally tears wet Nuela's face, wet the rock where she lay as she monitored the slow return of her strength. She wondered why she had never noticed before that tears had the taste of seawater.

Eventually dawn made a grey waste of the sky. Bruised, still weak, Nuela sat and gazed across the water. If only Tirin would come, if only he were safe— But he did not come, and fear and pain grew keener, more difficult to bear.

Slowly mists and clouds diffused the sun's first light, then melted into the air. Distant arches and monoliths became visible, standing blunt and dark above the sea's restless surface. Nuela stared at them, hugging herself against an inner cold—then caught a sharp breath, her heart leaping. There was color in the water, rippling below the surface. It moved swiftly toward her, changing as it came. Blue. Green. Yellow. Red.

She stood, breath held, and the darting body of color approached the base of the rock, broke through the surface—raised a dozen sleek heads and shook water from them, laughing in a dozen light voices.

It took Nuela moments to realize what she saw: a string of Haspipi setting small hands to the flank of the rock, laughing and chattering as they pulled themselves from the water. Girls and women, they were tiny, exquisitely made. Color continued to rush in cycles beneath their gleaming skin as they climbed, although it had faded to little more than a tinted flush. The Rameki stripes blazed at Nuela's wrists in response.

The Haspipi paused in unison, as if they became aware of Nuela's presence simultaneously. They raised wet heads and peered up, their dozen faces so alike in contour, in expression—

"Nuela!"

Sinjanne scrambled up the rock, abandoning the others. Laughing, crying, she caught Nuela in a swift embrace that smelled of salt and sea grass. Nuela froze, too startled at first to understand. Then her own laughter and tears came.

Sinjanne was truly safe. She had survived the second wave as well as the first. And more—she had found people she belonged among. Nuela clutched her sister's shoulders, holding her at arms' length. The rebellious child was gone, as was the frightened adolescent who had waited for the sea trail to open. Nuela held a Sinjanne at once profoundly and elusively different from the sister she had known.

"You're safe." And for the first time she was not frightened by Sinjanne's slightness, by the fragility of her bones. Nor by the brightness that burned in her. The same brightness burned in all the Haspipi who gathered on the tabled summit of the rock, their hair streaming.

Sinjanne laughed. "Of course I'm safe. I've come to pledge my school. Kirina is my guide. She came to Pahla's Nipple and she knew me. She knew I was to be a Haspipi when she saw me, Nu. And when I saw her—"

A tiny person little older than Sinjanne clasped both Nuela's hands. "I found your sister on the Nipple, and I called her away, and I guided her to the voices." She beamed with pride, with pleasure. "And since she is the first I have guided, she has brought me fully into my own voice."

"You're a caller." This tiny person held the same office Tirin held, the office Lienne wanted so desperately to attain.

"When I've spoken the pledging chant for Sinjanne, I can call myself that."

Nuela shook her head, wondering. Sinjanne had found a place with people so like herself she might have been born to them. And this child who clasped her hands was a caller, capable of invoking the voices and the dreams. She had led her string of girls and women safely across the unmarked sea, darting happily like small fish—soon would lead them safely back again.

She had not failed in her promise to her father. She could never have foreseen the shape of her sister's future, but now Sinjanne stepped happily, confidently into it. She had done what she could, and miraculously it had been enough.

Tears sprang to Nuela's eyes. She had seen Sinjanne safely into adulthood, and she had not guessed until this moment how heavily the responsibility had weighed.

Sinjanne drew back, frowning with quick concern. "Nu, you didn't come here alone?" She pressed exploring fingers to a large, purple bruise on Nuela's arm. "You're hurt. You were caught in the wave."

Kirina peered up at her in alarm. "You didn't come without a caller?" Her glance flicked anxiously over the empty sea.

Nuela drew a deep breath. Released it. "Tirin and I were thrown against the rocks when the wave came. Neither of us was badly hurt, but he—he was worried about someone we left behind. He went to see that she is safe. He will come back for me tonight."

Pray that he did. Clearly this was one of the brightest days of Sinjanne's life—of Kirina's as well. Nuela would not darken it unnecessarily. If Tirin had survived unhurt, he would come when he could. And if he was lost somewhere, injured, even these twelve bright she-fish would never find him in all the sea.

The Haspipi crowded near, concerned, touching her injuries with light fingers. "But are you certain you will be all right?" Kirina demanded.

"Yes, I'm sure. May I—is this the pledging rock?"

"Yes."

"May I stay? While you speak the pledging chant?"

For answer Kirina smiled beatifically and Sinjanne threw her arms around Nuela again. *"Please.* We've taken different schools, but you will always be my sister, Nu. Stay with me while I make my pledge."

And so she did, and no one knew why she cried as Kirina called the verses of the chant, as Sinjanne answered in a small, awed voice, as the sea itself murmured its own refrain. Sinjanne, Kirina, the other Haspipi thought Nuela's tears were as purely from joy as their own.

# Chapter Seventeen

Sɪɴᴊᴀɴɴᴇ ᴀɴᴅ ʜᴇʀ sᴄʜᴏᴏʟ sɪsᴛᴇʀs sᴡᴀᴍ ᴀᴡᴀʏ ᴀᴛ midmorning, their dozen lithe bodies streaking the bright water with color. Sinjanne turned before they vanished and raised both hands in parting salute. Nuela waved back and then, when she could see them no longer, slumped to her knees, hugging herself against sudden, wrenching sorrow.

They would always be sisters. Sinjanne had promised that. She had not renounced blood for seawater. But they would never share a room again. Perhaps they would not even sit down together again for a meal. Certainly Nuela would never again stand at the center of Sinjanne's life, the one person she could come to, could rely upon.

And Sinjanne's going had left a gaping cavity at the center of her own life. This morning one long stage of her life had come to a close. What did the next hold?

The sea rocked restlessly at the base of the rock, reaching foaming fingers for her. Rising, she plunged in and stroked toward the place where she had seen Tirin last.

She swam among black spires, rocky arches, rugged monoliths. She searched the rocks themselves, dived to search their hidden foundations. She found no sign of Tirin.

A single mela-mela approached and accompanied her in her search, occasionally whistling softly, nudging her for attention. She dared not take its back. If Tirin had survived the wave, he would return to the pledging rock to find her. If he came and she was not there . . .

She whistled the three notes of his signature whistle to the mela-mela, stroking its smooth head. It answered with the notes of her own call and nudged her again, whistling plaintively.

Finally, the morning gone, she returned to the pledging rock and sat staring again over the sea. She made a light meal of pods and crustaceans. Afterward she was drowsy, but she did not sleep. She sat hugging her knees to her chest, listening to the water, watching, as if by unceasing alertness she could coax Tirin from the sea.

He did not come. Did not come to study her with tolerant eyes, to talk with her, to offer guidance.

She choked back an angry sob. If the wave had not separated them, would she have listened to what he said?

She listened now, in the silence of her mind—listened to the things he would have wished of her. Listened hard, as if that could bring him back.

The decisions she faced were not easy ones. First— he would tell her—she must find the wisdom to choose her course. Then she must use will, not to suppress the voice of wisdom but to carry her along the course it prescribed.

And the wisdom itself—

She sat, tense, resistant, wishing she did not know so well where Tirin would direct her for that. Finally, biting her lip, she slipped from the pledging rock. She plunged beneath the surface of the water and found a cavity in the flank of the drowned mountainside. She hid herself there and drew water into her lungs.

And she promised herself, unreasonably, that if she listened carefully enough for wisdom, if she followed its dictates unflinchingly—Pahla would give Tirin back.

The dreams were brief, ephemeral. She slipped through them as through a morning haze, moving with no clear sense of time or direction. As she did so, sea-water found its way into her. Soon thunder growled deep in her bones. The Deep Voice spoke.

She let it. She did not try to wake herself, did not try to flee the wordless grumbling and rumbling. It did not matter that the moons were wrong, the world wrong. The Deep Voice had been bred into her. That was truth. That was reality as it existed, not as she wished it. Neptilis had shaped her. She was a Chahera. And so she let the voice rise, and she asked her simple question.

What must I do?

The answer was as simple as the question. It did not come in ordered syllables, in comprehensible words. It rose wordlessly from within her.

She must care for the great beasts Neptilis had given the Chahera. She must think of them as cherished kin. She must do for them as she would do for her own mother, sister, daughter.

She must do what was necessary.

She must do it now.

So very simple.

And probably impossible. Free the moon-whales from the star vessel when they offered no sign of living awareness? Take them to the north waters to replenish their stores of fat—how else were they to live?—when she did not even know if there were feeding grounds in the northern waters of this world? Protect them from predators when she had no weapon?

More, she must do these things secretly. Because if

the lucticetes died, no one must ever know. The delicate balance the schools had struck over the centuries must be preserved.

The waiting must go on.

No one must know that it was a futile waiting—a senseless waiting on the wrong world, beneath the wrong moons.

She made the Deep Voice speak its wisdom to her again. Again. The things it said were the same each time.

Care for the lucticetes.

Do what was necessary.

Do it now.

And the dreams had already told her what was necessary. That she seek northward for waters rich with the species the moon-whales fed upon.

The sky was grey when she released herself from the rocky crevice and kicked herself toward the water's surface. More time had passed than she had guessed. Oddly, the scarlet stripes of the Ra-meki ached at her wrists. She cleared her respiratory passages, gulped hungrily for fresh air—hung aching in the water, filled with unwelcome wisdom, unappeasable doubt—fear, grief, regret.

She thought of Aurlanis, of friends she would not see again, of quiet garden lanes where she would not swim again. She thought of the Greater Milminesa. If she did not go back to them, they would cut their mooring ropes. She could not prevent it.

And so she must let it happen. Because before she thought of anything else, she must care for the lucticetes.

It was near dawn when she reached the flat peak of the pledging rock. Her hair lay wet on her shoulders. Her limbs were heavy and cold. Before going into the water, she had shaped strands of sea grass into a message: *Wait for me.*

No one waited.

So there was to be no reprieve. Simply permitting the Deep Voice to speak had not been enough. Pahla had not relented and released Tirin. She must actually pursue the course wisdom dictated.

When she had . . .

It was irrational to think the sea could be propitiated. Yet that one thought governed everything Nuela did that day. If Tirin was dead, then she must grieve for him as he would have wanted, by doing the things he would have wanted her to do. But if he was alive . . .

Irrational, but if she could bring him back by doing as the Deep Voice told her, then she would do it.

When she had rested and eaten, she dived into the water again and coursed along the rocky wall of the basin, searching for the star vessel. Bright little fish flickered around her. Once a toothfish glided toward her, jagged teeth grinning broadly. For a moment Nuela could only stare helplessly, her pulse racing. The stripes of the Ra-meki blazed on her flesh. She displayed the bold pattern.

The predator studied her with black, cold eyes, then rippled past her and vanished into the dim water. Surfacing, Nuela drew deeply at the morning air. When she had quit trembling, she dived again.

Finally at midmorning she discovered a dimple in the sand that lined the bowl of the basin. She dug at the sand and a few minutes later found her way back into the star vessel. Kicking herself forward, bobbing against the corridor ceiling, she probed the smooth walls with her fingertips. She wondered about the material they were made of. The ship had been hidden here for hundreds of years, yet nothing had grown upon the walls.

She explored the vessel in darkness, only her fingertips to guide her. She worked systematically, drawing a diagram of the interior in her mind, adding to it and revising it as she went.

She found a small forward chamber heavily choked with sand, otherwise empty. Beyond it, down the corridor, lay the larger chamber where she had hidden from the wave. It was empty too. Exploring fingertips told her there was another chamber on the opposite side of the corridor, but the door refused to slide.

Finally she slipped again through the crevice into the chamber where the lucticetes waited. The cool, dark water had a still, waiting quality, as if the normal rhythms of the sea had never touched it. Nuela kicked herself forward hesitantly and encountered the first large body.

The lucticete's flesh was as dense, as cold, as lacking in resilience as when she had first discovered the star vessel. She hesitated, suddenly afraid to listen at its side. When she did, the faint, thready beat of its heart was not reassuring.

Troubled, uncertain, Nuela lingered beside the creature, stroking its unresponsive flesh, then groped her way from the ship to breathe.

It was no longer midmorning but midday, and the world was strangely bright after the darkness of the star vessel.

When Nuela returned to the ship, she attempted to measure the corridor, using her own body as a gauge. Then, slipping back into the lucticetes' chamber, she applied the same gauge to them.

There was a marked discrepancy in their sizes. One of the lucticetes was little more than half the length of the others. She lingered over the creature, trying to find some indication of its gender. Did its diminutive size mean that it was a female? Or simply that it was younger than the others? If there was sense in the world, at least one of the lucticetes would be female, at least one male.

If she had measured correctly, the beasts would fit through the corridor, but only because of their emaciated condition. Puzzled, Nuela explored the chamber and found a second door, substantially larger than the first. But if she had oriented herself correctly, it opened only upon the rocky wall of the basin.

She had no choice then but to take the lucticetes through the corridor. She surfaced again to breathe, to peer across the empty sea. Isolation, uncertainty, anxiety sat heavily in her chest and stomach.

When she returned to the ship, she went to the smallest lucticete and stroked and massaged its unresisting flesh, trying to rouse it. The weight in her stomach grew larger, colder when it failed to respond. She moved to the larger 'cetes, poking, prodding, rubbing—receiving no more response from them. Troubled, she tested the long stems that connected them to the chamber wall. Would it help if she removed the hard blisters that blocked their nostrils?

Returning to the surface, she sat for a long time on the pledging rock, staring over the sea, wishing for someone to share her confusion, her uncertainty with.

Then, diving again, she examined the blisters with her fingertips. Found to her surprise that they were held in place simply by suction. Pressing at the lucticetes' flesh, prying at the blisters, she popped them free. Each time, the stem contracted immediately, drawing the discarded blister back against the wall.

Nuela explored the exposed nostrils with careful fingers. They did not seem to be blocked. She moved among the creatures, massaging their sides, pummeling and stroking their nonresisting flesh, pausing occasionally to listen to the beat of their hearts.

There was no response. The creatures hung motionless in the dark water, hearts pulsing weakly.

From that point, Nuela worked with little more than dogged will to sustain her. The door that led to the corridor was jammed. She pressed against it with all her strength. Wiggled it. Rocked it. Braced herself against the jamb and pushed at the panel with her bare feet. Tumbled forward in a slow spin when suddenly the door panel yielded, sliding into the wall.

Abruptly too tired to continue, she returned to the surface and gulped for air. It was late afternoon. Her body ached with cold, fatigue, and hunger. But once she cleared some of the sand from the corridor, she would be ready to try to extricate the lucticetes from the vessel. And that much done, perhaps . . .

Irrationality.

Irrationality and stubbornly held hope drove her back into the vessel, down the corridor. Her fingers trailed along smooth walls. A single small, luminous fish darted directly at her, then spun away. Its afterimage lingered, a pale yellow streak.

She knew as soon as she reached the dark chamber that something had changed. She paused in the doorway, her stomach tightening. The rhythms of the sea had reached the chamber. She could feel the difference in water motion, in temperature. She felt another difference as well. A hesitant, muffled percussion she had hardly been aware of before was absent now.

Panic set her legs kicking the water. She pressed her ear to the largest lucticete's side. Found the hesitant beat of its heart. Turned to the second beast and found another tenuous beat.

Turned with slow, unwilling strokes to find the smallest lucticete. Freed from the connecting stem, it had drifted against the ceiling. She pressed her head to its side. There was no heartbeat.

Something in Nuela choked and died. She had done as the Deep Voice instructed her, to the best of her understanding—and the smallest 'cete had died. Not in open water, but in the dark chamber where it had waited so long to be discovered.

Because she had let the sea into the chamber? Because she had removed the blister? Or simply because the wavering spark of life had been destined to flicker out one afternoon near the end of the Year of the Sia-kepi?

There had been no promises. The Deep Voice had not told her that if she cared for the lucticetes, they would survive. Nor that if she freed them, the sea would give Tirin back to her. It had only instructed her to do for the lucticetes as she would for beloved kin. And she had done so.

She had done so out of the irrational conviction that at least one of those promises existed nevertheless.

She lingered beside the dead beast, touching its flesh with apologetic fingertips, speaking a few silent words for it—as she would have done for kin. And then she fled. If the other two were to die, they must do so alone. She had reached the end of strength and courage.

Perhaps she would regain them with morning. Perhaps she would not.

She was too tired to forage, almost too tired to haul herself up the flank of the pledging rock. She clung for a long time to its base, the sea skirling cold foam at her. Finally she picked her crabbed way up and collapsed.

Tomorrow . . .

There was no time to make herself promises. Cold, exhausted, alone, she slept.

Time passed. Stars and moons rose. The sea sang a soft, keening song. Nuela's hair, her swimshift dried. She moved in her sleep, her eyes briefly opening. The moons shone upon the water, casting pale reflections.

Pale reflections that glided toward her—like something she had seen once in a dream.

Pale reflections that glided toward her like great beasts from another world.

Startled fully awake, Nuela drew a shuddering breath and sat, staring up at the sky. It was late. Tuanne had already vanished beneath the horizon. Lomaire was poised to follow.

The moons that glowed upon the water were not reflections. Nor were they dreams. The lucticetes had roused themselves and found their way down the narrow corridor to open water. She could not see their eyes. She could make out little beyond the diffuse glow of their sacs and the dark silhouettes of their bodies. But it was apparent that they were aware of her—that they had come for her.

Nuela licked dry lips, too stunned at first to be either elated or stricken. For long moments, she was unable to move. Dream and reality had collided, and she was caught at the interface of the collision, unable to move forward or back.

At last her muscles responded. She stood, and the lucticetes immediately drew nearer. Waited in massive, glowing silence. Nuela gazed down at them. Hours passed. Days. Lifetimes. While at the horizon, three stars set. Finally, numbed, disbelieving, Nuela found her way down the rock and slid into the water.

The beasts came to her, stroking gently through the water, their presence massive, benign. Nuela extended one shaking hand.

She touched flesh born upon another world, and dream became reality—incredible reality. Turning, Nuela looked back up at the pledging rock, expecting to see a dark-cloaked figure outlined against the stars. But she needed no one to tell her what she must do.

Care for the lucticetes as she would for cherished kin.

Do for them what was necessary.

Do it now.

*Tonight.*

Without waiting longer for Tirin? If he had been injured, if he was recovering somewhere from his injuries—

*Tonight.*

And so she had come to the final moment of decision. She was not to wait. And the Deep Voice promised her nothing. If she obeyed, she did so for no reason but that she accepted what was bred into her—wholly, finally, without reservation.

*Care for the lucticetes.*

*Do what was necessary.*

*Do it now.*

Or go back to Aurlanis. Close herself forever against the sea and its voices, against the deeper currents of the Chahera heritage.

And whatever her choice, it might never make a difference to anyone other than herself. The sea was large, the lucticetes gaunt and visibly frail. However capably she guided and protected them, she could not ensure their survival.

If they were not one male and one female, their survival would make little ultimate difference to anyone anyway.

If they died, she would be left alone somewhere deep in the sea.

She could not even persuade herself, this time, that if she obeyed the Deep Voice, the sea might yield Tirin to her. If she accompanied the lucticetes, she did so without promises or the illusion of promises.

The nearer lucticete nudged her. She could see their eyes now, dark, depthless, unreadable. Their huge, dark faces were totally inexpressive. She felt their gentleness, their intelligence anyway. She knew their question.

The nearer beast touched her with a broad flipper, urging her toward its glowing sac. Nuela drew away, shaking her head. She glanced up, and the tears that rose in her eyes turned the stars to clusters of jewels. "No, I can't ride tonight. I must guide you. I must show you the way north."

By sun, by moons, by stars, she must find the way. The decision was made.

# Chapter Eighteen

THE DECISION WAS MADE. NUELA DID WHAT WAS NEC-
essary.

She set a northward course. Sometimes she swam
ahead of the lucticetes, guiding them. Sometimes she
rode upon their backs, watching the water for predators.
Occasionally she dozed fitfully, waking with a start to
an empty sea. Each time that happened, tears sprang to
her eyes. But she did not shed them. Nor did she enter
the lucticetes' sacs when they beckoned. She had come
to guide and protect them. She could do neither from
the isolation of a sac.

On the first day, she found a skeletal toothfish on the
sea bottom. She broke free a section of its jawbone and
used green wiregrass to fix it to a long, flexible wand
from a plant she could not identify.

She was ready then, the next day, when she looked
down from the larger lucticete's back and saw a dark
silhouette gliding just beneath the water's surface. She
froze for only a moment. Then scarlet blazed along her
arms, and she flung herself into the water. A single
slash and the predator vanished, its blood clouding the
water.

Returning to her steed, her breath short, her pulse

racing, Nuela knew from the quiver of its flesh that it understood something of what had happened.

How much else the lucticetes understood, Nuela could not be certain. At times their understanding seemed as mammoth, as silent as their very presence. At other times, they were little more than sick, disoriented animals. They swam slowly, pausing often to sink beneath the surface, leaving only their nostrils exposed. Each time the smaller, frailer 'cete sank to rest, Nuela felt a sick hollowness in the pit of her stomach. But each time, the 'cete roused itself and swam again.

Because the 'cetes were so frail, Nuela made a net of sea grass and fished for them, sliding her catch between the fibers of their straining plates with her fingers. Although the 'cetes released the larger fish to swim away, they accepted a few of the very smallest fish. But it was obvious that even if she fished all day each day, she could never provide adequately for them.

Nor could she be certain that she would find feeding grounds—to the north or anywhere.

They swam in an empty sea. The Deep Voice no longer grumbled at the edges of her awareness. Nor did the sea itself sing.

Three days.

Four. The lucticetes continued to open their sacs to her. She continued to refuse them. She could not permit herself to be lulled. She must guide and protect.

Waking on the fifth day, Nuela met the beasts' eyes and saw a sadness, an emptiness that mirrored her own. Because they understood finally that they had wakened to a world they did not know? Because they realized they would not swim familiar seas again?

Or because her own grief and unhappiness infected them?

It was a contagion she did not know how to contain. She had obeyed the Deep Voice. She had left everything she knew. She had not even waited to see if Tirin had survived the wave. And now not even the glint of sunlight on water could brighten her. Pods of mela-mela came to play. Their antics did nothing to leaven her mood.

The fifth day passed, a string of bright hours, and she saw only shadow. The lucticetes grew stiller, more sad, two great, starving shapes haunting the water behind her. They no longer attempted to coax her into their sacs.

She led them to the depths and tried to teach them to make their own catch. They refused to strain the sandy sea bottom. Refused as well to pursue the schoolfish that darted everywhere. Either they had no instinct for feeding upon unfamiliar species or they recognized that the energy expended would be greater than that taken in.

She abandoned the effort. And later, when she netted fish for them, the lucticetes let them swim away from between listless jaws.

Late afternoon came. Nuela met two pair of grieving eyes, and the conviction grew upon her that she had left something undone—something vital. Perhaps in the practical care of the lucticetes. Perhaps in the fulfillment of the Deep Voice's command. If she could return to the dreams—

She was reluctant to leave the lucticetes unguarded. But if she had overlooked something, she must discover what it was.

And so she left them as the stars rose. She lingered for a moment beside each, wishing she knew something to say, then kicked herself to the bottom and found a rocky crevice. She drew seawater into her lungs and squeezed her eyes shut. *Please,* she begged silently, *if there is more that I must do, tell me what it is.*

She did not remember, later, passing into the dreams. But after a while, she was enclosed in a lucticete's sac.

They glided through a moonlit sea, and the First Voice spoke in whispering tones.

*These great beasts who rise like moons from the night waters, these leviathans who bear us so willingly on their journeys and migrations, require little beyond our friendship and occasional protection against the sea's more vicious predators.*

*In this we enter into surrogacy with them. They serve as nurturing parents to us, we as protecting parents to them, each of us as affectionate child to the other.*

*Behave toward the lucticete as you would toward beloved human kin. Express your affection in ways that give pleasure. Offer care and protection as required. And accept graciously the gifts offered in return.*

But she had heard those words before. And she had honored them.

*These great beasts . . .* Again the murmured exhortation. She heard it through again to the end, clinging to each word. But how was the First Voice's instruction different in any essential way from the Deep Voice's command?

Care for the lucticetes as for cherished kin.

Do what is necessary.

Do it now.

Hadn't she done those things?

Again: *These great beasts who rise like moons from the night waters . . .*

Again: *Behave toward the lucticetes as you would toward beloved human kin. Express your affection . . .*

Beloved human kin?

Express . . .

Her affection?

And accept graciously—

*The gifts offered in return.*

And then Nuela was awake, kicking her way toward the surface. She had heard the necessary words, and at last she understood them.

What would she have done had Sinjanne wakened frightened, hungry and sick in a strange place? She would have done whatever was necessary. Yes. Of course. She would have given totally—not just of her physical energies, but of herself. And she would have recognized that affection and reassurance were first among the things she must give. Because Sinjanne was beloved kin.

And if Sinjanne had offered her some small gift—as she often had—Nuela would have accepted with open pleasure. Because she understood the need to give, understood the necessity that gifts be graciously accepted.

She had cared for the lucticetes, feeding them, guiding them, protecting them. But she had not *cared* for them. Not fully. Not deeply. She had not dared.

Now she must. And again, there were no promises. However much she let herself care for the lucticetes, however freely she gave herself to them, she might never bring them safely to the north waters. By caring, she might only bare herself to even more crushing grief if they died on the journey.

But she must care, and she must let them know that she cared.

She broke the surface and quickly expelled water from her lungs. Lomaire and Tuanne hung at the midpoint of the sky. The lucticetes glided near, moons that rose only for her. Nuela drew tremulously at the warm night air. Then, laughing jaggedly, she reached out, stroking first one broad nose, then the other.

*Beloved kin. Cherished mothers/daughters/sisters/ friends from another world. Now you belong to my world too.* She didn't utter the words aloud. She spoke them with her eyes, with her stroking hands. She spoke them in her laughter. And the lucticetes heard.

And this time, when they beckoned with broad flippers, Nuela let herself be drawn into the luminous sacs and cradled there. She let herself be lulled by the beat of first one great heart, then the other. She gave herself as surrogate child, sleeping enclosed and secure through the remaining hours of night—accepting graciously the gift the lucticetes offered. Accepting their caring and the form it took.

Dream and reality collided again, this time gently.

Morning came. Nuela emerged from the sac rested, and the sea uttered a hesitant trill. Diving, she netted small fish and stroked the lucticetes as she fed them. She spoke to them, and a new brightness touched them. She could see it in their eyes, in the way they carried their heads, their flukes.

After a while, the sea rocked silver, violet, green under a midday sun, and the lucticetes began to sing, uttering long calls and questioning notes that reached out through the water like rays.

Mela-mela came then in all their numbers. Came by the hundreds, sometimes it seemed by the thousands, drawn by the lucticetes' calls. They darted and leaped and whistled, adding their own joyous chorus to the songs of the afternoon.

The sixth day of the journey, the first day of Nuela's caring, ended noisily, happily. The sun drowned in the sea. The mela-mela went sporting away, and Nuela entered a warm sac to sleep. The lucticetes haunted the sea quietly with their night song.

Two things happened on the seventh day. Late in the morning, Nuela realized that many of the mela-mela that followed them whistled the three notes of a signature call. The signature call was Tirin's.

Nuela's heart sprang against her ribs, sending a strange, piercing pain through her entire body. She whistled her own name to the mela-mela, and they answered with both her name and Tirin's.

She began to hope.

The second thing: near dusk, she discovered an arc reef that had risen above the surface and captured a broad crescent of sand. Sighting it, she slid from the lucticete's back and swam toward the captive beach. Mela-mela darted at her and after her, whistling for attention. She dived beneath the surface and kicked herself eagerly forward.

And came to land.

The mela-mela, the lucticetes watched as she flung herself down and rolled, covering arms, legs, face, hair with sand. She threw golden grains into the air and let them rain upon her.

She settled finally to watch the sun set. To wait. To hope, the notes of Tirin's call on her lips.

Stars rose. The moons rose. He did not come. Yet her hope only grew stronger. Became conviction. When finally she lay down to sleep, Nuela knew she would see Tirin again. Knew the sea intended to give him back.

Dream and reality collided again, gently, joyfully. Sleeping beneath slowly moving stars, Nuela dreamed that Tirin came walking from the sea and knelt beside her. She dreamed that he bent over her and touched her shoulder. And when she opened her eyes, he smiled down at her, not dream but flesh. "How long did you intend me to wait?"

She stared up at him speechlessly. Drawing a long shuddering breath, she sat and reached eagerly for his hands. They were warm, firm, wet. The very touch of his fingers made her arms burn with color. "What?"

"I found your message on the pledging rock. How long did you intend me to wait?"

"Oh!" *Wait for me.* She had forgotten to throw the strands of sea grass back into the water. "I thought—I thought you had been hurt. I thought you might come back for me while—" She frowned, reaching to touch the jagged, dark mark at his temple. "You were hurt."

"Knocked and torn," he said lightly. "How long has it been since the wave?"

"Nine days. Ten tomorrow."

"Then the mela-mela carried me around for four days before I was well enough to navigate on my own. Once I recovered, I went back to the pledging rock and waited. For a while."

"And then you came to find me."

"With no luck at all until your friends sent out a call that drew every mela-mela in this quarter of the sea."

And the lucticetes had sent out their call because she had learned to care for them, because she had accepted the gift of their caring. Because they had found cause for celebration. She glanced past Tirin. The lucticetes had settled deep in the water, their light little more than a ghostly shimmer. She drew a long sighing breath. "You have seen them."

He nodded and sat beside her, gazing across the water with narrowed eyes. "I've seen them, I've touched them, I've talked to them. You're taking them—" He raised questioning brows, inviting her to speak.

"To the north. To feed." And when he only nodded and continued to wait with raised brows, she told him everything—eagerly, anxiously. Just as eagerly, just as anxiously, she weighed his reaction: surprise when she told him how and where she had found the lucticetes; pain when she told him of the 'cete that had died; agreement when she explained why she had set out for the north waters in secrecy; finally a greater, graver pain when she was done. Tirin closed his eyes and sat with head bowed. The sea whispered at the sand, leaving white foam to spark briefly, then vanish. Lomaire paused in her pursuit of Tuanne and gazed down in silent sympathy.

At last Tirin raised his head and met Nuela's questioning gaze. "Yes," he said.

He did not need to say more. Yes, he would come with her. He would abandon everything known and familiar, just as she had. Together they would swim the uncharted waters of a world that had no name, guiding and protecting the lucticetes. Perhaps they would find emptiness. Perhaps they would find wonder. If they were very fortunate, they would find a place where great ice cliffs towered over cold water rich with nutrients.

Perhaps the lucticetes would die in the quest. Perhaps she and Tirin would die.

But until they did, they would swim with the striae of the Ra-meki blazing upon their flesh. They would dart beneath sunlit waters. They would ride in enclosing sacs. They would laugh, they would play, they would take every pleasure Neptilis had bred into them.

And one day, perhaps they would return to school waters leading a pod of lucticetes.

Nuela sighed, seeing everything that could be, hoping.

Tirin touched her chin, raising her eyes to meet his. They were bright, smiling. "Tell me who you are, Nuela."

For a moment, gazing into the brilliance of his eyes, she did not know the answer. Then she did. "I am Chahera," she said. "Neptilis is my father." And her mother, the sea.

When SYDNEY J. VAN SCYOC graduated from high school in 1957, she discovered that being at the top of her class in math and science was not a plus for a young woman: several colleges refused to send her application forms when they learned she wanted to study in their engineering and technical writing programs. Realizing that she wasn't going to get a scholarship for science or math, she married and the next year acquired a venerable Underwood typewriter and started writing fiction. Early on she decided to submit her work under her first name, Sydney, because "Joyce was the individual who was refused college application forms." *Galaxy* published her first short story.

Currently, Ms. Van Scyoc and her husband live in Hayward, California, on the one-acre remnant of a dairy farm. She converted the milk processing shed into an office and reports, "There is a drain in one corner of the floor so I can hose away excess verbiage. I store old manuscripts in the odd construction we call the refrigerator-bump. The barn stands ten feet from my desk. If I forget to feed the pony before sitting down to work, she loudly reminds me."

Sydney J. Van Scyoc is the author of ten science fiction novels, among them *Darkchild, Bluesong,* and *Starsilk,* and most recently DEEPWATER DREAMS, which you are holding. FEATHER STROKE (Also available from Avon Books) is her very first fantasy.